Luke

Also by Cheyenne McCray

Romantic Suspense

Zack: Armed & Dangerous
Moving Target
Chosen Prey

Suspense

LEXI STEELE NOVELS
The First Sin
The Second Betrayal

Urban Fantasy

NIGHT TRACKER NOVELS
Demons Not Included

Paranormal Romance

Dark Magic
Shadow Magic
Wicked Magic
Seduced by Magic
Forbidden Magic

Erotica (WRITTEN AS C. MCCRAY)

Total Surrender

Anthologies

Real Men Last All Night
No Rest for the Witches

Luke

Armed and Dangerous

Cheyenne McCray

ST. MARTIN'S GRIFFIN ❧
NEW YORK

LUKE: ARMED AND DANGEROUS. Copyright © 2009 by Cheyenne McCray. All rights reserved. Printed in the United States of America. For information, address St. Martin's Press, 175 Fifth Avenue, New York, N.Y. 10010.

www.stmartins.com

Library of Congress Cataloging-in-Publication Data

McCray, Cheyenne.
    Luke : armed and dangerous / Cheyenne McCray. — 1st ed.
        p. cm.
    ISBN 978-0-312-38669-6
    1. Women ranchers—Fiction. 2. Cowboys—Fiction. 3. Arizona—Fiction.
I. Title.
PS3613.C38634L85 2009
813'.6—dc22

2009019942

First Edition: November 2009

10 9 8 7 6 5 4 3 2 1

To Anna Windsor. For everything.

To My Readers

Luke: Armed and Dangerous has its foundations in a novel I wrote several years ago for a small e-publisher. If you read that short novel, you will find this endeavor different. This novel is *almost twice* as long as the original book and richer with more action, adventure, and mystery.

You will be glad to know that you'll find "hot" scenes just as memorable as before (yes, that hot tub scene and Luke's chaps are as sexy as ever!), and you're in for a lot more danger and intrigue.

Along the lines of change, *much* has changed within the government since I originally wrote that shorter novel referred to above. Under the Department of Homeland Security, agencies and departments have been reorganized and restructured. I hope I have accurately reflected some of those changes in this novel.

Thanks to all of you *Armed and Dangerous* fans—the cowboy in the hot tub and the cowboy in chaps are for you.

Luke

Chapter 1

"Three kids with penny-ante possession charges across the last year. All from Cochise College—and not a one of them over nineteen."

Clay Wayland's voice was harsh and tight over the phone. The county sheriff sounded way rattled, and way past pissed as he continued. "We found the remains on a tip, in an old warehouse. The place has been shut down for two decades, but the vat of lye was new."

Wayland paused, and Drug Enforcement Agency Special Agent Luke Denver gripped his miniature secure cell so forcefully he was afraid he'd crack the battery. Most of the road between Douglas and Bisbee was reasonably straight and flat, which was a good thing, since his mind had gotten stuck on three dead teenagers who would never come home for Christmas break.

No doubt the kids were running drugs, probably small stuff, maybe to the campus or even to local high schools. It was a common way to make extra bucks these days—stupid as hell, but they didn't deserve to get murdered and left to dissolve in a vat of lye like exterminated rats.

"I think we've got ourselves a turf war," Wayland said. "But who in Christ would be stupid enough to poach on Guerrero's territory?"

Denver guided his classic turquoise-and-white '69 Chevy truck west as fast as he dared to push the limit. "We must have weakened Guerrero when we took down the cattle rustling part of his operation near the MacKenna ranch. Had to hurt when we wiped out their inside contact in local law enforcement. Now some other group thinks it can move in while Guerrero's cartel is distracted."

"Perfect." The sound of Wayland smacking something with his fist made Denver wince. "Fucking perfect. This little Christmas charity bash you're headed to better turn up some good intel, or a shitload more people are gonna get dead in Douglas before New Year's Day."

"I'll call Rios when it's over, and he'll be in touch." Denver punched off and tucked the small cell into its hiding place in his black duster. His gut churned as he covered the last few miles into town, then drove the truck up the winding rain-soaked street and into the last remaining parking spot below Nevaeh's Bed-and-Breakfast.

Nevaeh's was situated just off Main Street in Old Bisbee, on one of the sloping hills that reminded him of San Francisco. He'd heard that at one time, Bisbee had been called little San Francisco. Under normal circumstances, he'd enjoy the view.

He shifted into first, cut the engine and the lights, and firmly set the parking brake—he sure as hell didn't want that truck taking a journey of its own. The old Chevy had been his grandpa's pride and joy, and shortly before he died, the old man had given it to Luke. He didn't have much that mattered to him other than his job and that old Chevy.

Luke sat for a second or two, reminding himself of the basic details of his cover ID of Luke Rider.

Rider.

Who the hell came up with these undercover names?

Had to be some soap-opera-obsessed technician in Accounting.

For better or worse, whoever named him, he was Luke Rider, ranch foreman on the Flying M. He worked for Skylar MacKenna Hunter and her new husband, Zack Hunter. Zack was an Immigration and Customs Enforcement—ICE—agent who recently moved back to Douglas, his hometown.

Thanks to the cattle rustling bust, Zack and Skylar knew about Luke's real identity and purpose, but they were one hundred percent on board with helping him continue in his role. With any luck, the ongoing and intense joint efforts of just about every local and federal law enforcement agency in the region might yield enough intel, leads, data, and arrests to bring down Guerrero's operation.

As he reached for the Chevy's door handle, Luke caught the familiar vibration of his phone. It was powerful enough that he felt it from within the hidden pocket in his specially designed gun holster sewn to the inside of his duster. He reached under the black duster, slipped the phone out from below his firearm, and checked the caller ID.

It was his partner, Cruz Rios, who'd managed to get himself hired on as a ranch hand at Coyote Pass Ranch about a week ago. Rios was busy getting info on Wade Larson, owner of Coyote Pass, among others in the area—rancher, lawman, and cowhand alike.

Coyote Pass Ranch bordered the Flying M, and after that came a short string of border ranches also owned by longtime Douglas ranchers. All of them would eventually have to be investigated.

"Denver," Luke answered in his slow and easy Texas drawl. Luke's and Rios's cell phones had such sensitive reception that he could hear, as clear as day, cows lowing in the background and the chirrup of crickets.

"Trouble at Larson's," Rios said.

Luke pressed the phone harder against his ear. "Yeah?"

"I've got cut fences and footprints," Rios said, "but get this—the tracks lead *onto* the ranch, not off it. It's not illegals. Wrong direction. And it's not Guerrero mules, either. These guys didn't seem to know where they were going, or maybe they weren't sure about what they were doing."

Rios coughed, and Luke heard him spit on the ground. Not a good sign. Rios only spit when he was worried.

Luke's partner continued. "When I followed the trail, I found blood—a lot of it, but no body."

"Shit." Luke clenched his free hand. "Larson?"

"Safe in his house. All the hands, too." Rios paused, and Luke could almost smell the man's frustration over the encrypted digital connection. "Looks like the bastards turned on one of their own. We may never find what's left of him—or her. But I think this makes Larson a less likely target for our investigation. Even an idiot wouldn't kill somebody on their own spread and leave the evidence in plain view."

Luke didn't like Larson, especially after he'd watched the man try to possess Skylar MacKenna when she didn't want him, but he knew Rios was right. Skylar had been a suspect, too, way back before the rustling investigation exploded, but Luke knew she was clean. Larson had helped them bring down the cattle-rustling operation along with bringing down the rogue deputy running it—and Larson was probably clean, too.

Luke gave Rios the short on the dead kids the sheriff had discovered in Douglas, and listened to Rios swear for a full thirty seconds before the words came out of his mouth. "Turf war."

A shitload more people are gonna get dead before New Year's Day . . .

"Call the sheriff's office and our field office—get some extra officers out there to search Larson's ranch and the surrounding area," Luke said. "See if you can find where they dumped the body. We need some clue who's moving in, and why they think they can start a war with Guerrero's cartel and win."

"We need to take down the rest of Guerrero's operation, and right now," Rios said. "That's the fastest way to find out who the new players are. You get into that charity party and make nice with Francisco Guerrero. And don't shoot the fucker unless he draws on you first."

Rios punched off.

Luke glanced through the rain-speckled windshield, to the upper story of Nevaeh's B & B, and saw a woman's curvaceous silhouette pause in front of the sheer curtains. Two floors below, in the living room window, a second outline appeared, this one tall and heavily muscled, topped with an unmistakable hat. Luke couldn't see the hat, but he could call the make and model—O'Farrell, a Cheyenne Pinch, probably black, pure beaver, and with a beaded edge.

That hat cost more than most people made in a month.

And Luke Rider had been helping to investigate the bastard wearing it for the better part of a year.

Francisco Guerrero.

The youngest son of the worst drug lord ever to cross the border.

Francisco Guerrero was a relatively new player in the family operation, brought into the fold by his two older brothers a little over three years ago, when the old man died.

Guerrero, the youngest, had a pre-law degree from Cornell, an impeccable set of American manners, and a thin but glossy patina of respectability thanks to owning a string of auto dealerships throughout Cochise County. He was slowly buying up businesses and property in the Douglas-Bisbee area, digging himself and his family operation so deep into Douglas that it would be pure hell rooting him out.

Since Guerrero had come to Douglas, the drug trade volume had doubled, never mind the body count. New ideas, new methods of illegal operation all the law enforcement agencies were just beginning to sort out—the bastard was a real game changer.

Luke got out of his truck, all too aware of the weight of his Glock against his leg.

"Look out, sugar," he said to the woman in the upstairs window, then glanced back at Guerrero's outline. "Wouldn't want you to get caught in the crossfire."

Chapter 2

Trinity MacKenna peeked through the bedroom's filmy curtains and stared out into the drenched December evening. Goose bumps pebbled her skin, the colorful glow of Christmas decorations on each of the power poles somehow mesmerizing her.

The sight brought back countless memories of her childhood, of celebrating the holidays with her sister, Skylar, and of her parents before their mother died.

There were some not-so-happy times after cancer stole their mother away from them. Then there had been some worse times in her teen years when she tried—and failed—to live up to her beautiful, popular, older sister's reputation and successes, but Trinity preferred to think about joyous days, or at least the warm and happy moments.

Below the B & B, the door of a classic pickup truck swung open, and Trinity watched as a man climbed out. In a fluid athletic motion he put on a dark cowboy hat and shut the door of the truck. With his long black duster swirling around his legs, he looked dark and dangerous, like an Old West gunslinger who'd come to town to track down his prey.

The man tilted his head up, his face shadowed by the cowboy hat, and for a moment she could have sworn he was looking right at her. It was as though he could see through the curtain and straight through the tiny dress her friend had talked her into wearing. Trinity's heart pounded and heat swept across every curve and swell of her body.

She swallowed hard, knowing she needed to back away from the window, to break the electric current that seemed to connect her to the mysterious cowboy, but she couldn't move.

"Trinity, are you ready to come downstairs and join the party?" Nevaeh's voice sliced through that charged connection, snapping Trinity's attention away from the man and to her friend.

"Just about." Trinity cut her gaze to Nevaeh, her gorgeous friend who was peeking through the bedroom door. "I need to fix my hair and that should do it."

Nevaeh came in, her blue evening dress shimmering in the light as she shut the door behind her with a thump. "Here, let me help."

"Are you sure?" Trinity moved away from the window and to the old-fashioned vanity mirror. "You already have guests."

"These people are party veterans." Nevaeh—whose name was "heaven" spelled backward even though she liked to tell people hell forgot to come looking for her—gave Trinity her locally famous grin. "They'll amuse themselves."

"Thanks." Trinity frowned at her reflection while she yanked down on the very short lipstick-red dress. "But this thing is ridiculous on me."

Nevaeh rolled her eyes. "You look fabulous."

Trinity cut her friend a skeptical glance. The darn dress barely covered her ass, and her nipples poked against the silky material like mini-torpedoes, especially after her sort-of-encounter with Mr. Tall-and-Gorgeous Cowboy when she caught sight of him through the gap in the curtains. The neckline plunged halfway to her belly button, showing the full curve of her breasts from the inside for cripes sake. "I can't wear this to your Christmas Charity Extravaganza, Nev. They'll think I'm a high-class call girl."

"Hey, with this bunch, you could make a fortune." Nevaeh's grin was mischievous in her reflection.

Trinity turned from the mirror to glare at her best friend and pointed to the three-inch heeled sandals on her feet. "And where did you find these? If you had a better memory, you'd remember I'm a bit of a klutz."

"You're not a klutz. Well, maybe you used to be." Nevaeh's blue-green eyes glittered mischief. "And I'd say that dress was made for you. Those long legs, cute little butt . . ."

Trinity snorted. "Stop looking at my butt."

"Can't help it." Nevaeh backed up, propped her hands on her full hips as she checked out Trinity's figure. "I just can't get over how much you've changed in the last four years. No more glasses, and you're so . . . *tiny*. I didn't even recognize you when you first came to the door, even though we talked on the phone through every five-pound increment. Those pictures you e-mailed me don't even come close to doing you justice."

With a self-conscious smile, Trinity studied her best friend since her first year at Cochise Community College, and on up through their fourth year at the University of Arizona.

Before Trinity had taken off for Europe, she and Nevaeh had

been tighter than sisters . . . certainly closer than Trinity had been to her real sister, Skylar. Those last few years, anyway, when Skylar's heart was broken, from her breakup with Zack, she just stopped talking to everyone—even the little sister who needed her more than anyone.

"It's all still kind of weird to me." Trinity raked her fingers through her hair as she spoke. "Having IntraLASIK performed on my eyes was the best thing I've done for myself." She smiled. "Other than losing those ten dress sizes, that is."

Nevaeh cocked her head. "And you took it off in a great way. Healthy eating, all that kickboxing. You really changed your habits. Your whole life. Sweetie, you'll never be Meaty MacKenna again."

Trinity shrugged and tried to smile again, but that old nickname stabbed deep. God, how she hated the mention of it. It was one reason she had ditched her first name, Madeline, the minute she left home and started going by her more unusual middle name. A clean break. Leaving behind that life, that sadness, this place . . .

"That's my goal," she said, feeling more absurd than ever in the tiny dress. "All the exercise makes a world of difference for me."

"And what a difference." Nevaeh grinned. "Can't wait for our old classmates to get a load of you now. They'll flip—never mind all the major money of Douglas and Bisbee that'll be at this party."

"You'd think I'd be used to it." Trinity smoothed her hands over the silky material of the dress and glanced down at her hips. "I've never had hip bones—well, not that I could ever see." She cut her eyes back to Nevaeh and pointed to her own shoulder. "And look at this. Shoulder bones!"

Nevaeh laughed and hugged Trinity, her friendly embrace and soft baby powder scent bringing back memories of their college days. "I'm so proud of you, Trinity." Nevaeh pulled away and smiled. "As far as I'm concerned, you've always been gorgeous. But now . . . *wow*. You're a knockout."

"Yeah, right." Trinity turned back to the mirror and pushed her strawberry blond hair on top of her head to see if it would look better up, and frowned at her reflection. The row of gold hoop earrings down her left ear glittered in the room's soft lighting. While she was in England, just to be different and a little quirky, she'd had five piercings done on her left ear, with only two on her right.

It felt like a step out of Skylar's shadow, and a big leap away from the shy, awful days of Meaty MacKenna.

It's old stuff, Trin. Grow up.

But coming home again . . .

Yeah. Coming home brought back the specter of that quiet, hurting large girl who barely made it out of Arizona alive.

Truth be told, if Trinity hadn't been changing jobs, and if Skylar hadn't e-mailed her to tell her about the rustling troubles at the MacKenna ranch, she never would have come home.

Since she got here and found out the rustling problem was over, Trinity still hadn't been able to bring herself to call Skylar or see her. After a combined ICE–DEA operation, Skylar and the Flying M were safe again—but the place didn't feel safe to return to Trinity in so many ways.

Trinity knew she needed to force herself to visit her sister, but it felt so horribly much like stepping back in time, like surrendering all the progress she had made in life.

Trinity sighed. "Skylar's always been the beautiful one in the family. The thinnest, the smartest—even the best barrel racer."

"Being a rodeo queen doesn't make Skylar MacKenna royalty," Nevaeh said, looking more serious than Trinity had seen her since she got back to town. "Let me take you downstairs, and we'll see who gets the royal treatment from every eligible male in the room—and half the ineligible ones, too."

Nevaeh slapped Trinity's ass hard enough to make her jump.

"Hey." She rubbed her stinging butt cheek with one hand and glared at Nevaeh over her shoulder. "You're not acquiring an ass fetish, are you?"

Shaking her head, Nevaeh scooped up a gold hairclip from the antique vanity table. "Sooner or later, you've got to stop comparing yourself to your sister. Now sit." Nevaeh placed her hands on Trinity's shoulders and firmly pushed her down onto the bench in front of the vanity mirror. "Look at all you've accomplished."

Trinity shrugged. "No big deal."

Nevaeh narrowed her gaze at Trinity's reflection. "Graduated with honors from U of A. Hired by Wildgames—only the best software company in the world. Never mind jetting all over Europe and shooting up the corporate ladder. Hell, you practically ran Wildgames's software development until they got bought out last month—and DropCaps Digital snapped you up with a giant bonus *and* a month off."

She gathered Trinity's hair into the clip and didn't even stop for a breath. "And don't forget the best part. You're still dating an English god."

Trinity knew better than to interrupt Nevaeh on a rant, even to tell her she wasn't sure about her long-distance relationship with Race Bentham. Her friend barreled along like a boulder rolling downhill when she had a point to make, and she'd freak if Trinity mentioned she might be dumping a handsome, wealthy business-man with a Ferrari *and* a way-hot British accent.

"And now you look incredible," Nevaeh finished as she fluffed the soft cloud of curls left out of the clip. "Like you walked out of *Cosmopolitan.*"

Trinity couldn't help but smile at her friend's enthusiastic sup-port. "It's funny how confident and successful I've felt since I left home." Her smile faded a bit. "Until my airplane landed in Tucson. Now . . . I don't know. Time warp. I feel like I'm the old Trinity instead of the new Trinity."

"Close your eyes." Nevaeh held up the hairspray can.

Trinity obeyed and held her breath as the spray hissed and a wet mist surrounded her. When she heard the can clunk on the dresser, she opened her eyes again and saw Nevaeh's reflection. She had her arms folded, her blue-green gaze focused on Trinity in the mirror.

"You know what I see?" Nevaeh asked.

Trinity gave her friend an impish grin as she waved away the lin-gering smell of melon-scented hairspray. "A redhead in a too-small red dress with no bra?"

"Turn." Nevaeh didn't even crack a smile as Trinity slid around on the polished bench to face her friend.

"Don't tell me." Trinity scrunched her nose as though she was seriously considering Nevaeh's question. "A girl with strawberry blond hair and freckles?"

"I see the same Trinity MacKenna that I've known and loved—only with bright, beautiful wings." Nevaeh crouched so that she was eye level with Trinity and rested her hands on the bench to either side of Trinity's hips. "Honey, you've always been a butterfly. You just finally had a chance to come out of your cocoon."

Warmth rushed through Trinity and she bit the inside of her lip before saying, "You're wonderful, you know that? You always know the right things to say."

Nevaeh adjusted the spaghetti strap of Trinity's dress, a no-nonsense look on her stunning features. "Hush up and get that tiny ass downstairs. It's time to soar, Ms. Butterfly. Besides, I want to see which of my moneybags charity donors falls all over himself first."

Chapter 3

Luke hitched one hip against the bar while he nursed his fancy imported beer—twenty dollars a mug for charity's sake—and studied the crowded reception room of Bisbee's best-known bed-and-breakfast.

According to Skylar MacKenna, Nevaeh always threw one hell of a holiday party in the name of toys and medical care for the towns' orphans. It looked like everyone with a sizeable bank account in Bisbee and Douglas had turned out for it again this year. Especially the people he was most interested in seeing.

Skylar played a good ranch "boss" to help his cover, even though she now knew he was DEA and not just a damn good foreman. Too bad Zack Hunter had showed back up when he did and swept Skylar off her feet. If he hadn't, Luke would have asked the woman out, rules be damned.

Not going there tonight.

Not with three dead college kids on his mind, a bunch of blood on the Larson ranch, and a turf war exploding along a stretch of border land not big enough to hold that level of violence. Time to get down to business. The job had been his life anyway, for so long he'd forgotten what it felt like to do something other than work.

There was no way the Guerrero operation was running so smoothly in a place like Douglas without some local help. The DEA had long believed there had to be somebody cooperating, somebody with a ranching pedigree and some border land, or another front or cover that made it easier for the Guerrero cartel to move their drugs into the United States.

This person wouldn't have been born into a drug dynasty like Francisco Guerrero, and this person might screw up and leave a trail to follow. Whoever was making Douglas hospitable to the cartel might be the key to tearing down Guerrero's perfect little world.

Luke took another swig of his beer, then strode directly up to the next suspect on the list the DEA had developed in its year of research before sending Luke and Rios into the field.

Bull Fenning, wearing pressed jeans and a crisp red flannel shirt despite the more formal occasion, claimed his scotch on the rocks from the bartender just as Luke drew even with him. He turned toward Luke, and he caught a flicker of surprise in the big man's frost-gray eyes.

Fenning's thick white eyebrows lifted, and the lines in his weathered face tightened as he said, "Well, now, Mr. Rider. This party's steep for a ranch hand."

"Foreman." Luke offered his hand for Fenning to shake despite the dig. "But you're right. I'm here representing the Flying M, since Skylar MacKenna couldn't come."

"I forgot. Still on her honeymoon, even though she's back in town." Fenning grinned, but his expression remained wary.

Luke gave a smile in return, just enough to keep some sort of rapport with Fenning. The old man was a big-time rancher in the area who had a big-time grudge against undocumented aliens—UDAs—for damaging his fence line.

He'd lost thousands of dollars' worth of cattle off his Bar F Ranch in the rustling operation Luke had helped to bust, and then he lost even more when the fences got cut. The cattle strayed out and died after getting into some bad feed.

But Fenning had recovered quickly. Maybe too quickly. DEA financial snoops were doing their best to figure out where Fenning's stream of cash came from, since his insurance and the income from his stock weren't sufficient to cover that kind of disaster.

"Glad to see the Bar F made it back so fast from losing so much of your herd." Luke kept his tone conversational, relying on his cover as a ranch hand to make him nonthreatening. "Skylar said she'd never have been able to come back from a hit that big."

"Skylar trusts banks. The government." Fenning drank his scotch in one gulp, then set his glass on the bar for a refill. His cheeks flushed maroon—maybe from emotion, maybe from alcohol. "My daddy taught me not to put all my bullets in one gun."

Luke responded with a practiced silence, but he widened his eyes, playing his role as a younger man interested in Fenning's wisdom.

Fenning picked up his refilled scotch. "Diversity. That's the key. You want to stay in business, you better know how to diversify. Always have one stream of income that won't let you down, and a stash of cash the government can't touch." He killed the drink, and his face turned redder as his expression relaxed.

Luke shifted his weight back and opened his stance to give the appearance of even greater interest. "So, if I get to the point where I can buy my own ranch and run my own cattle, what other streams of income should I think about?"

The hard wariness came back in a rush, and Fenning answered with a snort. "Son, if you disappeared from Douglas tomorrow, I wouldn't miss you. What makes you think I'm ready to tell you my business secrets?"

Luke shrugged, as if to say, *fair enough*. "Maybe down the road, I can do some work for you—show you what I'm worth."

"I got myself a good foreman," the old man grumbled, but Luke heard the hint of interest. Fenning's foreman, Brad Taylor, was infamous in the community of ranch hands for partying hard, staying out late just about every night, and barely getting to work on time. Luke also heard that Taylor had a penchant for twins . . . at the same time. Maybe Fenning found that interesting enough to keep Taylor around.

"If something changes, let me know." Luke gave a short nod then took a drink of his beer as he moved away from Bull Fenning before he overplayed his hand. Every detail of the conversation was recorded in his mind to share with Rios.

Diversity. Secrets. Cash the government didn't know about. Definitely merited more digging—though the old man might be making his bucks filming Taylor's exploits.

Luke made his way across the room to Gina Garcia, a statuesque blond who had bought the old Karchner K, a couple miles north of the Bar F. Drug activity had escalated since her arrival in the area, and some big busts had been made in a corridor discovered between the Bar F and the K & K. Luke's gut instinct told him that the single mother had nothing to do with Guerrero or the new operation that was starting the turf war, but it wouldn't hurt to question her and check out the K & K for good measure.

Gina was decked out in a long green dress and a glittering gold locket. Classy. Definitely easy on the eyes. Looked like she was born to wear evening gowns and sip champagne—so why was she so nervous she was picking lint off a branch on the Christmas tree?

"Evening," he said as he approached her, then felt bad when she jumped.

Gina's long fingers fluttered against her chest. Her green eyes went wide, but she seemed to relax when she saw who was speaking. "Luke. What are you—oh. Skylar MacKenna couldn't come because she just got married."

Luke nodded. "Skylar says every ranch owner around Douglas has to do their part for this shindig to work. But yeah. She wasn't ready to give up her alone time with her new husband."

Gina's smile trembled. "I wish I had an excuse. Especially a good one like that."

When her voice faltered, Luke realized she was about to cry.

Ah, hell.

Did he have a handkerchief?

With his free hand, he felt the back pocket of his pants through his duster, but he hadn't come prepared for this.

"I mean, it's just—well." Gina's voice dropped. "Everything's so expensive. I didn't realize I'd have to pay for more than the tickets. But it's charity. And like Skylar said, if you own a ranch around Douglas or Bisbee, it's expected."

Luke thought he was beginning to understand. "If it's too much for you, Ms. Garcia, you don't have to stay."

"Gina, please." She lowered her hand, and seemed to relax even more. She wasn't flirting with him, not really, but Luke could tell flirting was a natural habit she was suppressing—probably because it seemed out of place at a highbrow event like this.

"It's hard, getting in with the ranching and business crowd in Douglas, Luke." Gina nodded toward Bull Fenning, who was terrorizing the bartender, who apparently didn't want to serve him another drink so quickly. "My herd's small, but the stock's strong. I need them to know I'm going to keep building—and that I can hold my own."

Luke took a taste of his beer. "Got it. Tough for a woman to make it as a rancher, even in the twenty-first century."

"Skylar's doing it. I can, too. No matter what it takes." Gina's anxiety shifted to anger so quickly Luke almost raised his eyebrows. "My daughter deserves a fresh start and a good home. She's only eight. I have to show her how to be strong."

Fresh start—now that's interesting.

How far would this woman go for her daughter's welfare?

Guerrero's people were opportunistic and ruthless as hell. Luke wouldn't put it past them to use a child to get what they wanted from the girl's mother.

We need to put more surveillance on the old K & K.

He was about to offer to help Gina feign illness and make her exit before she bankrupted herself for a soft drink when a loud female voice intruded into their conversation.

"Hello, there. You are one fine slice of cowboy." A good-looking gray-eyed brunette edged up beside Gina Garcia, smiling at Luke and sticking her chest in his direction. The curve of her breasts was halfway to obscene through her thin black dress, and her manner left no doubt she'd be a willing roll in the hay.

Luke tipped back his beer bottle for another swallow. He had no interest in women who were that obvious. A little chase was more interesting.

"I'm Joyce Butler," the woman said, extending her hand.

Luke made himself give her fingers a squeeze, but only because Ms. Joyce Butler was on his list. Rich father, politically connected. Her family had a massive amount of border land on the outskirts of Douglas—and Butler's Rocking B hooked on the old K & K ranch. More importantly, Joyce Butler had reportedly been tight with Gary Woods, the sheriff's deputy who went bad, rustled cattle for Guerrero, and tried to kill Skylar. Joyce Butler had dated the bastard at one time, and she might have information about the Guerrero operation, whether she knew it or not.

When Joyce Butler gave him a quick wink, Luke sighed and took another drink of his overpriced beer. Damn. He'd bet his Stetson she was already planning a make-out session in the corner, or imagining that they'd do it right on the dance floor.

Gina Garcia mumbled a few excuses, then hurried away into the crowd, abandoning Luke with Joyce.

"Who are you, handsome?" Joyce's voice had a rich, silky quality.

"Hired help," he said, hoping it would back her off a step. "I'm here for Skylar MacKenna."

Joyce pushed a strand of her curly hair behind one ear and moved even closer to him. "Then you're Luke Rider. Her foreman. I've heard half the girls in town talking about you."

"Guilty," Luke admitted, making note of all the potential exits in the room.

"A foreman." Joyce brushed her chest against his, then moved back, like it might have been an accident. "I'm sure you know how to ride."

Luke went to take a drink of his beer, but he'd already drained it. Fast as a flash, Joyce had his empty bottle out of his hand, trailing her nails over his knuckles as she took it away from him. Then she was off toward the bar, her hips bouncing back and forth like somebody was hitting drums and cymbals to keep the rhythm.

She works it well, but I don't want that.

But, hell. He didn't know what he really wanted anymore. His dedication to his work had cost him every important relationship he'd ever managed to build, so he'd stopped bothering to try. Skylar MacKenna—yeah, she had piqued his interest before Zack Hunter had come back, but he'd never acted on it.

And then there was Rylie Thorn—a real spitfire friend of Skylar's. Now, that woman might have sparked Luke's libido if she hadn't reminded him so much of his younger sister.

Luke watched as Joyce passed by Cochise County's new sheriff, Clay Wayland. Wayland was at the buffet table, talking to a sexy cowgirl with brown hair and blue eyes, who owned a ranch just east of Douglas.

New man in town, around the same time as the new competition for the Guerreros. Despite Luke's earlier conversation with Wayland, the fact the sheriff could be involved had potential, though Luke couldn't imagine two crooked lawmen in the same small town. By and large, those who swore to serve and protect did exactly that.

Wayland's attention was on the cowgirl—was he just being polite or horny, or was he investigating some lead or other? As Luke watched, Wayland excused himself from the woman and took a call. A few seconds later, the man left without looking back, and

Luke figured he'd gotten the call about the trouble at the Larson ranch that Rios had informed Luke of earlier.

Too bad.

That little cowgirl looked like she might have some spirit. Clay Wayland probably just lost out on a night of fun and relaxation.

The mellow malt flavor of beer lingered in Luke's throat as he contemplated the fact it had been too long for his liking since he'd enjoyed the company of a fine woman. He'd known his share of ladies, but in the past few years, since he gave up trying anything serious, he hadn't met any ladies who could keep his attention for more than a night or two of good, hard sex.

Past few years?

Hell. If he got honest with himself, he'd have to admit that had been a problem most of his life.

He was more attached to his truck than most people. Probably a consequence of growing up hard and alone, then going into law enforcement. Like Clay Wayland, he rarely got a night of uninterrupted fun. And until he brought down the Guerrero operation and whoever it was starting a war with them, he'd be too busy for any kind of involvement.

That whole cattle bullshit Woods had arranged for Guerrero had just been a distraction, a sleight of hand, and a little more cash for the asshole. The real scheme involved smuggling drugs in from Mexico using illegal immigrants, UDAs, for Guerrero mules.

Noah Ralston of Customs and Border Protection had been notified of the UDA's and immediately took over that aspect of the investigation. Ralston and the CBP had subsequently called the DEA. What CBP hadn't known was that Luke and his agency had already been sniffing around Guerrero.

Luke sure would like to know what that weasel Woods knew, but the bastard wouldn't say a word even to cut his potential prison time. The men that Clay Wayland, Zack Hunter, and Luke had rounded up with Woods had been damn near worthless as far as information on the Guerrero operation.

Gritting his teeth, Luke clenched and unclenched his fists. No sign of Joyce. She was lost in the crowd at the bar. For half a second, he wished he could take the night off and have some fun, get the edge off, but time was one thing he—and Douglas—didn't have. And Joyce wasn't the type of woman he'd like to sink into to take that edge off.

Just as he was about to go looking for his own beer, he saw a woman coming down the stairs who had to be Nevaeh, by Skylar's description. Pretty, vivacious, bright and intelligent eyes. And—

Damn.

The woman beside Nevaeh.

Any thought he had about finding any other woman evaporated like water on a desert rock.

Nevaeh said something that caused the woman to laugh, and her lips curved into a radiant smile that met her beautiful green eyes.

Eyes that seemed vaguely familiar to him. Yet he knew he'd never seen this woman before, and he never forgot a face. Ever.

Luke's sharpened senses took in every detail of the woman and came up with a puzzle. She appeared strong, sexy, and confident, yet there was a contradicting air of vulnerability about her.

Intrigued, he watched her stroll into the room, her movements smooth and graceful. Her strawberry blond hair was piled on top of her head in a sexy just-got-out-of-bed style, and her jade green eyes were big, giving her an innocent look.

Yet the tiny red dress she wore was made for sin. It hugged her figure, showing off her generous breasts, small waist, and curvy hips. Definitely a dress designed to drive a man to his knees. And those high heels she was wearing—*damn*.

A vision came to him—having the woman beneath him, sliding between her thighs while her desire-filled green eyes focused entirely on him.

Luke's groin tightened and he shifted his position.

Looked like this night might get real interesting.

How the hell was he supposed to keep his mind on business now?

Chapter 4

"I'm going to have to hire a bodyguard just to beat the guys off of you," Nevaeh said as she and Trinity headed down the stairs and into the enormous recreation room of the bed-and-breakfast. "You're a man magnet. I swear every male in this place is watching you." She pointed to the Doberman resting at the foot of the stairs. "Even Killer, my dog. Look at him staring at you—he's in love."

Trinity laughed. "More than likely Killer just wants to sink his teeth into these stilts you call shoes," she said, while at the same time trying not to tumble down the staircase. She could just picture herself landing in a heap, this ridiculously small red dress up around her waist. Now *that* would certainly get some attention.

Why had she let Nevaeh talk her into wearing this outfit, anyway? This was more Nevaeh's wild style than Trinity's. The blue backless dress Nevaeh was wearing hugged her generous figure perfectly, outlining every beautiful curve. And the daring slit on one side went straight up to her hip bone. Nevaeh carried it off with elegance and style. Unlike Trinity, Nevaeh never tripped or spilled anything.

Nevaeh greeted guests with a wave and a brilliant smile as they descended. "Too bad you're engaged," she said to Trinity.

"I'm not *exactly* engaged." Trinity gave a little shrug as they reached the landing. "Race just hinted, rather strongly, that he plans to ask me when we get together for Christmas in a few weeks."

Guiding Trinity to the lavishly spread snack table, Nevaeh said, "Close enough. And it's a real shame."

"I don't know that I'm going to say yes, Nev."

Trinity braced for Nevaeh's reaction, but her friend didn't say a word. Trinity glanced from Nevaeh's frozen smile to the vat of red Christmas punch with the fifteen-dollar-a-cup price tag.

Oh, so not.

Red punch, white carpet—not happening.

She checked out the bottles of wine and decided on a twenty-dollar glass of Chardonnay. At least that way if she spilled it on the carpet, it wouldn't stain. She paid the bartender, took the wineglass, and cocked an eyebrow at Nevaeh, who was still smiling like she hadn't heard Trinity.

"Nev, I just told you that a rich, gorgeous man with a sports car and a British accent is going to propose to me and I might say no, and you didn't even scream. What the hell is wrong with you?"

"Would you look at that cowboy?" Nevaeh leaned close, and Trinity caught her powdery scent. "The man is to die for. That's a man who could rock somebody's world."

Laughing, Trinity rolled her eyes. "You and cowboys. I never did go for the big-hat-and-horse types myself."

"Let's at least find out his name." Nevaeh put her hand on Trinity's arm. "If you don't want him, I might. Seriously. That's one gorgeous hunk of cowboy."

Trinity shook her head so hard it was a wonder her hair didn't tumble out of its clip. "I left boots and spurs behind four years ago. Even if I was free, and even if something ever came of it, I'm not about to settle down here, where I went through the worst years of my life."

"Mmmm-hmmm." Nevaeh rolled her eyes. "DropCaps would let you work anywhere. And you can take the cowgirl out of the ranch, but—"

"Madeline, is that you?" a man's voice cut in, and Trinity winced at the name before she looked up to see Noah Ralston, one of the nicest as well as one of the most drop-dead gorgeous cowboys she'd ever known growing up. At over six feet with that chestnut brown hair mussed all over his head, he looked like he'd just come in from a long trail ride. Sexy bastard.

"Noah!" Trinity reached up and gave him a quick one-armed hug, being careful not to spill her wine. "Dang, but it's good to see you."

"Well, hell. I hardly recognized you." He tweaked a tendril of Trinity's hair and gave her his easy grin. "Probably wouldn't have if Nevaeh here hadn't told me you were coming, and that you'd changed. You're all grown up now."

Trinity felt heat creep up her neck and she shook her head. "Thanks, big guy. You don't look so bad yourself." And he didn't. The tall, well-built man was a good eight years older than she, but she'd sure had a crush on him back when she was a teenager, until he'd gotten married. He'd always been more like a teasing older brother, one of the few guys in town who hadn't tormented her, and she'd come to appreciate him as a good friend. It had been a real shame when his wife was killed in that car accident, leaving him a widower and a single parent.

A faint ringing sound met Trinity's ears over the Christmas music. Noah gave Nevaeh and Trinity a sheepish grin as he dug the phone out of his pocket and checked the caller ID. "Sorry, ladies. I'm on call and I've got to take this."

"No problem." Trinity smiled and waved him off. "We'll do some more catching up later."

Noah nodded and put the phone to his ear as he headed up the stairs, probably to someplace where it was a little more quiet.

"You know that Noah's an intelligence agent with Customs and Border Protection, don't you?" Nevaeh's smile turned into a frown as she started to add, "He's here with——" She stopped as the caterer rushed up and interrupted, telling Nevaeh she was urgently needed upstairs in the kitchen.

"All right, all right." Nevaeh sighed and waved the caterer off. "Be right there." She turned to Trinity. "Think you can fight off all the men while I go handle this mini crisis?"

"Sure." Trinity laughed and raised her wineglass. "I'll do my best to stay out of trouble." Her gaze cut to Killer. "And I've got my buddy right here."

"Go talk to that cowboy," Nevaeh said, pointing into the growing, well-dressed, and talkative crowd.

Trinity glanced in the direction Nevaeh pointed, but saw no one special. Lots of fancy suits, lots of strong, expensive cologne to make her eyes water. Heavy cologne was such a turnoff. She loved a man's true scent—most of the time.

She lifted the goblet to her lips. A devilishly adorable guy with jet-black hair and a neat moustache was gazing at her as he sipped a majorly expensive mixed drink. Black Armani suit, expensive black hat with a beaded edge, silver cuff links, nice diamond ring on his pinky—now this one screamed big money and big trouble, didn't he?

He nodded to Trinity.

She managed to nod back, but felt her cheeks coloring. Old Trinity was still hard at war with New Trinity.

She let her gaze drift over the party guests, trying to calm herself. It had been good to see Noah, as well as other old friends. Her thoughts turned to her first days back in the United States, when she'd stayed a few days with another good friend, Chloë Somerville.

Two years ago, Chloë had interviewed Trinity about the software projects she was supervising for Wildgames, and they'd hit it right off. Chloë was a journalist with a popular San Francisco magazine, but she was going through one hell of a messy divorce. Her ex-husband was a cheating bastard. Damn, but Chloë needed a good man.

Holiday music and laughter filled the room, and Trinity smiled as she watched couples dancing to a country-western tune. The room glittered with all the women dressed in brilliant sequined dresses and from the hundreds of Christmas lights and decorations.

Scents of pine, cinnamon, and hot wine punch started to compete with the cologne, along with the smell of burning mesquite wood in the fire blazing in the corner hearth. Sounds, sights, and smells of holidays that reminded Trinity of growing up in Arizona, and made her feel like she was home.

Home . . .

No. Home was wherever she decided to go—and that would probably be straight back to England, one of the hubs for Drop-Caps. And home would be with Race once he got around to asking her about sharing his life forever.

If she said yes.

Trinity sighed and tasted her wine again.

Why wasn't she sure about Race? They'd be good together. She'd never want for anything, never have to worry about her security—so why did the word NO keep flashing through her mind in pink neon whenever she thought about tying the knot with him?

Was it fear of commitment?

Inability to accept who she was now instead of who she had been?

"You look like a lady with much on her mind," said a low, enticing, accented voice to her right.

Trinity startled, and her wine nearly sloshed over the edge of her glass.

The gorgeous man with the dark hair, expensive suit, and obviously expensive hat caught her elbow and held it steady. "Careful. That is very good wine."

His accent was light, but definitely Hispanic, and his dark eyes sparkled as he smiled at her. "My name is Francisco Guerrero, though my friends call me *Cao*. I very much hope you will be my friend."

Trinity felt the man's gentle grip on her elbow, and the reality of his touch made her cheeks flush even more. "*Cao*. Doesn't that mean *gardener*?"

"One of the interpretations, yes." The man's smile would have dazzled even a seasoned harpy.

In England, she would have been enjoying this exchange, taking control of it—but here, she was folding like a cheap lawn chair.

Old Trinity.

God, she was starting to hate herself all over again.

"I'm clumsy with my glass sometimes." She tried to smile as she extracted herself from his warm fingers. "Well, I'm clumsy with a lot of things."

"I find that hard to believe," Guerrero said, and he sounded like he meant it.

Hair prickled at Trinity's nape, as though she was being watched from a totally different location, and a slight shiver skittered down her spine. She knew she was acting slightly rude to Guerrero, but she couldn't help pivoting, searching for the source of the sensation—and she came to an abrupt stop.

Caught her breath.

Heard Nevaeh's voice bouncing through her mind, whispering, *One gorgeous hunk of cowboy.*

Okay, yeah, this must be the guy.

Because he was the most rugged, most handsome cowboy she'd ever had the pleasure of viewing.

He was standing a few yards away from her, sometimes hidden from view by the flow of the crowd. The look on his face was nothing short of feral.

Instinctively she took a step back, bumping into Guerrero, who caught her and her wine both this time. He didn't keep hold of her, and Trinity noticed that he seemed angered by the cowboy's scrutiny.

"My apologies," Guerrero murmured. "I had no idea you were attached. Please forgive my boldness."

He was gone before Trinity could correct the mistake, not that she could have managed a single word with the cowboy staring at her so intently.

She raised a trembling hand and drained her wine.

The cowboy moved toward her.

Was it her imagination, or was the crowd parting for him?

You're losing your mind, Trin.

He came closer, closer, a few feet away from her. Now a few inches. She tried to back away again, but in a quick movement he caught her wrist, drawing her closer to him. Her flesh burned where he held her, and her mind went entirely blank. She would have dropped her wineglass if the cowboy hadn't slipped it from her limp hand and placed it on a server's tray.

His expression was so intense that Trinity's knees almost gave out. And those blue eyes—God, the way he was looking at her made her feel like he was making love to her right on the spot.

She tried to pull her wrist out of his iron grasp. "I—let go."

The man shook his head, the look in his eyes possessive and untamed. "No, sugar," he murmured, his liquid-hot Texan drawl flowing over her. "You're not going anywhere."

Chapter 5

Sensual heat scorched Trinity in a rush. It shot up her thighs and waist, straight to her breasts, and on up to the roots of her hair. He had to be the one she'd seen getting out of the truck earlier. Even without the cowboy hat and duster, he seemed just as dark and dangerous. Maybe even more.

Dang, the man was tall. sexy. He had a strong, angular jawline shadowed by dark stubble, and the most intense gaze that refused to let her go. God but he smelled good. Like the clean scent of soap, a hint of malt beer, and 100% Grade A male. The way the man was looking at her, she could just imagine his touch, his mouth—

Hold on. Who the heck did he think he was, telling her she wasn't going anywhere?

Yet she couldn't speak. Couldn't move.

Like a deer trapped by headlights . . . only what had captured her was a pair of wicked blue eyes and a steel vise grip on her wrist.

"You keep some hazardous company, sugar."

"Excuse me?"

"Guerrero." The man nodded in the direction Guerrero had taken. "All hat and no cattle—but lots of guns and drugs."

The man's expression faltered, as if he hadn't meant to say exactly that. Then he seemed to come to some decision, and added, "Francisco Guerrero is a dangerous man. If I were you, I'd stay far away from him."

The man's expression was so earnest and fierce that Trinity actually felt a thrill of fear. "I—I never met him before tonight."

The man's eyebrows lifted. "Is that so?"

"Are you a detective or something?" Trinity studied the man, searching for any clue that might help her get a grip.

"I'm a ranch foreman," he said, and Trinity almost laughed, despite the fact his fingers seemed to be burning straight into her skin.

"Yeah. At *this* party?"

His expression looked tense again. Very nearly rattled. He cleared his throat. "I'm standing in for my boss. Now, back to Guerrero. You think about what I said, sugar." He smiled in a way that could be called nothing short of possessive. "Tell me your name."

Trinity swallowed and mustered a defiant look. "Well, it's not Sugar." Her voice came out sounding small and hesitant, and she forced herself to put some muscle into her tone. "Let me go."

"Name's Luke Rider." His firm mouth curved into a sensual smile that met his eyes, and she thought for sure her knees were going to just up and give out on her. "It's most definitely my pleasure to meet you . . . *sugar*," he drawled, sounding every bit as lawless as he looked.

Oh. My. God. Trinity MacKenna had *never* come across a man that she wanted to jump, then slap, then jump all over again the moment she'd met him.

Uh . . . uh . . . uh . . . Take me now, I'm yours.

Okay, she'd set a new record. She'd become a complete and total idiot in less than two minutes.

The man—*Luke*—placed a possessive palm on her waist and took her other hand in his. Before she had gathered her thoughts, what few she had left, Luke drew her into the crowd of people dancing at the center of the room. "Do you two-step?" he asked, even as he led her.

"Uh, yeah." *Brilliant, Trinity.* "It's, ah, been awhile." She glanced down at their feet as they moved, and promptly imbedded her three-inch spiked heel into the leather toe of his boot, bringing them to a halt. Her gaze shot to his and to his credit he didn't even flinch. "A really *long* while."

He grinned, a dimple appearing in one cheek, and she instantly became a dithering idiot. Again.

A-*duh-duh-duh.*

"Well, then," he murmured, moving his mouth close to her ear, "we'll just have to keep at it till it all comes back to you. All right?"

"O—" Trinity shivered and almost moaned at the feel of his warm breath along her cheek. "Okay."

And can I have your babies, too?

What the heck was the matter with her, she wondered, as Luke drew her smoothly into the throng of dancers. Sure, she'd gone gaga over guys before—when she was a *teenager* for goodness sake. And those had been the ones in *Teen People* and *Bop* magazines. The adorable and unobtainable.

But this was a *man.* And God what a man. Certainly just as unobtainable as her childhood crushes. Including the fact she was spoken for. More or less.

Er, good ol' whatshisname . . .

Her pulse rate zoomed past the legal speed limit as they two-stepped to a country-western tune that had been popular back when she'd lived on the Flying M. Funny how she could still remember all the words. Yet right now she had a hard time remembering what her almost-fiancé looked like. All she could picture in her mind was this sexy hunk of cowboy whose mere presence had fried all the circuits to her brain.

Cowboy. Jeez! She didn't do cowboys. Well, not to mention she shouldn't be doing *anyone* but the man she'd been with for the last couple of years.

"Are you going to tell me more about you?" Luke's baritone rumbled as the tune came to an end and a much slower song started. "Or am I gonna just have to keep making things up in my imagination?"

Uh . . .

Trinity's whole body went on high alert as he brought her into his embrace for the slow dance. She placed her hands lightly on his shoulders—like she was afraid to touch him. His jeans-clad hips moved so close to hers that she felt the brush of denim through her silky skirt. She gulped and her gaze shot up to his. That couldn't be his . . . he couldn't be . . . it had to be her imagination. He wasn't aroused, was he?

Amusement glittered in Luke's blue eyes as he guided her in a slow and easy turn to the music. "Did you drop your voice into that incredible cleavage?" he murmured.

Trinity blinked and then smiled. "Now that's one I haven't heard before."

"Well, what do you know?" He gave her that sexy grin again. "The beautiful woman does remember how to speak."

Beautiful. Sheeee-yeah.

"I—I'm Trinity." Trinity gave her "new" name, her Europe name, wishing like hell she could find that newer, confident version of herself.

"Nice." Luke moved one hand to rest on her hip, but she didn't know if he was referring to her name or her body. His palm felt so hot that it was like he had it pressed to her bare skin, rather than against her dress. "Where have I seen you before, Trinity? You're not from 'round here, are you?"

She caught her breath as he twirled her to the song, and he somehow managed to bring her body even closer to his. "I used to live in this area, ages ago. I'm visiting."

"Very sexy." Luke brought one hand to her left ear and lightly ran his thumb down the row of earrings. His expression turned thoughtful. "Your eyes . . . I never forget a woman's eyes. Hell, I've never forgotten a face. So why are you so familiar, yet I can't place you?"

"We've definitely never met." Trinity managed a smile. "I'd remember you."

"Yeah?" He moved away from her and took her hand, his palm hard and callused against her softer skin. "And why's that?"

With a start Trinity realized Luke was drawing her through the open doors of the sunroom. "I really should get back to Nevaeh," she said, her words rushed and her heart beating furiously as he led her toward the Christmas tree in the corner. "She'll wonder where I am."

Chapter 6

Luke's cock strained against his jeans as he brought Trinity to a stop beside the decorated tree. Lights twinkled, the soft glow playing upon her delicate features and reflecting in her eyes.

He took both her hands in his, resisting the urge to grab her hips and press himself tight against her, letting her feel how badly he desired her. He wanted to dispense with the time it would take to get to know this beautiful woman, and get her straight into his bed.

But everything about her told him he'd have to take things a lot slower than he'd like to. And he found himself wanting to do that—take his time. There was something about Trinity, something that told him that this was a woman he'd have to possess on more than a casual basis.

Damn.

That instinct alone should have made him turn her loose, but turning her loose was the last thing he planned to do.

"Really, I should get back." Trinity avoided his gaze, looking instead toward the rec room.

Luke released one of her hands and caught her chin, forcing her to look at him. Her soft peaches-and-cream scent eased through his senses. "What are you afraid of?"

She licked her lips, her eyes focused on his. "You," she whispered.

The corner of his mouth turned up. "Not ten minutes ago the most dangerous criminal in Douglas was cozying up to you. Why would you be scared of me?"

"I—I shouldn't be here." She tried tugging her hand away, but he held on and raised her hand to his chest.

He pressed her palm against his shirt and rubbed his thumb over her fingers. "No ring." He frowned as he studied her jade green eyes. "You're not married, are you?"

"No." She swallowed, her throat visibly working. "But I'm in a long-term relationship. Two years now. I'm practically engaged."

The freight train of jealousy that slammed into Luke took him completely by surprise. "So where's your boyfriend?" he asked in a tone that was too calm for the fury churning his gut at the thought of another man with a claim on this woman.

"England." She brought her other hand up to his chest and pressed, as though trying to push him away. But the feel of her palms through his shirt only made him want her more. "We'll be seeing each other soon, though."

Nope. Wasn't happening. No way in hell was Luke letting another man have this woman. If she'd been married, he would have walked away, no matter the bitter regret that would have chapped his ass. But as far as he was concerned, if the guy in England hadn't staked his claim with a ring and a wedding vow, then the bastard wasn't man enough to keep her.

But he had to make sure.

Luke gritted his teeth. *"Practically* engaged?"

A fine blush tinted her cheeks. "He hinted that he's planning to ask me when we get together for Christmas."

Luke released his hold on her fingers and slid his palm onto her hip at the same time he cupped the back of her head with his other hand. "If the man hasn't made you his by now, then he doesn't deserve you."

Trinity's entire body vibrated, her skin alive in a way that she'd never felt before with—with, er . . .

Luke brought his face closer to hers, so close she could feel the warmth of his breath on her lips and she could almost imagine how he would taste. His spicy scent saturated her senses, his male presence hard and solid.

Everything about him was virile and sexy, dark and dangerous. Definitely dangerous, and definitely not part of the carefully arranged hand Trinity planned to play out, meticulously and cleanly, to win the stakes she'd set her sights on years ago. Good job, nice home, stable family a million miles away from faithless cowboys like the one who broke her sister's heart and her dreadful past as Meaty MacKenna—a man like this definitely wasn't part of the draw she needed. No, he was . . . a wild card.

An unexpected, unpredictable wild card who could win the game instantly—or wreck it forever.

He was waiting. Waiting for her to tell him no. But all she could think about was how badly she wanted him to kiss her.

No, Trinity. You can't do this.

Just one kiss. One little kiss.

Luke made a noise like the rumble of a bull, and a whimper slipped from Trinity. A sound of longing and desire.

His mouth crushed hers, his lips firm and possessive. She opened up to him, but he didn't slide his tongue into her mouth. Instead he nipped at her lower lip, small, untamed bites that made her burn in a way she'd never imagined.

Trinity moaned and clenched her hands in his shirt as she reached up, begging for more. Part of her couldn't believe what she was doing, couldn't believe what he was doing to her. And a part of her didn't give a darn. She just didn't want it to end.

Luke separated his mouth from hers, but kept his lips close to hers. "I've got to taste you, sugar. All of you."

Omigod. By the tone of his voice and the look in his eyes, he didn't just mean a kiss. He meant every part of her body. Her skin seemed to catch fire at the thought of his face pressed against her belly, his rough hands tracing every inch of her flesh.

What was she doing? She didn't even know Luke—she'd just met him what, twenty minutes ago? And now here she was, thinking of spreading a little Christmas cheer by making out with him in front of a roomful of people.

What about her plans, the man she thought she was going to marry?

I am a calm, rational software designer. I'm a project supervisor. A businesswoman. I am not a call girl at a Christmas party.

She gripped his shirt so tightly her knuckles ached. "Luke, I—"

He cut her off with another hard kiss. Only this time he plunged his tongue into her mouth, demanding and insistent.

Everything melted away. All thoughts of anything outside the feel of his stubble chafing her skin, the taste of him . . . a heady male flavor combined with a hint of malt beer.

Small purring sounds echoed in Trinity's ears, and she realized it was her making the sounds. A low *Mmmmmm* rose up within her, as if she was sampling the finest of chocolates and she couldn't get enough.

Right then she knew the kiss would *never* be enough. If she didn't put some distance between herself and this man right now, she'd never be able to walk away from him.

She tore her mouth from his, her breathing hard and uneven. Luke's chest rose and fell beneath her hands, and she knew he was as deeply aroused as she was.

"I, ah. . . ." Trinity unclenched her hands, releasing his shirt, her knuckles aching with the sudden flow of blood. "I need to use the ladies' room."

Luke ran the back of his hand along her cheek and smiled, his blue eyes dark with sensuality. "I'll get you something at the bar."

"Rum and Coke would be great." The conversation seemed inane considering the kiss they'd just shared and the wild lust pulsing between them in tangible waves. Impulsively she reached up and lightly kissed him. "I'll be right back."

She slipped away, refusing to look over her shoulder at him one last time, her lips still tingling. As she entered the rec room, she suddenly realized how she must look—her lipstick kissed off, her mouth red from the scrape of his stubble, her lips swollen from his kisses and bites.

He'd *bitten* her for cripes sake.

44 | Cheyenne McCray

In her state of total freak-out, she bumped into another woman carrying two beers, and the woman dropped both bottles. They made a thud and a fizzing sound as they hit the carpet.

Trinity's gaze shot up to meet the brunette's furious ice-gray eyes, and the apology died in Trinity's throat. "Joyce Butler?" Trinity said almost reflexively.

"Yeah." The woman's frown deepened. "Who the hell are you, a roller-derby queen?"

Madeline. The name almost popped out, but Trinity choked it back.

Madeline. Don't you remember?

It's me. Meaty MacKenna.

"Excuse me." Trinity dodged past the person who she'd once considered her worst enemy in high school. Joyce Butler, the vivacious beauty who had been one of the most popular girls in school.

And the bitch who'd given her the nickname she hated more than anything in life.

Joyce Butler had considered it her mission to make Trinity's life miserable all four years of high school, and even on into college. She couldn't even take satisfaction in the knowledge that Joyce hadn't recognized her.

No. If Joyce found out who Trinity was . . . *crap.* The woman would no doubt work to learn all about Trinity's existence now. Then make sure Race found out she had been kissing another man, or whatever other trouble she could stir up in Trinity's life.

The irony in the fact that Trinity had finally remembered Race's name almost made her burst into hysterical laughter.

Her face burned as she blindly rushed through the crowd. She stumbled over Killer, but regained her balance, sidestepped the dog, and hurried up the stairs.

She had to get out of here, as far away as she could get for the moment. But where—

Skylar. Of course. Her sister would hide her out until she could get her thoughts together.

Keep moving, she told herself, even though her body wanted to fling itself back through the bed-and-breakfast until she found Luke.

"Not happening," she said aloud.

She had to get to the Flying M, and *now*.

Chapter 7

Luke fisted his hands at his sides, lust raging through his body. He watched Trinity as she left, a gentle sway to her hips and a little wobble to her walk, like she wasn't entirely used to wearing shoes with heels the size of nail heads.

The corner of his mouth quirked into a smile. He could just picture those ankles around his neck as he slid into her . . . *damn.*

As he tried to clear his mind enough to have a thought not involving hours of steamy sex, Trinity bumped into the brunette with the big tits, Joyce Butler. Luke noted the beers in Butler's hands, and he watched them slip to the carpeted floor.

Oh, yeah. She went to get me a beer. Well, good. Now she'll have to go back for more.

Joyce Butler looked pissed, like she'd just swallowed an anthill.

Luke heard Trinity say, "Joyce Butler?" in a surprised tone, followed by a snappy, snarky question from Butler that Luke couldn't hear and that Trinity didn't answer.

A moment later, Trinity turned and slipped into the crowd, vanishing from his sight.

Right then his gut told him that she didn't intend to come back.

He'd see about that.

The way she'd kissed him, the way she had trembled in his arms, her passionate purr . . . all had made it clear as an Arizona sky that she wanted him as badly as he wanted her. Problem was she didn't know how to handle those desires.

He was just the man to teach her.

Since he was several inches taller than most of the folks at the party, Luke was able to search the crowd for the petite strawberry blonde, and spotted her at the top of the stairs just before she disappeared from view. Damn she was fast. He started after her, only to find Joyce Butler blocking his path. She already had fresh beers, and two servants were busy cleaning up the spill she had left behind.

"Thanks," he said, waving off the beer she offered. "I appreciate it, but something's come up. I'll have to get back to you." He tried to sidestep her.

She placed one hand on his bicep and deliberately moved in his way, her perfume as brazen as she was. "Not so fast, handsome."

Even though the woman was keeping Luke from going after Trinity, his upbringing and professional instincts kept him from being outright rude. His mama had raised him to always be polite to a lady. Besides, he still needed as much information as he could get from Joyce Butler on the Guerrero operation.

"Okay." He nodded and tried to move, but her hand tightened. "What can I do for you?"

"You at least owe me a dance, cowboy," she said as she brushed her breasts against his chest.

"I'd be obliged if you'd save a dance for me later." He gave her another slight nod and a tight smile. Before Joyce Butler could respond, he took her by the shoulders and gently removed her from his path.

Well, gently enough.

Luke barely heard Joyce's gasp of annoyance above the Christmas music as he walked away.

In a few strides he made it to the stairs and took them by threes. When he reached the B & B's front room that served as the lobby, he saw Nevaeh standing in front of the registration desk with a slip of paper in her hand.

"What the—" she said as her gaze cut to the desk clerk. "This is it? All she left?"

Luke didn't stop. He headed straight to the front door and yanked it open.

December's chill air rushed in, but outside all he could see were cars parked up and down Old Bisbee's Main Street. The rain-soaked blacktop reflected red, orange, blue, and green Christmas lights strung down the silent street—but nothing else. Not even a pair of taillights.

Ah, hell.

The click of Nevaeh's heels against the tile and her powdery perfume alerted Luke to her presence, even before she spoke. "I saw you with Trinity. Do you have something to do with her leaving? What's your name, anyway?"

"Luke." He shut the door a little too hard as he clenched his jaw and pivoted to face Nevaeh. "Where'd she go?"

"Her sister's." Nevaeh shook the note at Luke. "I'd told her to go meet you, but I sure never thought you'd scare her off like this. I haven't seen her in years."

Luke snatched the note from Nevaeh's hand.

Left for Skylar's. I'll call. T.M.

"Skylar . . ." His gaze shot up to meet Nevaeh's frustrated expression as it finally hit him. Where he'd seen Trinity's eyes before. Eyes that had been hidden behind glasses in pictures taken years ago. Photos he'd seen countless times at the Flying M. Eyes that had captured his attention the first time he'd seen them. Had made him wonder about the girl . . . the woman.

Shit.

"Trinity MacKenna." He shook his head. Some big bad DEA investigative agent he was. "Skylar's younger sister. But I thought her name was Madeline."

"She uses her middle name now," Nevaeh said. "*Madeline*—that one brings back bad memories."

"Madeline?" Joyce Butler's voice sounded loud and sarcastic from behind him. "You mean Meaty MacKenna? Last I heard, she was in England. What would you want with that heifer anyway?"

Both Luke and Nevaeh turned to face Joyce Butler. The woman had one hand on her hip as she tossed her dark hair over her shoulder.

Luke narrowed his eyes, but Nevaeh laid into the woman before he could open his mouth. "I don't care if your daddy is running for Congress. I wouldn't give a flying fuck if he was the President of the United States," Nevaeh said with fury in her voice as she pointed to the front door where Trinity had made her hasty exit. "If you *ever* talk about my best friend like that again, I'll kick your ass from here to Texas. You hear me?"

"*That* was Madeline MacKenna?" Recognition dawned in Joyce's eyes, but her tone turned cool as she glanced from Nevaeh to Luke. "The slut in the red dress?"

"You bitch." Nevaeh stepped forward, her fist raised, but Luke caught her by the shoulders and held her back. "Let me at her, damn it!"

"Not worth it," he responded in a controlled voice as he turned Nevaeh loose, his gaze fixed on Joyce Butler. *To hell with information.* "*She* is *definitely* not worth it."

"Now, now. We should keep this civil." Francisco Guerrero approached on Joyce's right, and took her elbow gently in his hand. "This event is for charity, after all."

Nevaeh mumbled under her breath, and Luke wanted to break his promise to Rios and shoot Guerrero on the spot.

Then he noted that Joyce Butler wasn't pulling away from Guerrero's grip. Her furious expression had softened to something like familiarity—or maybe even disguised fear.

Shit.

Maybe Joyce Butler was a lot more familiar with Guerrero than anyone had realized.

Guerrero's chilly gaze swept over Nevaeh, then settled on Luke. "If you let that magnificent creature get away, shame on you, Señor . . ."

"Rider," Luke supplied, though he had a gut-stabbing sensation the bastard knew exactly who he was.

Joyce Butler's frown settled into a harsh, pressed line, but she said nothing.

"Señor Rider." Guerrero's smile was as phony as Monopoly money.

Luke knew better than to push the issue. One wrong step, and his cover—not to mention a year-long DEA operation and even more complex investigations by a bunch of other branches of law enforcement—would get blown to shit.

"You're not welcome here," Nevaeh said to Joyce Butler. "No offense, Mr. Guerrero. If you hadn't come with Noah Ralston, Joyce, I'd never have let you through the front door."

Ralston. Thank God. Luke let out a short breath. Ralston would likely be able to get the skinny on Guerrero from Butler, since she'd no sooner spit than talk to Luke now. Good ol' Noah sure needed help with his taste in women, though. Luke had to say he'd never pictured Ralston as going for a woman such as Butler. Must be one hell of a story wrapped up in all that.

"Well, Nevaeh, you still have the hots for Noah, I see." Joyce Butler extracted her arm from Guerrero's fingers, and Luke caught the flash of anger in Guerrero's dark eyes. "I've got better places to be."

Chin up, Butler swayed her hips deliberately as she headed toward the main desk, took her belongings from the clerk, and walked to the front door. She skimmed her gaze over Guerrero and Luke before laying a particularly spiteful look on Nevaeh. "Give up on Noah, sweetie. He'd never go for a fat ass like you."

Guerrero stepped smoothly between Nevaeh and the front door as it slammed behind Joyce Butler.

Luke was grateful for the intervention, but he still had to grab Nevaeh's shoulders again. Her face was redder than a bullfighter's cape.

"Let me get out there and punch her once." Nevaeh's fists

clenched, and she struggled like a hellcat against his hold. "Just once."

It was Guerrero who said the obvious this time. "Señorita, you must not stoop to the level of a woman like that." He glanced at the closed front door, and Luke saw that flash-in-the-pan rage again, hot enough to peel paint. "We have a lovely party to return to. Might I escort you to greet some more of your guests?"

Nevaeh tensed, but Luke saw the truth on her face. Yes, she was frightened of Guerrero, and she also knew this was an invitation she shouldn't refuse. "Thank you," she murmured as Luke turned her loose again.

Francisco Guerrero put out his hand, and Nevaeh took it. Luke didn't like letting her walk away with Guerrero, but there was no way he could make a scene without sacrificing everything.

When they reached the bottom of the stairs, Guerrero kissed Nevaeh's hand, and as he lowered it, he locked eyes with Luke.

Luke tensed, calculating where his weapon was, how fast he could get to it, and how many people might get hurt in the crossfire.

What's he playing at?

Luke could almost smell the gunpowder-fire scent from hot pistol barrels.

Guerrero turned slowly toward the crowd, gesturing for the servants to start the Christmas music again, and leading Nevaeh forward to mingle with her better-mannered guests.

Christ.

Way to go, Denver. You really made a pal out of Guerrero. And kept a low profile, too. Great job.

Luke figured he had done enough damage for one night. The

most he could do at the bed-and-breakfast now was make a bigger mess.

He adjusted his duster and headed off to find Noah so he could take care of business, then get the hell out of Dodge.

Bisbee.

Hell, whatever.

Chapter 8

Trinity gripped the steering wheel of the sleek rented Mustang convertible while she headed into the night and out of Bisbee on the hour drive, past Douglas, to the Flying M.

Fortunately she'd packed her luggage in the trunk before the party to try to make herself go visit Skylar, so all she'd had to do was grab her purse and coat from the desk clerk and scribble a quick note to Nevaeh before she'd fled.

Blacktop and yellow highway markings scrolled by her headlights, glittering from the recent rain. Her thoughts whirled—she couldn't believe she'd just kissed another man.

Should she be up-front and tell Race? Or was it better left unsaid? A onetime mistake that wouldn't be repeated.

Yet her stomach flipped and her heart pounded harder as she remembered every moment in Luke's presence. The way he'd staked his claim on her, as though he intended to make her his. The way he'd brought his mouth to hers and paused, his breath warm on her lips, just waiting to see if she'd refuse him.

And oh, God. The way he kissed. The way fire had seared every part of her body, like flames burning just beneath her skin. She'd never felt such intensity with any other man. She was so worked up now she could almost scream. If she hadn't slipped away, would she have ended up in bed with him?

Would she have cheated on Race?

Her face grew hotter, but she couldn't tell if it was embarrassment at what she'd done . . . or the heat of desire from imagining what it would be like to make love to Luke.

Trinity flipped on the radio in an effort to get her mind on something else. The rich voice of the man singing a popular country-western tune only reminded her of Luke's deep baritone.

She tried to turn her thoughts to the deserted country highway, tried to get the cowboy out of her mind, but it was impossible. Her body ached for him, in every intimate place. The silk dress caressing her skin and her tight thong didn't help matters any. Considering the chilly desert night, she was burning hot.

Jeez. She couldn't get to Skylar's looking like this—decked out in this tiny little outfit, looking like she'd just made out with a guy. What was she thinking?

Trinity kept her eyes open for a dirt road and pulled the Mustang onto the first available one she spotted. Good thing this was a rural area. She could make a quick change and get back on the road.

After she made sure she was well off the highway, Trinity parked the car and turned off the ignition, but left the radio on. The blue glow from the dashboard was the only light in the car, but outside the moon slid from behind a scrap of moody clouds and washed the desert with its silvery radiance.

She leaned against the cool glass of the side window as she looked up at the incredible display above her, stars glittering in patches where clouds had retreated. She'd forgotten how bright the stars were out here in the country, far from any towns. It was beautiful. What would it be like to make love to Luke under these stars?

No, *Race*. She meant what would it be like to make love to *Race*. Yeah, right.

With a groan, Trinity moved and reached between the bucket seats to grab her duffel out of the back. From years of travel experience, she always kept a quick change of casual clothes in a carry-on bag, along with basic necessities, just in case her luggage was lost at the airport or stolen from the trunk of her car.

Her dress pulled against her breasts as she stretched her hand toward where the duffel rested on the floorboard, and one nipple popped free. It felt cool and erotic rubbing over the leather seat of the Mustang as she reached for her bag. Her thong slid into her folds, pressing harder against her.

Maybe what she needed was a good orgasm. It had been at least a couple of weeks or longer since she'd had sex with Race. He'd been tired from work one week, and the next had been an inconvenient time of the month for her, and then she'd left for the States a few days ago.

Then came an image of Luke, his big body spreading her thighs before he thrust hard and deep inside of her . . .

Trinity leaned forward and banged her forehead against the steering wheel. And then again.

It didn't work. The big, tall cowboy just wouldn't get out of her mind.

Chapter 9

"Yeah, I figure Joyce Butler knows Guerrero pretty well." Noah Ralston punched off his cell phone and stuffed it into his back pocket. He glanced around the main floor's sunroom, as if he was checking for anyone who might be listening. "And yeah, that's why I'm here with her, to see what she might share with me, for old time's sake."

Luke nodded and scuffed one boot heel against the hardwood floor. "At least that makes sense. Once I met her—well, she just didn't seem like your type."

"Back in the day, Joyce wasn't all bad. Mean as hell, insecure, but she had her reasons." Ralston's eyes got a little unfocused. "We used to be friends, Joyce and me. It was never more than that, even though she tried. I've just been thinking lately, seems like the lady could use a friend again."

Luke took a slow breath, sorting that statement out the best he could. The whole space smelled like a mixture of Christmas and chlorine from the hot tub under the sun roof and the decorated tree where Ralston was standing. Ralston didn't seem inclined to say much more about Joyce Butler, but Luke assumed the man wouldn't hold back anything essential.

Luke jerked his thumb over his shoulder. "Butler had a few words with Nevaeh a few minutes ago, after Butler insulted Trinity MacKenna."

The corner of Ralston's mouth quirked. "If I know Nev, I'd say she probably came out on top of any cat fight."

Luke grinned. "Would've laid into the b—, er, woman, if not for a little restraining on my part."

Raising an eyebrow, Ralston said, "I take it Joyce's gone."

"Just left the party. Guerrero tried to calm her down, too, but she wasn't having any of it."

"Good thing we drove separate vehicles." Noah sighed and shook his head. "She always did have a hell of a temper, but she came by it honest. Her mother was a flat-out spitfire before she died, and her dad—crooked politician, no time for the girl, except to run her into the ground."

"Is that why she took up with Guerrero? Some sort of daddy-payback thing?" With a wry smile, Luke added, "Sorry to interrogate you, but after I sided with Nevaeh in the fight, it's not likely I'll get anything out of Ms. Butler."

"I'd say that depends on what you're willing to give her in return." The CBP agent folded his arms across his chest.

"No thanks." Luke shook his head. "That one's definitely not my speed, either. Butler's full-throttle, damn the curves, and I'm thinking she doesn't much care what she drives."

Ralston's sigh said a lot. "It's sad, but that's how Joyce operates. The lady doesn't like spending nights alone."

Luke waited and watched Ralston shift through different emotions. The man's face finally settled into an expression that told Luke his loyalty to law enforcement was winning out over old friendships.

"To answer your question, no. I don't think Joyce planned to use Guerrero to jab at her father. I think she just wanted his company, his attention—but I get the feeling she got into something. Something way over her head. I think she's scared of the bastard now, but she won't admit it to me." Ralston's color darkened. "Even if she did admit that, I'm not sure she'd tell me why."

Luke took this in and waited some more, because gut instinct told him Ralston had a little bit more to say.

Ralston's frown turned deep and Luke got his first glimpse of a side of the man that wasn't laid-back at all. "I've got reason to believe Joyce knows a little about how Guerrero's getting his goods across the line—that she may have been helping him round up UDAs to use as mules. If he even needs mules." Ralston gestured to the door of the sunroom. "Hell, Joyce's family owns half the borderland in these parts. Guerrero could have tunnels on one of those properties."

Hooking his thumbs in his Wranglers, Luke rocked back on his heels. "Joyce Butler would have agreed to something like that?"

"Not if she had a choice—she's not stupid." Noah raked his fingers through his dark hair and grimaced. "But since Guerrero showed up, women I've known for years have left, or changed, or gone squirrely like Joyce. I wish I could figure that bastard's angle. I don't know how he gets them on his hook, or how he keeps them—but I know one thing for sure. Francisco Guerrero doesn't seem to give women many choices at all."

Gina Garcia, the pretty blond doing all she could to give her kid a good start in the world, drifted by the sunroom, looking as lost and frightened as a woman could look. Luke studied her wide eyes, her pale face, and the way she seemed cut off from anything safe and comfortable. "Yeah," he said to Ralston. "I'm beginning to get that impression."

Chapter 10

The knot in Trinity's belly grew tighter as she drove closer to the Flying M Ranch. She'd changed out of the wild made-for-Nevaeh-and-not-Trinity outfit, and into a pair of worn Levi's, a royal blue scoop-necked T-shirt, thick socks, and Nikes. She'd even taken a moment to tone down the blush on her cheeks with a tissue. Didn't have to worry about the lipstick—Luke had eaten that off.

Shivers skated along Trinity's skin at the mere thought. Cripes—when would she be able to push that kiss and that man to the back of her mind?

She guided the Mustang onto the dirt road leading to the MacKenna ranch. It'd been over four years since she'd been home. Four years since she'd stormed out and told Skylar she didn't care if she ever saw her again.

It had taken Trinity a long time to realize that Skylar had done the best job she could in raising Trinity. Sure, there were only a few years between the two of them, but Skylar had been there for everything when their mother died and their father drew away from them.

In Trinity's immaturity, she had seen only that Skylar had what she didn't—beauty, talent, intelligence . . . But one day, long after she'd established herself with Wildgames in Europe, it had hit Trinity that she did have all that Skylar did, she had just needed to recognize her own self-worth. Skylar had tried to tell her that time after time, but Trinity had let envy—*jealousy*—cloud their relationship.

Eventually, when Trinity had moved to England, she'd sent Skylar a letter, chatty and friendly, trying to reestablish their relationship. Skylar had been warm and receptive, just as always.

That had been a couple of years ago, and now, Trinity had come home. It really was time to make amends. To say the things she should have said long ago.

And to finally bury the old, insecure part of herself she should have laid to rest with her troubled childhood.

Meaty MacKenna . . .

Countless memories unraveled in Trinity's mind as the Mustang's wheels rattled over the cattle guard. She slowed the car down as she drove toward the house.

Toward her *home*.

She'd spent her entire life at the Flying M, up until her two years at the university and then the last four years in Europe. She'd practiced calf roping and barrel racing in those corrals to the northeast of the ranch house. Despite darkness shrouding the ranch she could easily make out the split-rail fencing and the water trough made from a fifty-gallon steel drum.

And over there, in that huge old barn, was where they kept

Dancer, Trinity's mare. Farther out back she could even see the bunkhouse where most of the ranch hands lived, and she smiled. When she was growing up on the ranch, she'd certainly had her fair share of crushes on hot cowboys.

At the thought of cowboys, one particularly tall and good-looking one came immediately to mind. Amazing—she'd finally been able to forget Luke Rider for all of what, three minutes?

As she brought the Mustang to a halt in front of the house and switched off the ignition, the knot in her belly rose into her chest, making even breathing difficult. Why was she so anxious about getting together with her sister after all this time? Maybe it was the combination of seeing Skylar, and what had happened earlier with Luke.

After she took a couple of deep breaths, Trinity climbed out of the car and slammed the door behind her. A dog barked from inside the house and the tawny glow of lights spilled through the kitchen's curtains.

She paused for a moment to look up at the now almost clear star-spattered sky. Wow. She'd missed the sight of all those stars. It was so dark out here in the middle of nowhere that stars were far more plentiful and brilliant, and the Milky Way was like white cotton candy spun across the universe.

Dirt and rocks crunched under her shoes as she made herself walk toward the house. Rain-fresh desert air filled her senses, along with the instantly familiar ranch smells of cattle and horses. The weeping willows and oaks had sure grown in the past four years.

Wooden stairs squeaked as she jogged up them to the plant-crowded porch, thick enough that it looked like a small jungle.

A porch light flicked on as Trinity reached the front door, and she blinked away the sudden brightness. The rattle of the doorknob caused the knots in her belly and chest to double. Then triple.

The door swung open, but Trinity couldn't make out the shadowed figure in the entrance, until the person stepped onto the porch.

Skylar. She hadn't changed much in four years—if anything she was more beautiful than ever. Her auburn hair flowed around her shoulders, her skin as flawless and perfect as it had always been.

Only she seemed *happy*. Happier than Trinity remembered ever seeing her.

"Yes?" Skylar cocked her head, a puzzled smile on her pretty face. "Can I—" Her jaw dropped and her eyes widened. "Trinity?"

Trinity gave her sister a little smile, pleased that Skylar had remembered to use that name and not Madeline. "Hey, Skylar."

"You brat!" In the next moment Skylar had her arms wrapped around Trinity, hugging her so tight that the air whooshed out of her lungs. Skylar still smelled of orange blossoms, and her embrace was warm and loving. "I missed you so much, knothead," Skylar whispered, her voice choked with emotion.

Trinity pulled away and smiled, swallowing hard and fighting back tears that she'd never expected. "I missed you, too, string bean. I didn't realize just how much till now."

"You look so—so *different*." Skylar shook her head as she held Trinity by the shoulders and looked her up and down. "I thought you had to be someone who'd gotten lost or something. Until I saw your eyes. You have Mom's eyes, you know."

A dog barked as though in agreement, and Trinity reached down to pet the black-and-white Border Collie. "That's Blue," Skylar said as Trinity rubbed the dog behind his ears.

"What a gorgeous boy you are," Trinity crooned.

"Think you might like to let her in out of the cold, Sky?" a masculine voice asked. Only one man had ever called Skylar "Sky."

Trinity's gaze shot up to see Zack Hunter standing just behind Skylar. "*Zack?*" was all Trinity could manage as she stood straight and looked at the man who had once been her sister's boyfriend—about ten years ago..

"I was saving this as a surprise, for the next time we talked." Skylar grinned up at Zack before looking back to Trinity. "Come on in and say hello to my husband."

"Your *husband?*" Trinity stumbled across the threshold as she followed Skylar, Zack, and Blue into the ranch house, and let the door swing shut behind her. "You're *married?*"

"Almost two months." Skylar held up her left hand, the marquis stone in her wedding band glittering in the light. To each side of the diamond a peridot was set in the gold band. "It happened too fast to send out invitations and do all the formalities."

"Wow." Trinity sighed with admiration at the ring. "It's gorgeous."

"Welcome home." Zack settled his arm around Trinity's shoulders and gave her a quick squeeze. "Sky, why don't I leave you ladies to catch up while I head to the study?" he said as he released her.

"To watch the end of the football game no doubt." Skylar grabbed him by his shirt collar and reached up to brush her lips over his.

"Watch it, woman." Zack's voice rumbled as he wrapped his arms around Skylar's waist. "I might just throw you over my shoulder and cart you off to the bedroom, reunion with your sister be damned."

"Mmmm," Skylar murmured against his lips. "Promises."

Zack gave Skylar a smoldering look that reminded Trinity of the way Luke had looked at her earlier. Hot, sensual, and possessive. The kind of look that curled a woman's toes.

I've. Got. To. Stop.

No more. No more about Luke.

Zack gave Skylar a hard kiss and then winked at Trinity before walking past the enormous Christmas tree and striding down the hall toward the study.

For a moment Trinity had to stand and absorb the living room of the place that had been her home since her birth until she left for Europe. There had been some changes in the past four years. Lots more house plants filled the room that was decorated in a Southwestern motif. Navajo rugs were scattered across the tile floor and the walls were covered with a combination of Southwestern oil paintings and family portraits. Skylar still had all the pictures of Trinity and other members of the family on the end tables, as well as lots of new ones that she'd have to spend time looking at later.

The room smelled of pine from the Christmas tree, and of leather from the overstuffed chairs and couches. And there was that old rocker that their mom used to rock them in when they were little, long before she'd died.

When Trinity's eyes met Skylar's, her sister flashed a grin and motioned toward the kitchen. "Let's fill one another in over our favorite chatty food."

"Rocky road?" Trinity laughed as her sister headed toward the freezer with Blue at their heels. "Remember all the times we'd sit at the table with a half gallon of the stuff and eat it straight from the carton with a spoon?"

"Ohhhh, do I ever." Skylar yanked open the freezer door, then dug out the ice cream carton.

After grabbing a couple of clean spoons out of the dishwasher, Skylar and Trinity settled at the table in the breakfast nook, while

Blue curled up at Skylar's feet. A peridot heart pendant sparkled at Skylar's throat, and Trinity shook her head, remembering all those years ago when Skylar had said she'd never wear it again.

Incredible how things change. How people change.

The carton made a sucking sound as Trinity popped off the lid. "You bought this just because I was coming home, I'll bet."

Skylar stuck her spoon into the container and scooped out a spoonful. "Uh-huh." Her gaze lighted on Trinity's left ear, and then she tilted her head and looked at Trinity's right. "Very cool. Definitely suits your sexy new image."

Trinity shook her head and laughed. Thinking of herself as sexy was taking some getting used to.

The sisters spent the next three hours bringing one another up to date on their lives. Skylar told Trinity how Zack had come back, determined to make up for lost time. "And have we *ever*," she said with a laugh.

Trinity shared with Skylar all she'd done while living abroad, the places she'd been, the people she worked with, and even a bit about Race. She was surprised at her reluctance to talk about the man she's been with for two years. She couldn't bring herself to tell Skylar that she thought he was going to give her an engagement ring for Christmas.

And she definitely couldn't bring up the cowboy she'd met tonight. No, that was better left unsaid.

One kiss, one night, end of story.

Even after the sisters had hugged and said good night, and Trinity had crawled into the four poster bed in her old bedroom, she couldn't get Luke Rider off her mind.

Instead she stared up at the canopy, looking at the patterns of colorful light on the white fabric that were reflected there from her Tiffany lamp with the stained-glass shade. In place of the colors, she saw Luke, reliving every touch of his hands, his lips, his body.

Trinity pulled her nightgown over her head and tossed it on the floor before she shimmied out of her thong and ditched it, too. She brought her hands up to her breasts and pinched the bare nipples. Instead of the one man she'd had sex with for the past two years, she could only visualize Luke. Could only imagine his hands caressing her, flicking his thumbs over her nipples.

Her nipples beaded even tighter in the bedroom's cool air. Her pulse picked up at the thought of Luke's mouth on her nipples, licking and sucking, and *biting* her the same way he'd kissed her.

Slipping one hand between her thighs, Trinity ran her fingertips along her folds and shivered. She'd never been so wet before. So *hot*.

Trinity let go of the guilt, let go of everything but the fantasy of letting that cowboy make her his own. She slid her fingers into her drenched folds and gasped when she stroked herself. She was so close to exploding, when it usually took her awhile to reach orgasm.

With her free hand she cupped one breast and raised it up while lowering her mouth. Her breasts were big enough that she could flick her tongue against her nipple while she fingered herself.

She closed her eyes, imagining it was Luke who licked her nipples. Luke rubbing his cock against her before sliding deep inside her. And how it would feel to have Luke driving into her. She could still feel that long hard length of his cock as he'd pressed up against her on the dance floor. Oh, God. He'd take her so deep and hard, rough and wild, and he'd make her scream.

Trinity bit back a cry as her orgasm spiked through her, and her eyes flew open. Her hips rocked against her hand as she drew out her orgasm as long as she possibly could, enjoying every electrifying jolt.

When she could catch her breath, she rolled over and switched off the Tiffany lamp and tried to relax on her pillow.

She turned one way. Tossed the other. Kicked off her covers. Pulled them back up.

Wasn't happening.

She'd never get to sleep with Luke constantly in her thoughts.

Only a kiss, she told herself as she closed her eyes. *It was only a kiss.*

That was a lie, wasn't it?

Trinity sighed.

She might be a lot of things—confused, insecure, worried about her homecoming—but she wasn't stupid.

The way she'd enjoyed Luke Rider's touch, it might not mean a thing about where she'd go with that cowboy, but it damn sure meant a lot about where she should go with Race.

And where she shouldn't.

Trinity turned on her lamp again, and estimated the time in England.

Not optimal, but then, it never would be, would it?

She got up naked, feeling half out of her own body as she made her way to her purse and pulled out her cell phone.

Her heart thudded as she realized what she was about to do. She was going to dump the man she'd been with for two years, a man she was close to being engaged to.

For what? A kiss by a cowboy she might never see again?

The thudding of her heart slowed and she was surprised at how calm she felt when she heard Race's familiar, cultured voice answer on the other end of the line.

Two years together, yet it only took a few minutes to tell him it was over between them.

Race was far too much of a gentleman to pitch a fit over getting dumped, even suddenly, and long-distance instead of face-to-face.

Trinity almost wished he would have made a little fuss, fought for her in some way—even threatened to fly straight to the States and talk sense into her. But of course, he didn't, and that really summed up her problems with Race.

He was hurt. Polite. And in the end, cool and distant. The man had absolutely no fire at all, at least not for her.

By the time Trinity turned off her phone and slipped back into bed, she was positive she'd done the right thing. She knew she'd be able to sleep, maybe better than she had in months.

Her hand moved back to the warm, damp place between her legs, and she closed her eyes.

First, though—another fantasy.

This time, without a drop of guilt . . .

Chapter 11

After the party, Luke headed back to the Flying M Ranch, refusing to let himself consider that Trinity MacKenna was staying in the main house. She was practically close enough he could smell her, if he let himself go sniffing.

Which he damned sure didn't need to do.

Luke bypassed the main house. He saw the strange Mustang convertible and knew the sweet little treasure was tucked somewhere inside the house. His pulse throbbed in a vein at his throat to know she must really be there as he made his way to the foreman's cabin behind the bunkhouse. Shit. He had to get his mind on his job. For now.

Out of habit ingrained from years of training, he made sure the building was secure before he let himself into the small cabin. He'd installed his own security locks on the front and back doors, as well as pull-down shades at the windows, and he always chose a different means of identifying if anyone had been in his quarters in his absence. Today the almost invisible threads had still been intact at both the front and rear entrances, and he found nothing suspicious.

Once he'd made a quick round of the living room, single bedroom, bathroom, and kitchen, he slung his duster on the coatrack beside the door. He tossed his Stetson on the knobby top, where it rocked back and forth for a moment before going still.

From out of his duster pocket he withdrew his PDA—a slim palm device. From the holster he pulled out his cell phone and switched it so that it would hum instead of vibrate, and then kicked back in the comfortable leather recliner in the cabin's small living room. The room always smelled of mesquite wood from the pile stacked next to the old woodstove and of leather from the worn couch and armchairs.

The furnishings weren't much to look at, but it was neat and clean. A pair of ancient deer antlers was mounted on the wall beside the black stovepipe of the old woodstove. A few throw rugs were scattered around the tiled floor and the room had been paneled in a rustic knotty pine.

On one of the wooden tables perched a small potted Christmas tree with miniature decorations, courtesy of Skylar who figured all her ranch hands needed something Christmassy in their quarters. The tree she'd put in the bunkhouse had been a little too big for his tastes, but the men had gotten a kick out of it.

Luke managed to keep his mind off Trinity MacKenna—sort of—as he set to work. He turned on his palm device and used the stylus to tab through the pages of notes he'd made during the cattle rustling case, until he came to his short list of subjects and suspects, people he thought might be players in the Guerrero operation, or potential competitors.

He added in Joyce Butler and Gina Garcia, though he wasn't

happy about it. Ralston thought Guerrero was using more than his charm to rope women into doing his dirty work—and Ralston's instincts had proven pretty sharp in the past. As for Guerrero, damn, but that bastard deserved something worse than a bullet between the eyes.

Maybe he and Rios could accidentally castrate the fucker when they took him down?

Luke wanted to smack the PDA on the table, but stopped himself before he destroyed the little piece of technology. He needed to get the sociopathic drug lord out of circulation, and fast, but he hated the idea of having to lean on scared, vulnerable women to get the information he needed.

Guerrero probably knew that, too.

Tomorrow Luke had plans to head down to the county hospital to interview a UDA who'd been used as a mule to smuggle drugs in from Mexico. The man had been beaten half to death by the *coyotes* who had been loosely connected to the cattle rustling they'd stopped at this ranch a few months back. Maybe he'd get enough information from the mule to leave Butler and Garcia out of the picture.

The hum of his cell phone snapped Luke out of his consideration of the suspects to date. He picked up the phone from the end table and saw by the caller ID that it was Rios.

"Denver," Luke said into the phone at the same time he shut off the PDA.

"Just talked with Miguel Cotiño," Rios said.

"The Special Ops supervisor over at CBP?"

"Yeah." A feminine giggle could be heard in the background and Rios's voice lowered. "Said to not bother heading to the hospital to interrogate that mule. He's dead."

"Shit." Luke ground his teeth and thumped the PDA onto the end table after all. "Anything else?"

"Nah. Catch you tomorrow. I got me a hot little thing waiting for me."

"Lucky bastard," Luke said before punching the phone off and setting it back down.

At least Rios was getting some tonight. He could use a distraction himself, like Trinity MacKenna. That was about as likely as a tornado in Arizona.

With a frustrated sigh, Luke got up from the recliner. Damn the *coyotes*. Damn, damn, damn. Without the mule, what did he have, other than suspicions and scared women?

Scrubbing his hand over his stubbled face, Luke considered what to do next. He'd never get to sleep feeling as restless and edgy as he was.

And as for distractions—well, he could go into town, but he didn't think generic hookups would work so well, due to one sexy little strawberry blonde he couldn't get off his mind.

Didn't help that he was sure she was only a few yards away from him.

It took only a few minutes to lock up and secure the cabin. Luke found himself striding through the dark night and toward the MacKenna house without any real purpose or plan. Just on the hope of seeing Trinity, maybe catching her outside or in the kitchen, and getting to talk to her for a few minutes.

He passed by the corrals and barn, the sounds of a horse whickering, the low of a cow, and the singsong of crickets filling the night.

Luke knew the sounds well. He'd visited Douglas dozens of times as a kid, to see his favorite aunt on her little ranch that had been sold years ago. Not to mention he was a native Texan. He owned his own nice spread near Houston, full of its own cows and crickets. Once this case was closed and cleaned up, he intended to head back there.

Although he enjoyed his work, he was accustomed to family dropping in, big get-togethers with his folks, his grandma, his sisters and brothers, and all his nieces and nephews. It had been months since he'd seen them, and he could sure use some of his mom's blueberry pie, straight from the oven, with a scoop of homemade vanilla ice cream right on top.

He might even talk to his mom about Trinity.

Luke almost stopped walking, because that thought caught him totally by surprise.

Not smart. Don't even start thinking that way.

Yeah, he knew how this movie ended, and the story never worked out neat and pretty. Best to go back to his cabin—but before he knew it, he was standing in front of the ranch house and near the room he knew had belonged to Trinity MacKenna when she was growing up here. No doubt it would be where she'd be sleeping.

What are you going to do, Denver? Throw rocks at her window?

He bit back a wave of frustration and embarrassment. But then, why the hell not? Maybe she'd get a kick out of it, of him showing her his teenage-feeling interest.

Around the corner at the back of the house, hidden within a closed-in yard, he could hear the pulsing of the hot tub jets as well as Zack's and Skylar's voices. By the sound of Skylar's gasps and Zack's groans, Luke suspected they were more than enjoying themselves.

Better move on from that. Private things were private—though to hear Rylie Thorn talk, she wouldn't have thought twice about it.

That little hellcat would have pulled up a front-row seat and wouldn't be the least embarrassed to admit it.

Luke had never been much for voyeurism, except for once in his teen years, when a kid could be forgiven for being desperate. With a wry smile, he bent and picked up a few pebbles from the yard. Then, he eased behind the trees that obscured the room's window from sight and looked in.

Covert operations was something he'd done often, although nothing like this . . . spying on a woman he was dying to get his hands on, with the intent of grabbing her attention with a pebble or two.

I'm losing my damned mind. And I don't spy on women I'm interested in.

All right, except for that time when he was thirteen and he had peeked into Maggie Jensen's window while she was dressing. She'd been eighteen and built like a brick shithouse—one of those figures that gave all teenage boys wet dreams. It'd been the first time he'd seen a live pair of breasts and a woman's hair-covered mound. Afterward, he'd masturbated more than a time or two over the image of her naked, imagining what she'd feel like.

But now he was an adult, with a raging hard-on for a woman who he couldn't get off his mind.

A few tosses. If she doesn't answer, I'll go on back home.

He melted into the shadows behind the tree as he peered through the parted curtains. Good. The window was closed. He raised his hand for the first pebble toss just about the time he saw Trinity.

She was lying on her back, staring up at the canopy of the bed. The light beside her bed was on, its stained-glass shade casting rainbow fragments across her face and the pale blue nightgown she wore.

Luke hesitated, hand at the ready, the pebble feeling warm and solid between his fingers.

That gown had thin little straps that would easily break if he tugged on them, and he was sure the silky-looking material would feel soft beneath his hands, just like her skin. The nightgown was hiked up to the top of her thighs, but not quite high enough for him to see anything more than her shapely legs.

Her thighs were squeezed together tightly, and she squirmed a little, as though trying to alleviate an ache there. But in the next moment she reached her hands up and pulled off her nightgown.

Luke dropped his arm back to his side. The pebble—hell, all the pebbles—fell out of his hands.

The woman had damn perfect breasts with cherry dark nipples just begging for his mouth.

His cock bucked against the denim of his jeans. He knew he should have some moral battle inside, but the reaction was too strong, too deep. This woman, oh, yeah, she was his. He had claimed her at Nevaeh's, and he was claiming her again, right there under her sister's tree.

He unbuckled his belt, unzipped his jeans, and released his aching erection. With slow familiar strokes he moved his hand up and down the length of his cock as he watched Trinity shimmy out of her thong before she cupped her breasts and squeezed her nipples.

"That's it, sugar," he murmured as she slipped one hand down and then she spread her legs wide as though welcoming him between her thighs.

"You're beautiful," he said softly as he worked his cock. "Can't wait to get to know you better."

Trinity's fingers slipped between her folds and she began rubbing herself in a slow, circular motion. With her free hand she pushed up one of her generous breasts and flicked her tongue against her own nipple.

Damn but that turned him on. He'd never watched a woman licking and sucking her own nipples, and the sight was fucking arousing.

Her fingers grew more frantic and his strokes more intense.

When she came, she threw back her head, and she bit her lip as though to keep from crying out. Her body trembled and vibrated, and she kept rubbing herself until she came a second time.

As her body relaxed, a dreamy expression covered her face, and he only hoped she'd been imagining that he was the one making her so happy. She raised her fingers to her nose as though to smell her juices, and that was enough to make Luke's climax hit him in a rush.

He bit the inside of his cheek as it took him, and went on, and went on a little longer. Damn that had felt good. But the real thing was going to feel a whole lot better.

Luke fixed his belt and jeans, as he forced himself to turn away. For a moment, he stood there, wondering what the hell he'd just done. He'd had no intentions of spying on Trinity MacKenna and had ended up masturbating while he watched her do the same.

Fuck.

He was losing his goddamned mind.

Over one beautiful woman.

Luke slipped away from the house and faded into the night.

Chapter 12

Trinity couldn't remember being so hungry in years.

How could breaking up with the perfect boyfriend and having wild sweaty dreams about a cowboy—a cowboy, for God's sake—get her stomach growling this loudly?

Skylar rattled her omelet pan on the stove, and the sizzle of onions filled the air. The whole kitchen smelled like them, and eggs and peppers and rich, melting cheese, and bacon—oh, man. Skylar flipped two omelets onto her plate, walked to the table, and plopped down across from Trinity, right next to Zack. With a grin, she slid her second omelet onto Trinity's plate, and Trinity's stomach growled again.

Damn it, midnight breakups and all the hunger in the world didn't change the fact that Trinity didn't do cowboys. She never had, never planned to—because cowboys tied women to places like Douglas. She wasn't about to make that mistake.

She glanced across the breakfast table and caught another glimpse of the pictures her new brother-in-law had been studying.

He'd been hard at work since she started stuffing down the first excellent omelet Skylar had cooked for her.

Trinity made herself swallow a delicious bite of fresh, hot cheesy eggs before asking, "Are those pictures of footprints?"

"Yeah." Zack acted as if he wanted to slide the pictures back into the folder he was guarding with his elbow, and Trinity realized the photos had to be related to some investigation. Interesting. Zack worked for Immigration and Customs Enforcement and Skylar had told Trinity the border and drug smuggling issues in Douglas had heated up so badly that lots of agencies were working together now.

Alcohol, Tobacco, and Firearms—ATF—for one, along with DEA, ICE, CBP, and the local sheriff and police forces. Just about everybody had joined the fight. The violence and risk scared Trinity a little, but she found the science of it fascinating.

"Sorry, Sky." Zack gave Skylar a guilty look.

Skylar ate a bite from a strip of bacon and shrugged. "Just don't drag out the blood and gore shots, okay? I want to enjoy my breakfast for once."

Trinity craned her neck to see the photos, which appeared to be multiple shots of human footprints, set in dirt or sand. Some dark stuff had been splashed all around the prints—oh. Trinity swallowed a little harder this time. That was probably the blood Skylar didn't want to see.

Trinity put her fork down and focused all her attention on Zack. "Does your office use footprint analysis?"

Zack's brows pulled together above his gray eyes. "For individual prints? Of course."

"I mean for the overall pattern of all the tracks." Trinity couldn't help herself. She picked up her fork and started eating again, barely getting her bite swallowed before she continued talking. "You know, to figure out who came and went first and second and third, and likely points of origin—that sort of thing."

Zack put his fork down. "Whether or not we can do it by sight depends on how clear and how fresh the trail is when we find it."

"I mean afterward, from photographs." Trinity glanced from Zack to Skylar, who took another huge bite of omelet and didn't seem to mind them talking about Zack's work. "It's similar to some of the gaming software for one of the products I supervised," Trinity said. "The designer used a trail analysis algorithm to help spaceships target off-screen enemies who were shooting at them."

Zack studied her. "Go on."

Trinity chewed up another bite of bacon and swallowed, wishing Skylar had fried another pound. "If you leave me a copy of that photo, of all the photos showing footprints—and show me due north on the crime scene, I might be able to give you some information."

Zack put a hand on his folder full of photos. "Like . . ."

"Like which set of prints arrived first, which set left the scene first—which direction they took, and maybe even which direction they came from." Trinity dug into the last of her second omelet. "If that would help."

Zack gave Skylar a mock frown. "You didn't tell me she grew up and got useful."

"Don't give her any pictures with body parts, damn it." Skylar pointed her fork at Zack's nose. "I don't want her having nightmares and leaving. I don't want her leaving at all."

Trinity's stomach gave a big lurch, and it was all she could do to keep a smile stapled across her face.

I don't want her leaving . . .

Skylar's words bounced through Trinity's mind, driving away the scents and flavors from the wonderful breakfast.

Okay, so, she'd known her sister wanted her around, wanted her to visit, even wanted her to stay, but hearing it out loud like this, here, now, as they all sat around the breakfast table eating eggs and bacon like a real family—ouch.

Skylar wants me here.

Trinity tried to make herself take her last bite as Zack riffled through his folder and picked out photos, but she couldn't lift the fork to her mouth.

Skylar wants us like this—a family again.

Talk about insta-guilt.

Or were all the knots in her stomach really fear, instead?

What am I afraid of?

That I want to stay in Douglas?

Get real.

She had a job. A future that had nothing to do with Meaty MacKenna or any of her old pains. She had a life, a boyfriend, a—

Oh, wait.

The reality that she broke it off with Race last night came slamming home, and for a few moments, Trinity felt completely cut loose from reality. She felt like old Trinity.

Madeline . . .

Stop it.

"These ought to be a good start." Zack slid four photos of footprints across the table.

From a thousand miles back in her own mind, Trinity noted that the bloodstained prints had been decorated with dozens of tiny evidence markers. The markers gave millimeters and centimeters, indicating depth and distance from each other.

"Are you okay, honey?" Skylar's warm, loving voice jerked Trinity back from the strange, distant place she'd gone.

"Fine." Trinity gathered up the photos, trying not to let her hands shake. "Just thinking about what I need to do with the software to prove I *did* grow up and get useful."

"Silly." Skylar went back to her omelet as Trinity slid out of her chair. "You've always been a lot more than just useful, especially to me. You're my only sister, and the best one in the world."

Trinity managed a smile, then picked up the photos and left the kitchen before she could freak out again. She made it around the corner and leaned against the wall, closing her eyes to settle herself for a second.

Skylar and Zack had started talking to each other, voices low and loving, sounding oddly right in the stillness of the ranch house.

This had become a happy place, a healthy place. A place Trinity could get used to, for sure, but she knew she couldn't have it both ways. She had to choose between staying away from Douglas except for visits and keeping her new, confident healthy self—or coming back to this town and house and life, and maybe drowning in her old, scared, helpless self.

Trinity opened her eyes, her mind sharper now. As much as Skylar meant to her, that choice wasn't really a choice at all. Trinity needed to get Zack's photos taken care of, then get hold of Drop-Caps to finalize their arrangements, stay the hell away from dangerously sexy cowboys—and get the hell out of Douglas.

Chapter 13

The helicopter swept low, stirring a shitload of dust across the dilapidated piece of border fencing between Bull Fenning's ranch and the edge of Gina Garcia's property.

Luke shifted his position to get a better look at the images on Noah Ralston's radar screen as they covered more territory. Ralston guided the 'copter on another sweep, as close to the ground as he dared.

Ralston shook his head, and Luke gave the pilot a signal to pull off and make another pass to the south, fully over the eastern edge of the K & K. They were still well out of visual range from the main house, though.

"The radar's only good to about forty feet." Ralston sat back from the wavy lines and colors on his screen. "If the tunnels are deeper than that, we'll never see them."

Luke nodded. Even the older version of ground-penetrating radar, which still had to be mounted on the bottom of military vehicles or towed in a cart, gave a lot of false positives. This new version that could be focused from low-flying helicopters helped with searching more territory. Problem was that the depth was shallow at best, and about half the signals they investigated turned out to be nothing, or naturally occurring pockets in the earth. Microgravity sensors would be a hell of a lot more effective in tunnel detection—but thousands of times more expensive, too.

Tunnel hunting had been a long shot, but what the hell. Luke figured he might as well be useful while he waited for Rios to get his ass back from the autopsy of the body—well, body pieces—they'd finally located on Wade Larson's ranch. It kept him busy, and it kept him away from Trinity MacKenna.

Who might be back at Skylar's house, naked in her bed, touching herself . . .

God help me.

Luke clenched his jaw so hard he almost cracked a tooth.

"You seem distracted," Ralston called over the dull roar of the chopper's whirling blades. "Not on the same planet distracted."

"Yeah." Luke tried to ignore the hard-on building at just the thought of seeing Trinity MacKenna with her fingers moving between her legs, of watching her flick that pretty pink tongue against her dark nipples.

I'm killing myself.

"You get anything from Joyce Butler yet?" he asked, mostly to refocus his own thoughts. Thinking about Joyce Butler definitely tamped his lust a few notches.

"We talked all of two minutes, at the most, after the Christmas party." Ralston squinted at his screen again, but didn't act as if he was seeing anything important. "Joyce left town early this morning to help with her father's campaign. We did a fairly thorough flyover of her boundaries after she was gone, and came up empty."

"Why don't you touch down and let me off over there?" Luke pointed to a flat stretch of packed sand and rock to the east. "My truck's close enough to K and K for me to pay a visit to Ms. Garcia and walk from there."

The walk would definitely do me good.

When Luke looked at Ralston, the CBP agent had a big smirking grin on his face. "You like Gina Garcia? Is that where your head's been?"

Luke shook his head. "I want to poke around a little, see what she's scared of—because she's definitely nervous about something."

"Uh-huh." Ralston kept grinning even as he guided the 'copter down. "Well, if it's not Gina, it's some other woman."

"You need a girlfriend, Ralston." Luke waited for the bird to touch ground before he jumped out, keeping his head low. "Your fantasies are getting the better of you."

Ralston shook his head, still smiling, as Luke moved clear of the rotors.

The chopper picked up in a swirl of dust and pebbles, leaving him alone for a few long minutes before he started walking.

Luke glanced around.

No cold streams to dive into, damn it. This was Douglas. The desert. Right now, an arctic shower might have been helpful.

He dusted off his jeans and Western shirt and figured he'd better start walking the few miles to the K & K's main house. The exercise would have to be enough to burn off his interest in Trinity MacKenna.

For now.

The old K & K ranch house looked a lot like Luke remembered it when he'd visited it as a kid—all white boards and angles, with a big porch and a bigger barn. The flower boxes in the windows added a soft touch, and the tire swing hanging from a wooden strut off the barn's side door—that looked new.

The kid in the tire swing with the long blond braids—she was definitely a new addition. The little girl had big wide eyes that got even wider when she saw Luke coming across the field toward the house.

Before he could call out to her, the girl jumped from the swing and ran for the house. She yelled for her mother, spooking about thirty white hens and a couple of roosters into loud squawking as she pelted across the driveway.

Good girl, Luke thought as he let himself through the field's back gate into the K & K's sprawling back lot. *You stay safe.*

A minute or so later, Gina Garcia met him on the porch, looking nothing like she had at the Christmas benefit. Today she had her hair pulled up in a messy ponytail, and her white tank top had more purple stains than clean fabric. Probably blackberry or blueberry juice, Luke realized. Gina had left the back door ajar when she came out, setting free a tantalizing smell of baking pies.

The girl was nowhere to be seen, and Gina followed Luke's glance into the kitchen. "She took off to her bedroom." Gina dusted flour-covered hands against faded jeans and studied Luke with wary green eyes. "Lola gets nervous easily, and you scared her, coming in the back way like you did."

"Sorry." He relaxed against one of the porch's wooden columns. "Wasn't my intention, but you've got her trained well."

"I've been homeschooling her since—we came here." Gina reached behind her and pulled at the back door until Luke heard it click shut, masking the delicious smells of home baked pies. "I think I'll let her try school next year. She'll be in fourth grade. What are you doing here, Luke Rider?"

Luke appraised Gina's steady, emotionless face. Not nervous today, at least not on her own turf, with her baby to protect.

Easy, mama bear. I'm not a threat to your cub. "I was out with a friend and left my truck nearby. Thought I'd check by on my way to get it and see how you're doing, since you didn't seem too happy or comfortable at Nevaeh's Christmas gig."

This made her mouth twitch, there and gone, just a flicker of movement. "Neither did you."

"True." Luke had to smile. He liked it when people were direct. She wasn't finished with the direct thing yet, either.

"I'm not in the market for a foreman, or a husband, or even a boyfriend." Gina's voice took on a furious edge, sharp enough that Luke raised both hands as he continued to lean against one of the back porch's columns.

"Not trying to sell you anything like that. Seriously, I'm just checking on you."

Gina's green eyes turned as hard as her voice. "Why? I've got pies baking and a kid already fifteen minutes late on starting her mathematics for the day, so if you've got something to ask me, spit it out."

Direct.

No kidding.

Bulls could take lessons in basic self-defense from this woman. Maybe he'd read her completely wrong at the Christmas party. She didn't look like someone who needed anybody's support or protection.

Luke met her stony gaze with his, and tried a little directness of his own. "Francisco Guerrero seems to have scared a lot of women around here, according to some of my friends. Are you one of them?"

Gina's mouth came open, and her eyes misted so fast Luke blinked.

Well, hell. I pushed a button.

He felt like shit for spooking her, and the kid, too. Before he could apologize, Gina appeared to collect herself. When she straightened up and lifted her chin, she looked like a woman who should have on an evening gown again, and be drifting from high society party to high society party instead of baking pies on a ranch outside of Douglas.

"I'm not afraid of Francisco Guerrero," she said, but Luke heard it in her voice.

She wasn't scared at all. She was terrified.

His fists clenched as he wondered why, wondered what had happened. What had that fucker managed to do to her?

He tried to relax his fists. "If you need help, Gina, I know people."

Gina closed her mouth, then let out a laugh that didn't sound convincing. "You're a ranch foreman, Luke."

"A ranch foreman with a lot of friends." He pushed away from the porch column, careful not to crowd her.

Gina studied him in absolute silence, hands frozen against her hips, and her expression unreadable. The glint in her eyes seemed like anger mixed with fear mixed with—

What?

Hope?

Interest?

Luke took a chance on the last two emotions. "If you know anything you need to tell somebody, my friends could keep you and Lola safe."

Gina kept on staring at him, weighing and measuring. This time obviously considering what he said, and considering it very seriously. Her eyes drifted toward the barn, then snapped back to Luke's face.

"Thanks," she said, backing up toward the kitchen door. From somewhere inside, a timer went off, beeping, and beeping and beeping. "I'll keep that in mind. You have a good day, Luke."

She opened the kitchen door and had it closed behind her so fast Luke barely saw her move. He heard the dead bolt thump into place. A few seconds later, the beeping timer went quiet.

If Luke had less regard for laws and procedures and women in general, he would have searched her barn right then, or banged on her door and demanded more information.

Something wasn't right.

Gina was scared to death, and he'd made it worse just by coming here.

Luke didn't even let himself glance toward the barn.

If anybody was in there watching, he didn't want to give a hint that Gina might have tipped him off.

He left the porch, walking toward his truck, slow at first as if he was just out for a stroll.

A mile or so down the road, he picked up his pace and placed a call to the county sheriff, Clay Wayland, and asked for a favor.

"Can you find out everything on Gina Garcia and her background, as well as the K and K's boundaries and history?" As he spoke with the sheriff, Luke glanced at the sky as he walked, aware that Ralston had to be on the ground somewhere, since he didn't hear the chopper overhead. "I'd like the schematics on the barn if anybody filed construction or plumbing and electrical permits for it."

"Got something?" Wayland sounded like he might be writing the info down, to be sure he kept it straight.

"Could be my office can help out. You know the number—I'll get Rios on it when he gets back, too."

Wayland's voice went a little crackly, like he had moved his mouth closer to the phone. "Tell me what's up."

"I'll let you know. Nothing I can get a warrant for."

"Too damned bad."

Luke thought about Gina and her little girl. "Yeah. No shit."

Chapter 14

Three days after the Christmas party at Nevaeh's, Trinity waved her sister and new brother-in-law off as Zack's black truck sped down the dusty road away from the ranch house. They had a holiday party to attend in Tucson, and had decided to spend the night at a resort there, rather than making the hundred-plus mile drive back the same night.

Skylar had wanted Trinity to come, but Trinity had begged off, telling her sister that she still needed to recover from jetlag—never mind the half-zillion or so photos Zack had dumped on her once he saw the initial output from her first rudimentary tracking algorithm. She needed to get those scanned into her laptop, and factor them into her equations. And she needed to e-mail Chloë and Nev about the whole Race situation to get all the screaming and are-you-crazy's over with.

For a moment she stayed on the porch, enjoying what was left of the early evening sunshine. The December desert air smelled so fresh and clean. Over the Mule Mountains to the west, the sun hung low, teasing the sky with wisps of lavender, peach, and mauve. Skylar's Border collie raised his head and sniffed the wind, then trotted off toward the barn.

Trinity turned her gaze to the east, to the rocky Chiricahua mountains rising behind the ranch. She'd explored parts of those mountains many times with her sister when they were younger. Memories of the fun times they'd shared returned clear and crisp, like they'd happened last week instead of years ago. Light glinted off a certain special spot on the slopes, where Skylar and Zack always used to sneak off to carry on, like they thought Trinity wouldn't know.

Trinity had to fight not to cry, and she knew she really couldn't stay here much longer at all, even if she kept putting off the call to DropCaps.

Because it's already happening. My old life is already sneaking down those slopes, ready to pounce on me and try to keep me here.

She ran her palms up and down her upper arms, rubbing away the evening chill as she headed back into the house. After she shut the door tightly behind her, the complete quiet of the house settled over Trinity, reminding her of times she'd been home alone as a teenager, and Skylar had been off working the ranch. Would she ever get over the guilt of having left all the ranch's responsibilities to Skylar?

Pausing in mid-step, Trinity's gaze drifted over family photographs displayed prominently around the room. Pictures of her with Skylar, of both the two of them alone, and with their parents. After their father took off with his new wife and left them alone, Trinity had refused to contact him. He never took the time to see how she was doing, so why should she bother?

Trinity moved to one of the end tables, stopped in front of her senior photo, and slid her fingers along the wooden frame. In the picture her face was pudgy, her smile soft and wistful. Despite the wire-framed glasses she used to wear, her green eyes were bright and full of hope for the future.

Next to her senior photo was a recent picture of Skylar and Zack. She was standing in his embrace, her face tilted up to his, and the way he was looking at her with so much love, it made Trinity's heart ache with both pleasure for her sister, and envy for herself.

She still couldn't believe Skylar was married to Zack, after all these years. Trinity had to admit they made the perfect couple now, as they had a decade ago. There was so much fire and passion between the two of them then, and now . . . *wow*. To have sparks like that. Trinity hadn't thought that kind of passion between a man and a woman could possibly be real—just something she'd read about in romance novels.

That was, until she'd met Luke.

With a groan of frustration, Trinity jerked herself away from the photographs, skirted the Christmas tree, and started down the hall. Why the hell did that cowboy keep popping into her mind? Maybe what she needed was a nice, long, relaxing bath.

Better yet, an evening dip in the hot tub would be perfect. They'd always kept it heated and used it year-round. Knowing Skylar, it still would be ready for use.

In her bedroom, Trinity kicked off her Nikes and yanked off her socks, then ditched her jeans and T-shirt. After she'd donned a short terry robe over her bra and underwear, she grabbed a thick towel and headed out to the hot tub in the enclosed backyard.

The French doors squeaked as she opened them, and then

again as she closed the doors behind her. There was a coolness to the air, and the steam rising off the top of the water in the sunken tub was a welcome sign. Thank goodness Skylar had the outdoor heaters set up close to the hot tub to take the chill out of the air. The pole heaters were easily six feet tall with tops that looked like woks turned upside down.

Trinity tossed her towel onto a deck chair and flipped on the heaters. In moments their elements began to glow rich orange-red, the same color as the sun sinking in the west. After she turned on the whirlpool jets, Trinity dropped her robe onto a lounge chair. For a moment she stood on the redwood decking in only her royal-blue satin bra and panties. With one little adjustment of her hair clip, she piled her hair up on top of her head so that it would stay out of the water.

The whirlpool bubbled and frothed like a witch's cauldron—even the lights beneath the surface appeared green and eerie, as though it truly was a magical potion. She started forward then hesitated.

What the hell? She was alone—the backyard was completely enclosed. It was secluded and hidden from view by countless trees and bushes, so no one could see her. And Skylar and Zack would be gone till tomorrow.

Trinity stripped out of her bra and bikini underwear, her nipples growing painfully hard in the cool air. When she walked in front of one heater, its warmth radiated along one side, the chilly air brushing her other side.

She stepped down into the hot tub and sighed in complete bliss as she sank into the warmth and settled onto the underwater bench. Jets of water pulsated along her skin while she breathed deep of the clear and clean country evening air. She'd forgotten how dry the Arizona desert was—it felt somehow lighter here than in England.

While she relaxed, for the millionth time her thoughts returned to the other night.

To Luke Rider.

Everything about the man screamed sex. Rough, wild, and hard . . . all that Race couldn't begin to give her.

No, Race couldn't be considered wild about anything. Anything other than Wildgames, that is. He was a shrewd businessman, but he'd been calm and refined as a boyfriend and as a lover. There'd never been any fireworks with him, but it had always been comfortable and enjoyable.

All the guys she'd dated—pretty much the same story.

I've never known it wild.

Is that what I want?

Trinity rolled her gaze heavenward and stared into the darkening sky and sighed.

When she thought of that cowboy there was nothing remotely calm or unemotional about how he'd made her feel. In just that short time she'd been with him, he'd made her feel sexy and *alive.*

Infatuation, Trinity, that's all it is. Not that you'll ever see him again, anyway.

She closed her eyes and focused on the feel of the heaters warming the back of her head, the water bubbling at her nipples and jets pulsating along her legs. Spreading her thighs, she adjusted her hips so that one of the jets aimed right where it mattered. *Mmmm, yeah.* That felt so good. She could almost imagine Luke licking her right where the water pulsed. Maybe he'd bite her there. Not too hard, but enough that it would drive her even crazier for want and need of him.

Trinity slipped the fingers of one hand between her thighs. Even through the water she could feel her own desire.

She brought her other hand to her breast and kneaded and plucked her nipple. Eyes still closed, she fantasized about sucking her own nipples while Luke devoured her. She raised her breast and flicked her tongue across the hard nub. A pleasant warm lick that immediately chilled in the night air until she licked it again.

Her fingers aided the jets, stroking her harder and harder, her tongue flicking again and again over her nipple, urging her closer and closer to climax. Imagining Luke's tongue all over her body. Imagining Luke sliding into her—

The squeak of the French doors jolted Trinity from her fantasy.

Her eyes snapped open. She jerked her head up and her heart started to pound.

The large figure of a man. He stood beside the hot tub, his face shadowed by a dark cowboy hat.

"Welcome home, Trinity MacKenna," he murmured.

Chapter 15

Luke.

Trinity would recognize that deep, sensual drawl anywhere.

Omigod.

Heated embarrassment prickled her skin. She wanted to die from humiliation at being caught masturbating—by the very man she'd been fantasizing about. And darn it if her brain and mouth hadn't taken another vacation.

Her cheeks burning as hot as the heat lamps, she slid farther beneath the water so that her breasts were hidden by the bubbles and crossed her arms over her chest for good measure.

"I—I—" She couldn't find any words that made sense. She needed to tell him to back off, to get out and let her get herself covered and decent. She needed to say something, didn't she? Anything?

"Who were you fantasizing about, sugar?" His eyes were shadowed by his hat and his voice was rough. "The man who hasn't had the sense to claim you by now?"

Trinity didn't know what to say, then what came out was, "I broke up with him. My boyfriend."

Damn.

I have totally lost my ever-lovin' mind.

The rough, aroused look on Luke's face seemed to catch fire, burning her deep inside, and convincing her yes, yes, she was crazy, completely and totally.

Trinity slid farther into the water.

"Uh-uh." Luke crouched down beside the hot tub and pushed his Stetson up with one finger. She could clearly see his roguish blue eyes in the waning evening light. "Keep going, sugar."

"What—" She swallowed, her throat incredibly dry. "Ah, what are you doing here, Luke? How did you find me?"

"Later." He reached out his hand and ran his thumb along her lower lip, causing more warmth to spread throughout her—but this time it was from arousal. "Right now you're gonna touch yourself, just like you were doing when I walked in here."

Trinity sucked in her breath. "You want me to . . . in front of you?"

"Oh, yeah." His sensual smile and the way his finger moved on her skin almost made her climax on the spot. "I want you to touch yourself while I watch. But first you're going to move up a little higher to give me a better view."

Face burning impossibly hotter, she shook her head, pulling away from him. "I—I can't, um, do it in front of you."

"You can." Luke caught her chin in his hand and forced her to look at him. "And you will."

Trinity trembled, yet managed to ask, "And if I don't?"

His eyes glittered with dark sensuality. "I'll pull you out of that hot tub, lay you across my knee, and spank your naked, sexy ass."

Oh. My. God.

At the visualization of him doing just that, Trinity's eyes nearly crossed, her whole body aching with a wild urgency. The need to have Luke inside her, and to have him *now,* exploded through her like a storm.

But she couldn't have sex with this man, this cowboy—although for the life of her, she wasn't able to remember why not.

Like, she didn't even know the man?

What was that again?

His fingers slid in a slow and sensuous movement from her chin along her jawline. "Now what'll it be?"

She was almost tempted to let him spank her—the thought was strangely erotic.

Trembling with nervousness and desire, Trinity eased up until she was sitting on the redwood decking, her feet still in the frothing waters of the hot tub. Her nipples chilled as hard as gold nuggets, and goose bumps roughened her flesh. She quickly warmed from the heaters at her back, but it was mostly Luke's touch that set her on fire as his fingertips skated from her lips and down her neck to the hollow of her throat where he lightly caressed the soft skin.

The night smelled of desert air and of Luke's masculine scent and his spicy aftershave, and her senses whirled. Her blood thrummed even harder in her veins, the sound loud enough to nearly drown out the pulsing of the hot tub.

She held her breath as he moved his hand along her collarbone, and over the gentle rise of her breast. "Spread your legs," he said in that drawl that made her throb.

Trinity widened her thighs, her feet dangling in the churning waters, while keeping her gaze focused on Luke. It was as if she had no choice but to do as he commanded. No will of her own. Or was it that his will *was* the same as hers? What she really wanted.

"Sweet." Luke settled on one knee as he cupped her breast with his large hand, his powerful T-shirt-clad chest brushing against her arm. "Touch yourself."

Shivers raced through her as she braced herself with one palm behind her on the decking, and slipped the fingers of her other hand through the soft curls of her mound and into the slick heat of her wet folds.

"Yeah, that's it." His voice rumbled as he caressed her nipple with his thumb.

She trembled, so close to exploding like a bunch of firecrackers on Independence Day. Just a little more—

"Stop." At his command her fingers came to a halt and she wanted to scream. "Not just yet." He moved his hand to her other breast. "Slide two fingers into yourself and hold them there."

Oh, God, this man was going to kill her.

Trinity's whole body vibrated as she obeyed and pressed her knuckles against her folds. The feelings were so intense it was as if Luke's fingers were inside her.

With his free hand, he took off his Stetson and tossed it onto a deck chair. "Arch your back so that I can get a real good look at your breasts."

Two fingers still deep inside herself, Trinity obeyed. Her nipples had hardened to such sensitive nubs that the lightest brush of his fingers sent lightning bolts of sensation through her. "Luke, I can't take any more."

"We've just gotten started." His hand moved away from her breasts and he stood in a quick, fluid movement. She lifted her chin to watch him as he jerked his T-shirt over his head and tossed it onto the deck chair beside his hat.

Dang, but that man had a fine chest. Chiseled muscles that made her want to run her fingers over every sculpted contour down to his flat, hard, six-pack abs. Thick veins ran along his bulging biceps to his large hands, hands that she wanted all over her. She'd never seen a man so up close and personal with such a fine body.

His hands moved to his Western buckle, and in no time he'd unfastened it and set the belt aside, then toed off his boots and peeled off his socks.

Oh jeez. Oh cripes. He was going to get completely naked.

Hurry, darn it.

As if he'd heard her thoughts, Luke smiled and unfastened his jeans and slid them down over his hips. His thick, luscious cock sprang out at full attention as he pushed his jeans past his heavily muscled thighs.

Wow, wow, wow. His cock was even bigger than she'd thought when she'd felt it pressed against her at the Christmas party. Dang but that would feel good.

A sense of light-headedness swept over Trinity and she realized she was holding her breath. She gulped in the fresh evening air, her heart beating faster and faster as Luke slid out of his jeans and briefs. She watched the ripple and play of his muscles while he strode toward her and stepped into the hot tub.

When he was waist-deep in the water, he moved between her thighs, pressing her knees apart, and braced his hands on the decking at either side of her hips. He pushed his cock against her hand, forcing her own fingers deeper.

She couldn't. She could. She wanted. She shouldn't.

"We don't have protection," she finally whispered.

"I can satisfy you in more ways than you can imagine." He leaned forward and nuzzled her ear, and then ran his hot tongue along the row of earrings. "Now," he murmured, "back to where we left off."

That's all the man had to do—talk in that deep, sensual drawl, and she'd do just about anything for him.

Anything at all.

"Stroke yourself." He lowered his head and nuzzled her breast, his warm breath fanning across her nipple as he spoke. "Nice 'n slow."

She slid her fingers out of her core, slick with her juices, and stroked her tight nub. Luke flicked his tongue over her nipple and Trinity arched her back toward him, needing him to take her deeper into his mouth.

He moved to her other nipple and scraped his stubble over the sensitive flesh. "While you're fingering yourself," he murmured, "imagine that I'm sliding into you."

Trinity's breathing came quick and uneven. As her finger rubbed faster, her eyelids drifted shut. She was a trigger-pull away from climaxing.

"Look at me," he demanded and her eyes popped open. He smiled, and with one hand he caught the back of her head and brought her toward him. With a flick of his wrist, he pulled out her hair clip, allowing her hair to tumble down around her shoulders and to slide below her shoulder blades like a sensual caress.

The clip clattered on the decking as Luke cupped the back of her head. Her fingers continued to stroke her sensitive center as he brought his mouth above hers. She tasted his warm breath upon her lips, bringing back a rush of memories of that incredible first kiss from the night at Nevaeh's.

"When I take you, sugar," he said, his gaze locked with hers, "you're gonna watch me slide into you. You're gonna watch me possess you. I'll fuck you so deep you'll feel it in your throat."

His words magnified Trinity's arousal. She gasped and started to cry out as her orgasm began to ripple through her. But Luke brought his mouth down hard and kissed her with such savage intensity that her orgasm multiplied. Her hips rocked against her hand, his cock rubbing her knuckles as he pressed himself to her. Trinity's world and thoughts spun as he devoured her in a kiss she never wanted to end.

When she finally stopped convulsing, he broke away. Trinity could only stare at him, tasting him on her tongue, her face burning from the scrape of his stubble, her fingers still lodged between her thighs.

He took her hand, slipping her fingers into her folds and then out, and brought it to his face. He breathed deep, and a pained expression crossed his rugged features. "I've got to sample you," he said and then slid her fingers into his mouth, licking her juices from them with sensual swirls of his tongue.

Oh my God, was all Trinity could think. *Oh, my God.*

Luke's cock strained toward Trinity, dying to get inside her slick heat. Her unique flavor only made him want her more, and he gritted his teeth to hold himself in check. He wanted to take her right out here in the hot tub and drive into her till she couldn't walk for a month of Sundays.

The way she was looking at him, her jade eyes an even darker green, her skin flushed from her orgasm, and her body trembling with desire . . . he had no doubt she'd let him in.

If this was any woman but Trinity MacKenna, he'd slide into her now and make her moan.

But Trinity was different. He'd known it from the first time he'd seen her photo in the MacKenna living room. And when he'd met her, even when he hadn't recognized her by her appearance, he'd known this was one special woman.

Luke had no doubt in his mind that he'd have her—he just had to make sure that she was ready, and there wouldn't be a single regret when he made her his.

Only his.

But for now, he had to taste her—thoroughly.

Kneeling on the hot tub's underwater bench, he placed his palms on the inside of her pale thighs and pressed.

"Luke." His name was a gasp on her lips as she slid her hands into his hair.

He breathed deeply of her scent as he nuzzled the soft curls of her mound. "Damn you smell good," he said, then trailed his tongue over the fine hair to the sensitive skin between her sex and her ass.

She clung to him as he held her thighs tightly in his hands. He licked the inside of each of her thighs then gave the soft flesh gentle bites.

He was feeling anything but gentle. It was all he could do to continue his slow seduction. A sexy woman like Trinity would enjoy some hard and fast loving, but Luke wanted to give her more than that—and take more, too. In fact, he wanted her heart, because he aimed to keep her.

The thought surprised him, yet at the same time he didn't question it.

Trinity's soft moans became louder and more urgent as Luke worked his way back to her drenched folds. Her fingers clenched tighter in his hair as he dipped his tongue into her, tasting her full potency.

Her thighs trembled as he flicked his tongue over her center, and then pulled away. "Not yet," he said against her flesh, and then thrust his tongue into her hot core.

That purring sound rose up from Trinity as he licked and sucked. Her taste and smell, the feel of her body beneath his hands, all made his cock so hard he could probably bench-press with it. All he'd have to do was rise up and plunge into her heat. He could more than imagine how it would feel to be buried inside her.

His rampant thoughts added fuel to the intensity of his desire for Trinity. He plunged two fingers inside her, and as she cried out he nipped at her swollen heat.

She screamed. Her body rocked, and she gripped his hair like she was busting a bronc. He pressed his face even harder against her, licking and sucking her as she bucked, coming again and yet again.

"I want you to stand with your back to me now," Luke said while she was still trembling with her orgasm.

Trinity audibly caught her breath. "I don't know if I can."

"Sure you can, sugar. I've got to see that beautiful ass of yours." He could barely keep his hands off her as she turned and stood on the underwater bench, facing away from him, her ass well out of the water. "That's real nice," he murmured as he cupped her smooth cheeks with his palms. "Brace your hands on the decking."

His hands spread her ass cheeks apart so that he could see her puckered anus, and he could just imagine sliding into that tight rear hole. He slipped his fingers through her slick juices and smoothed them back.

"Oh . . . my . . ." Trinity's voice wavered as he circled her anus, and then she gasped as he slid the tip of his middle finger inside.

Tight, but not too tight. She'd be a nice fit. "How does that feel?" he said as he slowly pushed his finger all the way to his knuckle.

"Good." She let out a soft moan as he slowly moved his finger in and out of her anus. "Really, really good."

"You've done it this way before?" he asked, then gritted his teeth at the thought of any other man sharing this with her.

"Never." Trinity shook her head, her hair sliding over her back with the movement. "But I—I have fantasized about it."

Luke relaxed. He'd damn sure be the only man who'd do it, too. He increased the motion of his finger, and she rocked her hips back and forth and rode his hand. "You've played with toys like this . . . haven't you?" he asked, and stopped the motion of his finger but kept it lodged inside her.

"Yes." A whimper escaped Trinity's throat that she couldn't hold back. "Don't stop, Luke."

"I'm not through with you yet." Luke slipped his finger out and then in the next instant, he scooped Trinity up.

She gasped as she found herself on her back in his embrace, and she threw her arms around his neck. "What are you doing?"

Instead of answering her question, he eased onto the underwater bench in the hot tub and cradled her in his lap. He fondled one of her nipples with his thumb, and she squirmed on his lap. "Why'd you run out on me at Nevaeh's?"

Trinity moaned, so incredibly aroused from what he'd been doing to her just seconds ago. "I—dang. I can't even think when you do that."

Luke gave a soft chuckle. "Try."

"Fear." She swallowed, her eyes heavy-lidded as her arousal grew. "I was afraid if I stayed around you, something would happen. Something like this."

"What's wrong with what we're doing?" he asked softly.

"You know." She could feel heat rise in her cheeks. "A few nights ago, this would have been cheating. That kiss at Nevaeh's—it *was* cheating."

The blaze in his eyes nearly made her come unglued. "And tonight?"

"Tonight, it's not." Trinity let out a moan from his touches. She couldn't help it. "I told you, it's over with him. I called him and told him I wasn't going to see him anymore."

"Damn good thing." He held her tighter with one arm and continued his exploration of her body with his other hand. "He's not right for you."

Her gaze met his as she tried to straighten in his arms. "You've never even met Race."

Luke grinned at the bastard's name. "Race?"

Trinity tilted her head up and glared at him. "He's a great guy. Kind, gentle, thoughtful."

"You're too passionate a woman for kind and gentle." Luke slid his palm down her flat belly toward her mound and felt her tremble beneath his touch. "After awhile you'd feel bored and trapped. Wouldn't be fair to either one of you."

Frowning, she placed her palm on his bare chest, like she was bracing herself. "You don't even know me."

"Better than you think." One hand rested on her belly as he slipped the other into her hair and rubbed the base of her scalp in a slow, sensuous movement. "You're confident in your work, but insecure in yourself. You're sexy and gorgeous, but you don't even realize how beautiful you are." When she dropped her jaw in surprise, he gave her a smile. "The time I first saw your eyes, it was plain as day."

Trinity stared at Luke, amazed and unable to speak for a moment. The churning waters of the hot tub filled her ears along with the sound of her own heartbeat. "We just met."

"The pictures Skylar keeps in the family room." He gently continued massaging the back of her head as the jets caressed her body. "Months ago when I saw those photos of you, I thought you'd be worth getting to know real well."

Prickles raced along her skin. "Who *are* you?"

"Foreman for the Flying M." He shrugged. "Been here 'bout six months."

"You live and work here?" Trinity clenched her fist against his chest, her thoughts spinning. "At the ranch?"

The corner of his mouth quirked and he nodded. "Uh-huh."

Oh, lord.

"That's just great." She rested her head against his muscled chest. "That's like leaving Eve in the garden of Eden not far from the apple tree. Irresistible temptation within walking distance."

Luke chuckled, his chest vibrating beneath her ear. "Irresistible, huh?"

Shifting on his lap, she felt the hard insistence of his cock pressed against her ass, and could hardly form a coherent thought for a moment. What if he slid into her tight rear hole and took her now?

Taking a deep breath, she said, "I don't know what it is, but you make me forget everything." She leaned back and tilted her head to look at him. "Except you. All I can think about is you. And I barely even know you, Luke Rider."

"That's as good a start as any." He adjusted her in his lap, turning her so that she was straddling him, his cock pressed against the soft curls of her mound. "For now I want to see you climax again."

She laced her fingers around his neck and arched her back as he leaned down to flick his tongue over her nipple. The damp ends of her hair rubbed over her back as she moaned and squirmed on his lap, against his erection . . . dying to feel him inside her, yet hesitating to take that step, to cross that boundary.

Luke slid his forefinger between her thighs as he licked and sucked and gently bit her nipples. Harder he stroked her, bringing her closer to yet another orgasm.

"I can hardly wait to be inside you, Trinity," he murmured against one nipple. "I want you so bad I can taste it."

"Yes," Trinity whispered as she rode his fingers. "You're so big. You'll feel so good."

He groaned and bit harder at her nipple, causing Trinity to cry out with the pleasure and the pain of his teeth sinking into her soft flesh. His cock pressed against her belly as his hand worked between her thighs, and she wondered when he was going to slide inside her.

Deep. Hard. Fast.

Just the thought was enough to push her over the edge.

A furious climax stole her breath and all her senses, going on and on until she collapsed against his chest.

She expected him to raise her up, to drive his cock into her core.

Instead it sounded as though he was speaking through clenched teeth as he said, "I've got to go before I lose what's left of my control."

"What?" Trinity rose up to look at him, but he grasped her waist with his big hands, moved her aside, and set her on the bench. "What are you doing?" she asked as he stepped out of the hot tub.

He snatched the towel off the deck chair and rubbed it over his body. Even while she was confused by his sudden actions, she couldn't help but admire his muscled body.

Talk about prime choice cowboy ass!

When he started to yank on his jeans, she scrambled out of the hot tub to stand beside him, water trailing over her body and trickling to her feet.

"You're gonna catch a chill," he muttered, taking the now damp towel and rubbing it over her shoulders. "I intended to grab a fresh towel for you."

Conflicting emotions stormed through her. Was he rejecting her now that he knew she wanted him? Was that why he was leaving? Yet he was rubbing the towel over her so gently, and instinctively she knew this man didn't play games.

"Why are you getting dressed?" she asked as he dried her thighs, the soft hair of her mound, and on down to her calves.

"If I stay around you any longer I'm going to take you, sugar," he all but growled. "Right here and right now."

"Isn't that what we both want?" she whispered.

Only the sound of the bubbling hot tub and a smattering of

chirping crickets were her response. Luke stood, grabbed her bath-robe off the deck chair, helped her slip it on, then tied the sash with a rough tug.

"When I make love to you," he finally said, his voice still rough with desire, "you're gonna be sure it's what you want—and I mean all the way sure." He caught her cheeks in his callused palms and forced her to look at him. "No lingering feelings for some man in England. No rebound issues. No doubts. No fears. No regrets. You're gonna be ready for me. For us. Understand?"

Trinity nodded, unable to speak. Barely able to think.

"I want you to meet me this week for lunch." He brushed her lips with his. "I'll call you."

"Lunch." Trinity had a wild image of herself naked on a restaurant table with a red checkered tablecloth, legs spread wide, with Luke pounding into her until the damned wooden legs of the table snapped underneath them.

She was so far into the fantasy, she wasn't sure she was really speaking out loud. "Sure. That'd be great."

Luke gave her a quick, fierce kiss, then grabbed his boots and T-shirt and strode into the house without looking back.

Chapter 16

"Wayland and his people haven't turned up anything on Gina Garcia yet." Rios slid a folder marked INVOICES down the bar toward Luke as the Watering Hole jukebox kicked up with some old country tune Luke didn't know. "We're coming up empty, too—I say we pass on your suspicions and we turn her and her barn over to Wayland. Local law enforcement'll come closer to getting a warrant than we will."

Luke frowned. He didn't want to get a warrant and beat down the woman's door, or her barn door, but he was beginning to wonder if that wouldn't be the best thing.

He took the folder Rios had given him, then had to fight back a yawn as he opened it. He hadn't been sleeping well, thinking about Trinity, but now wasn't any time to doze on the job.

He'd be seeing her for lunch in a few, the first time he'd actually be with her since the night in the hot tub. He'd force himself to wait and indulge in his fantasies when he was looking into her green eyes.

He and Rios used this ranch hand gathering place to cover their own meetings. During their time off from their ranch cover jobs, they both pretended to be fairly heavy beer drinkers, starting early and finishing late, like the five or six guys already here before lunch.

The bartender knew how to keep his distance, too, and never approached unless they waved him over—which Rios had done twice already. The man's dark face already had a little flush to both cheeks.

Luke ignored the sour sawdust-and-sweat stench of the place and gave his beer a fake swig. At the same time, he looked at the autopsy report on the UDA from Wade Larson's place.

His eyes swept over the incidental findings, major issues, cause of death, and—

"No drugs in his system, no traces on the skin—but a chainsaw cut him up? Shit." Luke closed the folder. "What happened to the vats of lye they used in Douglas?"

Rios downed a third of his beer. "This may be a separate issue. Doc said the guy was already dead—and already dead for a while—when some sick fuck turned on the spinning saw blades. All the shit on the ground around the prints—cow's blood, to make it look like a new kill site." Rios tapped the autopsy report. "This guy, he'd been on ice somewhere. Literally."

Shit.

A turf war. UDAs out of control and surging across the border. Coyotes, mules, and drug lords. Scared women with barn issues. And now a freak-job with a chainsaw cutting up an unknown kid and going to huge pains to dump the body—for what?

Welcome back to the new version of the wild, wild West. Luke shook his head and thought of Tombstone, not fifty miles northwest of here.

"What happened to the good ol' days like in Tombstone, when a man called out his enemy and shot him dead in the street? Or death by hanging. These bastards definitely deserve a public hanging."

Rios snorted back a laugh. "Reminds me of that old Toby Keith song, 'Beer for My Horses'." Rios faked a drunken man swaying on his bar stool and belted out, " 'Take all the rope in Texas, find a tall oak tree . . . ' "

Luke smiled, closed the folder, and passed it back to Rios. The DEA agent dropped pretenses and his dark eyes went serious as Luke asked, "Who was the victim?"

"No idea. No prints in the system, no identification." Rios drained the rest of his beer. "Harder, since we just found the pieces, no clothes."

Luke was very tempted to drink all of his own beer, but decided it wouldn't help him stay alert. "Somebody had Juan Doe in a freezer, pulled him out, cut him up, and staged a kill site on Larson's land."

Rios shrugged. "Or Larson had enough of the UDA traffic across his land, killed him, froze him, waited for a good dump time, and splat." He popped his palm against the bar. The hard smack made a big man at the far end of the bar raise his head.

Luke pretended to drain his own beer, surprised to recognize Bull Fenning. The big rancher had on rumpled, dirty clothes and a thick gray-white stubble that suggested he'd been a few days without a shave. He didn't seem to recognize Luke or Rios, and even if he'd seen them, he couldn't hear them from where he was sitting.

Damned odd, to see him in here, this time of day, looking like that.

Luke gave an almost imperceptible nod to Rios in the direction of Fenning. Rios followed his gaze until his eyebrows lifted a fraction.

"Wouldn't have taken that one for a drunk." He glanced toward Luke, then Fenning again. "Obnoxious, maybe. A little unhinged, but his accounts and ranch upkeep suggest he's taking care of his business."

"Maybe it's a binge thing, or recent." Luke studied Fenning, who had already gone back to nursing his drink, seemingly numb and oblivious to the bar around him. Something in his posture suggested to Luke that Fenning was very familiar with this place, with that seat, and with slumping over a drink before lunchtime. "Could even be some woman dumped him."

Fenning still had his big head down, toying with the edge of his glass. If Fenning spent a lot of time here doing close observation of shot glasses and highballs, who was really minding his store?

As if to answer that question, the door to the bar knocked open, spilling light across the dusty, empty dance floor. Luke recognized Brad Taylor by his height and build, and watched as Bull Fenning's foreman strode over to the old man.

They exchanged a few words, then Fenning got up and walked toward the door with Brad holding his arm to give him some support.

For a time, Luke and Rios just watched the men go, but as the door swung shut, Rios said, "Rumor says he does twins."

Luke glanced at his partner. "So I heard."

He sighed and filed the whole Bull Fenning–Brad Taylor situation in his mind for consideration, then went back to the autopsy report. "About the murder—there were a lot of tracks for it to be just Larson."

"A lot of tracks, from one man, going back and forth." Rios lifted a foot off his bar stool rung and pointed to the boot. "About the right shoe size for Larson, though we need to check that out for sure. Zack Hunter's got himself a computer expert analyzing the print patterns. The expert says it was just one guy, and our people confirmed that. Hunter's expert wants body temp info from the doc. Says maybe we can get a search grid based on how thawed the body was."

Luke pushed his nearly full beer toward Rios as he got up. "Sounds promising. Sick, but promising." He checked his watch. "Think Clay Wayland could find out Larson's shoe size for us?"

"Already called him." Rios took a look at his own watch. "Expect to hear from him in an hour or so. Want me to head out to Gina Garcia's and give winning her over a go?"

Luke shook his head. "She's already suspecting I'm more than a ranch hand. If you show up, too, asking similar questions, she'll be on to both of us. Let Wayland handle it."

Rios's normally friendly, open face tightened a notch, and Luke knew he was thinking about Gary Woods, the deputy who went bad and rustled cattle at Skylar's ranch, not to mention others in the area. "Are we sure about Wayland?"

"Sure as we can be about anybody in Douglas. Catch you this afternoon."

"Hot date?" Rios gave a low whistle behind Luke. "Give her a good one-two for me."

A blinding surge of protectiveness almost made Luke wheel around and punch his best friend and partner, which immediately made him remember the depth and level of shit he had stepped into with respect to one Trinity MacKenna.

Yeah, he had it pretty bad.

And in a few minutes, it was about to get worse.

Chapter 17

Warm, heated air brushed Trinity's cheeks as she sat at a table in the back section of Zappati's, the newest restaurant in Douglas.

Unusual these days for the border town, the place had a certain class to it, with low lighting, even at lunch, and clean, bright tablecloths—with, er, no red checkered pattern. The Mayan décor and motif gave the place a Mexican flavor, but the dining area smelled like fresh baked bread with a hint of spices and fruit, and the establishment served an eclectic menu.

What was a place like this doing in a dirty border town?

Trinity had allowed herself some cheese sticks to munch on while she worked on Zack's footprint analysis on her laptop and waited.

For Luke.

God, I'm really doing this.

She looked up from her computer screen and the folder of photos next to it and almost groaned. She still couldn't believe what had happened that night in the hot tub. Every time she thought about

Luke—naked and doing the things he'd been doing to her—her stomach twisted and her body had an instant reaction. She swore she was walking around with permanently damp panties and her nipples poking through her T-shirt like someone had stuck jelly beans in her bra.

Out of the corner of her eye she spotted a couple of cowboys trooping in for lunch, but she refused to look outright at the door to see if Luke might be there. Of course she knew she really didn't have to *see* him to know whether or not he was near. If he had been, she'd have been able to sense him, to *feel* his presence.

"Work, MacKenna," she told herself, and got lost in the calculations all over again.

It took her some time, but between chewing cheese sticks and mumbling curses at dark digital photographs, she finally managed to superimpose the footprint data over a satellite-generated topographical map of Douglas. For a touch of the bizarre, she added a wavy-looking pirate's X to mark the spot where the body pieces had been found. Now, when she got the temperature and weather information from Zack, she could—

"Señorita. What a pleasure it is to see you again."

Trinity jumped so hard at the smooth, lightly accented voice that she almost knocked her dish with its last half of a cheese stick onto the restaurant's stone floor.

The man standing beside her had on jeans and a white casual shirt with the sleeves rolled up and the collar open. His tanned skin and muscled build accented his dark hair and eyes, and in another place, in some other world, Trinity would have thought he was way past handsome.

As it was, Luke had warned her about this man, then Nevaeh and Skylar and Zack had taken turns doing the same thing.

Drug lord . . .

Bastard . . .

Scary son of Satan . . .

She'd heard enough to be a believer, and she just wanted to close her folder and computer without being too obvious. "Mr. Guerrero." She pushed down the lid of her laptop, hearing the motor rev, then switch off as the machine hibernated. "I remember you from the Christmas party."

"And you, you are unforgettable as well." The man's smile made him look like a heart-stealing movie star, but Trinity saw a hint of wolf in his gaze as his eyes roved over the pictures of footprints she was trying to slide back into the folder. "Forgive me, but do you work in law enforcement?"

Trinity managed a laugh that didn't sound too fake. "Me? No. I'm a software engineer. I work for a gaming manufacturer."

"Computer games." Guerrero didn't sound convinced. "And what does your boyfriend think of your work?"

"My boyfriend." Trinity almost gave an automatic response, that her boyfriend worked in the same field, but then she remembered. No more Race. No more comfortable, easy future with comfortable easy answers.

Next, she almost said she didn't have a boyfriend, but that wasn't true either, was it? Because she was meeting Luke here for lunch, because she intended to sleep with him as soon as humanly possible. More than once. All night long. All week if she could, before DropCaps called her back with moving plans.

Her lust didn't make Luke a boyfriend.

But since he'd touched her, since he'd kissed her—hell, since the first moment he'd *looked* at her, Trinity had felt . . . taken.

Claimed.

"He's—ah, we haven't talked about it that much." She picked up her piece of cheese stick, then laid it back down. "But I'm sure we will soon."

Guerrero's gaze turned more wolfish, and Trinity wished Luke would show up fast. To cover her own rising anxiety, she said, "So, yeah, computer games. That's what I do. Like Grand Theft Auto—oops, sorry. You own a luxury car dealership, right?"

"I do. And if I could be so bold, you would look splendid in our new Jaguar XK-5." Guerrero held up his hands to frame her face. "Black would accent your natural beauty, though silver would work well, too."

Trinity shifted in her seat, uncomfortable with how Guerrero was looking at her cleavage. "Do you come here often?"

"This is my restaurant now." Another meant-to-be-dazzling smile radiated from his angular face. "A recent acquisition. What are you driving, Ms. MacKenna?"

"A Mustang. It's rented—but it's a sweet ride."

Damn, that was stupid. He might not have known—but he could find out pretty easily, I bet.

Trinity had a sense she was in some sort of chess game, and losing. Badly.

"A Jaguar is infinitely faster than a Mustang. Much more powerful." Guerrero flexed one of his well-ripped arms, and his expression turned downright dangerous. "If you ever want to experience true speed, Ms. MacKenna, a thrill you cannot imagine—see me."

Coming from anybody else, Trinity would have found that line laughable, but nothing about Francisco Guerrero seemed humorous to her.

"Let me give you a ride," he said, moving closer to her table. "A ride you will never forget."

"If the lady needs a ride home, I'll be the one to take her."

Luke!

Trinity almost jumped to her feet and threw her arms around Luke's neck.

He was standing behind Guerrero, a quiet mountain made out of muscle, handsome as sin in his dark T-shirt and jeans. He laid his Stetson on the table but kept one hand on the top of the table's empty chair, like he was thinking about smashing it over Guerrero's head.

"Sorry I'm late, sugar." Luke's eyes swept over Trinity, and she heard how his voice vibrated with possessiveness and concern. When she saw the pain and death radiating from Luke's overly calm face, she almost jumped to her feet a second time, this time to throw herself between the two men before Luke did something to Guerrero that might land him in prison.

Guerrero wasn't giving an inch of ground, and his expression didn't look any friendlier than Luke's.

"You're not late, Luke," Trinity babbled, trying to diffuse the tension. "I came early to work on the new gaming program I've been trying to develop." She tapped her nails against her laptop as her pulse raced. "Made good progress, too. Are you thirsty? I could order us some tea."

"Have a seat, Mr. Rider." Guerrero gestured to the chair Luke still seemed to be considering as a weapon. "I trust you'll enjoy something on our menu."

"*Our* menu?" Luke's question came out low, through his teeth.

Trinity tried to catch Luke's eye as blood rushed in her ears. "He bought the restaurant."

Luke's posture stayed hair-trigger tense, but he finally looked away from Guerrero. "I'm not that hungry. Want to get some air, sugar?" He smacked a bill on the table that was more than enough to cover her diet soda and cheese sticks.

"Sure." She got up so fast she jostled her water glass and had to snatch her laptop and the folder full of footprint pictures off the table. She barely got them stuffed in her laptop bag before Luke had her by the elbow, steering her toward Zappati's front door. He took the laptop bag and carried it in his free hand.

"I hope you will come back soon, Ms. MacKenna," Guerrero called after her, but Trinity didn't even turn around to tell him *no thanks*.

When she and Luke hit the sidewalk in front of the restaurant, the cool December air chilled her skin in a wake-up, calm-down sort of way. He gripped her hand and started walking down G Avenue where most of the businesses were. She could barely remember when the town was more alive and not so . . . dirty.

"I warned you about that man." Luke's low, angry voice didn't help Trinity's heart stop hammering, but she had her wits back enough to slow them down and pull free of Luke's grip. "I know your sister did, too."

"I didn't ask him to come snooping around my table." She stopped in front of a store with cheap dresses displayed in the window with circular racks lined up behind the display. "I was working. I didn't even see him standing there staring at what I was doing until it was too late." She rubbed her fingers over her eyes, willing her heart rate to slow back to normal. "Zack's probably gonna be pissed Guerrero got a look at those pictures."

"You mind?" Luke gripped her laptop bag like it wasn't really a question, he was just trying to be polite.

"Uh, sure," Trinity said as she studied Luke.

He reached into her bag, took the folder with the water stains, examined its contents, and frowned. In a too-quiet voice, he asked, "What does this have to do with designing computer games?"

"Patterns. Tracking." Trinity finally got a whole breath and took back the folder, stuffing it into her bag with her laptop. "We make all kinds of games, including mystery and detective scenarios. Space battles, car chases, Old West shootouts—you name it, and I've helped design most of the programs, or supervised their creations."

"And Zack asked you to use your software to analyze footprint patterns." Luke sounded six kinds of pissed off about that, and for a minute, he reminded Trinity of Skylar.

"I volunteered, but I haven't found much his own people couldn't tell him, except—" She broke off, not sure she should be talking about any of this, then deciding for the moment, she really didn't care. "I think the origin of these prints—most of them at least— might be the Bar F."

Luke's blue eyes flicked to the folder in her bag as he started carrying the bag for her again. "Bull Fenning's place."

Trinity heard the skeptical tone and nodded. "Doesn't make sense, I know, if it's UDAs. Not unless they got lost and walked east-west instead of south-north."

She looked up and sucked in another breath, because Luke was studying her so intensely she could feel his stare down to her toes.

"You should tell Hunter all this as soon as you see him. He'll want to look into it." Luke's slow drawl touched her as surely as his hands would, the minute she got him alone. "There's a lot I don't know about you, sugar."

"Likewise." She leaned against the stone wall of the Gadsden Hotel which had been built back in the early nineteen hundreds. She refused to look away from Luke. "How about we start with the basics? I like Mustangs better than Jaguars."

The corners of his mouth twitched. His shoulders relaxed, and some of the rage he'd been carrying since he showed up in Zappati's seemed to leave him. "Do you like your stallions wild?"

God, he was so sexy, she could ride him right here, right now. "I don't know," Trinity murmured. "Never tried to ride one that bucked. Skylar wouldn't let me."

Luke offered her his hand, and they started walking again, this time more slowly, allowing Trinity to enjoy the sun and the cool air.

"Did your sister raise you?" Luke's question came out sounding more normal, like he'd let go of the thought of killing Guerrero, at least for the moment.

"Yeah." Trinity squeezed his fingers. "It was just us."

Luke kept his gaze forward, and Trinity watched his eyes scan the street and everyone approaching them, like he was intent on looking out for her. "I hate that you were so alone. I had a big family—still have a big family. There's comfort in that."

"Big family?" Trinity hadn't expected that from a man who seemed like such a loner. "Where are they?"

Luke hesitated, then seem to make a decision. "Texas. But I had an aunt from around Douglas, so I know Douglas, Bisbee, and Tombstone pretty well from all my visits growing up."

She liked how it felt, walking with him, holding his hand, like they were courting the old-fashioned way, only without the chaperone. "How'd you start working on ranches?"

"I did a lot of that as a kid, too. Good money, and I seemed to have a talent with horses." His expression got a little tense again, but the pressure of his hand on hers never changed.

Trinity had a sense that she wasn't getting Luke's whole story, but then, he wasn't getting all of hers yet, either. That was okay for now.

He stopped them on a corner, and turned her to face him, taking her other hand. His eyes had gone gentle now, and when he looked at her, Trinity thought she could stare into them forever. "Tell me about it. What was it growing up that hurt you so badly?"

Her mouth came open, and her breath caught in her chest. Luke didn't force her to stand there, or push her. He gently pulled her forward, letting go of one of her hands, until they were walking again. Slow and easy, like he planned for them to walk up and down every street in the whole town, if that's what it took.

A few steps later, her fingers laced firmly in Luke's, Trinity found herself spilling out how their mother had passed on from cancer, and their father had walked away from them. She told him about her weight problems, and her torment in school, and all Skylar had done for her, and how badly she'd treated her sister.

"I just left her. I left her with everything." Trinity stopped them at a streetlight, and pictured in her mind the ranchland spreading out, a yellow grass carpet dotted with brown mesquite bushes. Then the Chiricahua Mountains guarding the end of the Flying

M's ranchlands. After a pause she added, "I abandoned Skylar to find myself, but I never stopped feeling guilty about it."

Luke gazed at her without judgment, open, understanding—and ran his thumb along her cheek. "You're back now, Trinity. That counts for a lot."

Her chest got so tight, she didn't know if she was dying or coming back to life again. When she spoke, her voice barely made it to a whisper.

"I can't stay here, Luke. Not even for Skylar."

Not even for you.

His blue eyes clouded, but his touch stayed steady and gentle. "Why not?"

"Because—because I'm scared my past will catch up to me." Trinity turned her cheek into his palm, and he pulled her against his chest and held her, then kissed the top of her head.

"You got skeletons in your closet, sugar? Ones you haven't told me about?"

"Skeletons." Trinity laughed into his T-shirt, drinking in his masculine scent of aftershave and soap, and that faint hint of malt beer. Fresh, and rich. All cowboy. All man. "More like blubber. All those bad memories of being Madeline, being the girl everyone pitied and laughed at."

"That's outside stuff." Luke pulled back from her and rested one hand on her chest. "I know it hurt like hell, but it's got no bearing on what's in here now. Childhood's over. I can promise you, you're all woman now."

The way he said that, the way Luke looked at her, Trinity could almost believe him. Almost.

"I can't stay in Douglas," she said again, maybe to convince herself instead of him.

"You can do anything you set your mind to, sugar. That's one thing about you that's obvious, even if you don't see it yet."

She expected him to keep going, to tell her that he wanted her to stay, or that she should stay, for Skylar, for him—but he didn't. He didn't ask anything of her, but he fought for her in a way Trinity didn't expect.

He kissed her, slow and easy, like they weren't standing in the middle of town, in the middle of the day. Like she was the only woman in Douglas, in the West, in the world, as far as he was concerned.

Damn, he tasted so good, and his arms around her—had she ever felt anything so perfect?

He pulled back from her again, and this time when he looked at her, she saw heat in the depths of his blue eyes that made her catch her breath.

Heat her body instantly answered, getting warm in every possible location.

"Come on." He released her before he caught hold of her fingers again and turned them toward the crosswalk. He pointed to a tiny building at the end of the street. "I know a couple of good hole-in-the-wall restaurants. That one serves the best damned barbecue I've ever had." His sexy drawl deepened as he smiled at her. "Considering I'm from Texas, that's saying a hell of a lot."

"Mmmm." Trinity grinned. "Now that's something they can't serve in Europe like they do here. A good old-fashioned platter of Western barbecue."

She kept a tight hold on Luke's hand, trying not to think too hard about her fantasy of breaking a table while he made love to her.

Oh, what the hell.

She let herself think about it.

Wonder if this barbecue place has checkered tablecloths . . .

Chapter 18

Trinity had hoped her lunch with Luke would end in barn-burning lovemaking, but he'd gotten a call at the end of the meal. He'd taken off to help with some emergency at another ranch where his friend Rios worked. She hadn't seen him the rest of the day, and by the time she was back at the ranch, Skylar and Zack had returned.

Trinity gave Zack what she had on the tracking program and she explained that the prints probably originated from the Bar F. Then she told him Guerrero had come up from behind her and had seen the same information on her computer screen. She also admitted she'd told Luke all about it. Zack had maintained a calm expression and didn't seem pissed, but Skylar did.

Trinity had ducked out of the house for some privacy in the barn before Skylar could chew Zack out for putting Trinity at risk, or doing something that might make her leave again. She couldn't take hearing that, not today, not after the jumble of emotions Luke had stirred on their walk.

When she reached the shadowed interior of the barn, Trinity paused for a moment to allow her eyes to become accustomed to the dark. The old-fashioned alarm bell still hung from its yoke where it always had been, right at the barn's entrance.

That thing would wake the dead, her dad had always said, before he left. It was cast iron and kind of looked like a church bell, only smaller. And much louder, according to her sister.

Maybe if she took the frayed rope and rang it as hard as she could, the clapper slapping against each side of the cast iron, it would bang some clarity into her own mind and heart.

Scents of alfalfa hay and sweet oats washed over her, along with odors of horse and liniment. Every smell was unique and brought back individual memories from all the years she'd grown up here.

When she'd come into the barn yesterday to practice her kickboxing in the storage room, and to see her old mare Dancer, she'd been surrounded by countless memories from her childhood. She'd worked up a good sweat while kickboxing, practicing her kicks, punches, and jabs, enjoying being back at the ranch. That feeling of being home had wrapped around her like a warm blanket, making her feel relaxed and secure, just like her walk in Douglas with Luke.

But England had been home for three years, and somewhere else was about to be home—San Francisco, or maybe Dallas—even New York City. Trinity knew she could go anywhere. She didn't *want* the Flying M to feel so comfortable.

Trinity wandered toward the ranch office that was close to the barn entrance and her thoughts turned to Luke.

Would he come home tonight?

Maybe he was too busy, or maybe he was having second thoughts about pursuing her.

Wow. Just the thought of that man pursuing her never failed to give her a little shiver down the small of her back. Somehow she didn't think he was the type to give up when he'd found something he wanted. And *wow*, he wanted *her.*

Trinity smiled at the Christmas wreath hanging on the door of the barn office as she let herself in. Skylar certainly got into the holiday spirit all over the ranch. The heavy oak door silently closed behind Trinity on well-oiled hinges as she headed to the huge desk.

That desk had been around since the days of the Old West, when her great-great grandpa MacKenna had claimed this stretch of land for the Flying M. The surface of the desk was glossy from years of use and smelled of lemon oil that her sister probably used to keep it in such beautiful condition.

The room was paneled in rich oak, and the leather couch and chair were all in a deep oxblood brown. It was much like it had always been, but she could see Skylar's touch in the gingham curtains at the room's only window, and in the small Christmas tree on the table between the couch and overstuffed chair. Family photos were in here, too, and it touched Trinity to see that her sister had pictures of all of them close to her when she worked.

To the left of the desk were a couple of huge filing cabinets, along with a computer station where Skylar kept all the ranch records and did payroll. Best of all, it had Internet access—but none of her work programs and business stuff crammed onto the desktop.

Playing on this computer would be like reading for pleasure. Fun and no demands.

Before Trinity sat down to check her e-mail, she reached for the bottle of hand lotion perched on one corner of the old oak desk. She squirted a generous amount of the thick stuff onto her hands and rubbed it into her dry skin. The lotion smelled like brown sugar and vanilla, a warm, comforting scent.

After she'd wiped the excess off her fingers with a tissue from a box on the desk, Trinity perched on the swivel chair in front of the computer workstation. Skylar had really brought the ranch a long way into the future. Their dad had never bothered with computers, but after Skylar went to college and came home to take over the ranch, she made some big changes—all for the better.

Trinity downloaded her e-mail and scanned her inbox. She bit her lower lip when she came to an e-mail from Race, sent just hours ago.

Why would he be e-mailing her now? Hadn't they settled everything the last time they spoke?

And why did it seem like years ago that she had dated the man in the first place?

This thing with Luke—it really was consuming her. And making it oh-so-obvious that she never, ever should have settled for a calm, rational man like Race.

She took a deep breath and opened the e-mail from Race and could almost hear his refined British accent in his post:

Dearest Trinity,
I miss you, love. I do respect everything you told me, and all you
said, but I find myself holding out hope that we can speak again. I

*would like the chance to rekindle the flame between us. I can't
fathom Christmas without you. Please, consider my request, and
respond if you see fit.*
R

Trinity stared at the message for a few moments, not really seeing it at all. In place of Race's aristocratic looks, sandy blond hair,
and his warm brown eyes, she saw a dark and dangerous man in a
black Stetson.

*Not meant to be, Race. I'm so sorry. Even if Luke didn't exist, coming
home might have made me figure this out. Somewhere down inside, I'm still
a cowgirl looking for her cowboy.*

Shaking her head, Trinity hit the reply button. She wasn't
ready to talk to Race on the phone again, and she didn't want to
string him along. She responded with a short e-mail, telling Race
he was a wonderful man, but she didn't believe it was possible to
rekindle anything. She wished him the best, and urged him to go
to his sister's down in Kent for the holidays, so he wouldn't be
alone.

She hit Send and hoped the message reached Race, even though
she figured it wouldn't make him feel any better. Then she ran
through the rest of her messages. All work-related e-mails she ignored, since she was on vacation, and just read the personal notes.
She was pleased to see one from Chloë Somerville, who sounded
positive despite the rough divorce she was going through. If anyone
deserved a good man, it was that girl.

Come to Arizona, she urged Chloë in her response. *You're a
reporter—you can report from anywhere! Stay with my sister for a while.
It's peaceful here, and different, and you could use a brand new start.*

Whenever I get settled where I'm going, you can come there next. Let go of the past, honey. Move on, like I'm doing.

She pressed Send on that one, and Luke's voice came back to her, telling her she could do anything she set her mind to.

God, was I just a hypocrite, telling her to let go of the past? Trinity's fingers hovered over the keyboard.

She *thought* that's what she had done, leaving Douglas, and staying away.

But if she had, then why was it so terrifying, being here, and even remotely considering staying for a while?

Trinity tried to shake off her doubts, and moved on to her friend Carly's note. She read it, and had to laugh out loud. Her next-door neighbor in London was a hoot, and she kept trying to get Trinity to read erotic romance books, In particular Anna Windsor's. Trinity hadn't had a chance to pick one out yet, but she'd just have to break down and do it. Especially after what she'd experienced with Luke.

Trinity closed her eyes for a moment, trying to block out those images, but it only made them stronger. Her fingers moved to her ear out of habit, and she played with her earrings as she visualized Luke and the night at the hot tub. She could almost smell his spicy aftershave, his unique masculine scent and could almost feel the heat of his body close to hers—

The door slammed shut behind Trinity, shattering her fantasy.

Her eyelids popped open and she swiveled on the seat and saw that it was her sister. The disappointment she felt that it wasn't Luke caught her off guard.

"No fair sneaking up on me like that," Trinity said.

With a mischievous grin, Skylar plopped down onto the overstuffed leather couch, and tossed a bundle of mail onto the cushion beside her. "Ran into Rylie at the Safeway grocery store in town. We figured a game of cards might be fun this Saturday night. Poker. You up for it?"

"Sure." Trinity tried to muster up some enthusiasm. At least it would get her mind off of Luke for a while.

Skylar glanced at the computer. "Checking in with your boyfriend?"

With a shrug, Trinity said, "Yeah. But, no. I sort of, um, broke up with Race."

Cocking her head to one side, Skylar said, "You . . . what?"

"I couldn't do it, Skylar. I couldn't let that relationship continue. Something was missing."

Please don't ask me if this means I'm staying.

But Skylar didn't go there. Her expression got distant for a few moments, and then she nodded. "It was like that for me, before Zack came back. I kept searching for something, but nothing satisfied me."

"You were meant to be with Zack, Skylar. Everyone's always known that." She leaned forward and propped her elbows beside the keyboard, staring at her sister. "My fate's a little less certain."

Skylar shook her head, not looking the least bit uncertain. "Somewhere out in the world, there's a man meant to steal your heart away, Trinity. A man who satisfies you so completely you couldn't imagine asking for anything more. I'm sure of it."

Yeah, me, too. Trinity sat back. *I'm just damned afraid he's right here on the ranch, near the town I never wanted to return to, and he wears a black Stetson.*

"Something wrong?" Skylar now had a worried expression. "You turned pale on me all of a sudden."

Trinity forced a smile and shook her head. "Just a little sad, I guess. Race wrote me and I had to sort of break up with him a second time."

"Why don't you get some rest?" Skylar scooped up the pile of mail and started flipping through the pieces as she spoke. "I don't need any help with the chores, and Zack's been killing you with all that computer mess when you're supposed to be on vacation. Besides, you already mucked out Satan's and Dancer's stalls, not to mention cleaning out the back storage room."

"Hey, Zack set up that punching bag for me there, so it was the least I could do." Trinity smiled. "And besides, it was kinda nice to do those things again."

The corner of Skylar's mouth quirked. "Then by all means . . ." Her voice trailed off and her expression looked puzzled as she held up a postcard. She flipped it over, and then her face turned the same shade of white as a new moon. Her fingers crept to her throat in that all-too-familiar movement that told Trinity her sister was upset about something.

"What's the matter?" Trinity said, even as she moved from her chair to slide onto the couch beside her sister.

"I'll have to tell Zack." Skylar shook her head, her lips pursed. "This is a bunch of bullshit."

Trinity reached for the card and Skylar let it slip from her fingers. As Trinity looked over the note, her sister got up and started pacing the floor.

On one side was a weird design of letters within letters. A capital B in red was a kind of border, and then a capital I in green was a little smaller in the middle, and then a T in blue a tad smaller than that. And to the left side of the T was a yellow C and to the right was an orange H . . .

BITCH.

Trinity's skin chilled, goose bumps pebbling her skin as she turned the card over.

In a messy black scrawl was written:

It's not over, you double-crossing whore.

"Shit," Skylar muttered, snapping Trinity's attention from the card and to her sister, who was still pacing the floor. "Woods. I bet it's Woods."

"Who?" Trinity tossed the card onto the couch like it was contaminated. "And why would he send something like this?"

Skylar stopped pacing and explained to Trinity how the former deputy sheriff had been caught red-handed stealing cattle from her ranch, and Wade Larson's, and other ranches, too. Then she explained how he'd been fixated on her, and almost taken her out.

"But if he's in jail, who sent you that piece of garbage?" Trinity pointed to the postcard.

Skylar shook her head. "My gut says Woods did it from behind bars. He probably paid somebody who was being released, or smuggled it out with some other prisoner's family or friends."

Trinity thought about the footprints in the photos she'd been working with, and the blood, and the pieces of dead body Zack and his law enforcement friends had been investigating.

"Maybe Woods still has friends on the outside. People Zack and the others didn't know about." Then she thought about Francisco Guerrero, and her stomach did a big flip. "Or maybe they do know about the bad guys, but they haven't been able to stop them. Yet."

"Whatever." Skylar glared at the postcard. "I'll give it to Zack, and then I'm not going to worry about it."

"Sky—"

"*You* don't worry about it." Skylar cut Trinity off, still shaking her head. "I mean it. Zack will handle this."

But Trinity could see the truth in Skylar's eyes.

Her sister had suffered a lot during the cattle rustling. She'd been scared then, and she was scared again now.

Skylar really does need me, Trinity realized with a start and a flood of dread—then the strangest sense of power and relief. *She needs her family around her for lots of reasons.*

"Come here." Trinity reached for Skylar, and pulled her sister into a fierce hug.

"You're supposed to be on vacation," Skylar whispered into her neck, and then she started to cry.

Trinity held on to her sister, not feeling like a little girl, or the baby of the family, not now. Not anymore. "I'm supposed to be right here, Skylar. This time, you don't have to do it alone."

Chapter 19

Luke stared into the muzzle of the shotgun and didn't twitch an eyebrow. Twitching anything would be a bad idea, right about now. He kept both hands raised, and his eyes straight ahead on the man who'd gotten the drop on him.

Brad Taylor stood in the front doorway of Bull Fenning's big stone ranch house with the shotgun leveled at Luke's nose. "I'm not asking you again, Rider. Why the hell have you been sniffing around my sister?"

Luke knew Taylor didn't have a clue he'd drawn a weapon on a DEA agent, and right now, he didn't think the man would give a shit. Taylor's short brown hair stuck up in sweaty spikes, and his brown eyes had the look of a grizzly protecting his territory.

But this sister thing—gun or no gun, Luke didn't know what to say to him other than, "Trinity's Skylar's sister, not yours."

"Trinity? What the hell are you talking about?" Taylor's gaze narrowed.

"That's who I'm—ah, sniffing around." Luke spoke slowly. Carefully. Making sure his lips and chin didn't move enough to touch the shotgun barrel. "Your words, not mine."

"Skylar MacKenna's sister?" Taylor sounded surprised on top of being a horseshoe toss away from crazy. "The one who just came home from England."

Luke kept his gaze on Taylor's trigger finger. "That's her."

The shotgun barrel moved back a fraction—not a lot, but enough that Luke could glance around and take in the big house's stone floor and wood paneling. The place smelled faintly of alcohol and cherry tobacco.

"You scared Gina shitless, showing up at her place a few days back." Brad's tone stayed hard.

"Gina Garcia." It was Luke's turn to sound surprised.

Brad frowned, but he finally lowered the damn shotgun. Luke allowed himself a complete breath of air, which he hadn't enjoyed since he knocked on the massive wooden door and Brad answered it with his say-hello-to-my-double-barreled-friend routine.

After lunch with Trinity, Luke had gotten the call from Rios. Apparently Taylor had an emergency at the Fenning ranch, and had asked for help, specifically from Luke. He'd thought that Taylor must have made him. Or maybe Bull Fenning's operation was in deep shit and Taylor actually needed another ranch foreman with some know-how.

He never figured on knocking on Fenning's door, and getting greeted by a gun in his face.

Taylor leaned the shotgun against the paneled wall beside the door. "Shit, Rider. You might as well come in for a minute."

"Yeah." Luke got to lower his arms and rub his elbows for a second. "Why don't I do that."

He took off his Stetson and followed Brad inside, trying to add up and sort out everything he'd just heard, but he couldn't make sense of it just yet.

Fenning's place was as big inside as it was out—high ceilings, wide, cavernous rooms, and big, heavy furniture. Paintings hung on every wall of women and children, and Luke realized that at one time, Fenning must have had a wife and kids in the home. By the look of it, he still had a boatload of grandkids in the mix.

"She's dead now." Brad nodded toward a massive oil painting of a robust woman with bright brown eyes. It was hanging over an equally massive mantelpiece, as if surveying the entire room. "Mrs. Fenning. Nice woman, from what I've heard. Now, tell me, what were you doing at Gina's?"

"Checking on her." Luke seated himself on the thick leather arm of one of Fenning's couches. "She seemed like she had a hard time at the Christmas party."

Taylor took a seat on the stone hearth of the fireplace, and kept his gaze on Luke's face. "You asked her about Guerrero, though."

Luke's fist clenched before he could get a handle on himself. "Guerrero's a bastard. Friend of mine told me he's been scaring women in Douglas, and I was afraid he'd come on to Gina—to your sister. That she might need a little help."

This seemed to appease Taylor a bit, but his tone stayed wary. "What she needs is to be left alone." He shook his head and stared at the stone floor. No dust, no dirt, no lint. Luke wondered if Taylor kept the place this clean, or if he hired help for Fenning. "If we'd known about Guerrero and all this drug bullshit, we never would have moved here."

Luke shifted on the couch arm. "Do I get to ask where you came from?"

Taylor opened his hands, as if to say *fair enough*. "I worked on a ranch in Colorado before I came here."

The man didn't say a word about Gina, and the way the afternoon light showed the tight line of his jaw, Luke figured he didn't intend to say anything, either. Fine. He wasn't about to push it, for now.

He wondered where Fenning was, then figured the old man was probably passed out, tucked into his room by Brad Taylor, who obviously had a history of taking care of people who needed him.

"So, Gina's had it rough." Luke didn't intend to pry. He hoped Taylor could understand that he just meant to be helpful to the woman. "I knew something was wrong. I just couldn't put my finger on what it was."

Taylor stayed way too tense, but Luke could tell the man was working to control himself. "My sister's known her share of bad guys. Let's leave it at that."

Luke shifted his grip on his Stetson. "Understood."

Taylor made eye contact with him again—no shotgun this time, but no less serious, either. "Don't ask her any more questions, Rider."

"Not a problem." Luke gave Taylor a long look. "But I do have a question for you."

"Guess I owe you an answer." Taylor's nod was slight as he spoke. "As long as it doesn't cause trouble for Gina."

Luke fiddled with his hat on purpose, keeping his gaze away from Taylor to make his inquiry as casual as he could. "The day I came to Gina's house, were you by any chance in the barn?"

"Yeah. When I'm not looking after stuff for Mr. Fenning, I have an apartment there." Taylor shrugged. "I fix things up for Gina, mend the fences and maintain her appliances—and make sure she and my niece are safe."

"Good." Luke thought about Lola on her tire swing. "I'm glad the little girl has an uncle on her side."

This seemed to put Taylor more at ease. "I try. She's a great kid."

Luke didn't ask about Lola's father, making a money bet to himself that Lola's dad might be who Gina was running from. "How's Fenning?"

Taylor's frown deepened, and now he looked tired on top of worried. "Rough."

Luke glanced around the huge living room again, at all the stone and wood and paintings and happy grandchildren—hints of how hard Fenning had worked in his life. "I didn't know he had a problem with drinking. Couldn't tell by the looks of this place."

"He'd been sober for years." Taylor glanced up at the portrait of the stately woman over the fireplace. "Cleaned up for her, and kept clean, but he fell off the wagon last month, around the anniversary of Mrs. Fenning's death."

Taylor glanced toward a room with a set of closed double doors. Fenning's study? "I'm hoping he'll get it out of his system soon," Taylor continued, "and I'm taking him to an AA meeting tomorrow night, if he's not passed out."

"Hope it does some good." Luke stood, intending to see himself out and get back to Trinity—after he made a phone call to Rios, and checked in with Ralston and Wayland.

Taylor got to his feet, too, and now the man looked bothered. A little guilty. "Rider, about the gun—"

"Forgotten." Luke waved him off. "Look after your sister and your niece—and good luck with Fenning."

The sound of tires on gravel made both of them look out one of the big front windows.

A silver Jag, an older XJ model, pulled to a hard stop at the edge of the paved driveway, spraying a cloud of rocks and dust as the tires popped off the side of the pavement.

What the hell?

Luke's pulse kicked up a notch, and he made a mental check. Phone in his left duster pocket. Glock in the holster behind his right hip.

Jags weren't common in this part of the country. This was truck- and SUV-navigated ranchlands. Was this Guerrero? One of his stooge-assholes?

But Taylor was hanging his head, looking like a dog that had been kicked real hard.

No man could make the guy look like that.

Nope.

Whoever was in that Jag—definitely female.

The minute the door opened, Luke saw an almost pained look of embarrassment claim Brad Taylor's face, and he understood. He didn't even have to see the long legs, the big chest, or the gray eyes as the pretty—but compared to Taylor, much older—brunette got out.

Couldn't be any doubt about who'd come calling.

"Joyce is a friend," Taylor said, a little too quickly. "With . . . benefits. As long as I keep her happy, she helps me keep Fenning's ranch running and in good shape. She's been out of town for a day or two, and—"

"You don't have to explain." Luke had already located the nearest back door. "I parked by the barn, so I don't think she saw my truck. I'll let myself out."

"Thanks." Taylor was already heading toward the front door to meet his *friend.*

Luke got out as best he could, and made his way to his truck, feeling like he needed more than a computer program to keep track of all of Douglas's secrets.

"Rios," he said into his phone a few minutes later, as he sped down the road toward the Flying M. "Find out who Brad Taylor really is, and follow up on his sister. It's Gina."

He waited for Rios to get over being surprised and get the info written down. "I think we need more eyes and radar on Joyce Butler's place. I know she's Ralston's childhood buddy, but something about that woman's just . . . not right. If he won't go for it, get our field office on it."

Without bringing attention to himself, Luke hitched one hip against the door frame of the MacKenna kitchen and folded his arms across his chest as he watched Trinity and Skylar prepare a taco dinner.

Zack Hunter came up beside him and stood, speaking so low only Luke could hear him. "I've sent the postcard that Sky received to check for prints, but you know we probably won't get much that's useful."

Luke knew a lot of people had handled that postcard, no doubt, since it got mailed from some little town upstate, nowhere near where Gary Woods and his rustling buddies were being held while they waited for their trials.

"Sky was pretty upset when they came in from the barn," Zack said. "Let's keep things light."

Luke nodded, and Zack headed to his office in another part of the sprawling ranch home.

One shotgun in his face—yeah, that was enough for any evening. Light, low-key, all of that was fine by Luke. Besides, he had to be very careful, since Skylar and Zack knew about his cover and real background, but Trinity didn't. He needed to tell her soon, but it wasn't that easy, or even that advisable, letting the information out at this point in the operation. One false move by anybody, with Guerrero already so damned suspicious, and he could find himself useless in the field, and Rios, too.

Still, after Guerrero's little stunt at the restaurant, and now the damned postcard, Luke didn't want Trinity too far out of his line of sight. Especially now that he knew Zack—damn him—had involved her in part of the investigation.

That night in the hot tub—Christ. He knew Trinity needed time to get her thoughts together, to get past her breakup and understand what she did and didn't want in her life, but he'd given her about all the time he could stand.

He could still taste her, from the flavor of her kisses and the juices between her thighs. Damn but she was sweet. His cock grew tight against his jeans and he shifted slightly, hoping nobody would notice he had a major hard-on.

Grease popped and crackled on the stovetop as Skylar dipped a corn tortilla into the hot liquid to make a taco shell. Warm aromas of seasoned meat, Mexican rice, and refried beans made Luke's stomach growl.

Neither of the women had noticed him yet, and it gave Luke a few more moments to study Trinity as she diced a tomato on a wooden cutting board. Wisps of strawberry blond hair fell into her eyes, shielding him from her vision, as she slid the knife into the tomato.

Luke itched to brush the strands behind her ear, to follow his fingers with his tongue and lick a trail down the row of gold earrings along her lobe. And then he'd bite her just below her lowest earring, a soft nip that would make her moan for more.

"Hey there, Luke." At the sound of Skylar's voice, Trinity's head shot up and her cheeks blushed a nice shade of rose as her eyes met his.

"Are you able to join us for dinner tonight, or are you going into town for some Friday-night action?" Skylar asked.

"Depends." Luke gave Trinity a slow smile. "If Trinity here is up for dancing, we could head on over to Sierra Vista."

Trinity's eyes widened and she blushed a richer red. "I, uh, can't. Dance, I mean."

"Guess I'll just stay for dinner then." Luke winked then turned his attention to Skylar. "Need a hand?"

"You're not flirting with my little sister, are you?" Skylar cocked an eyebrow, the corner of her mouth quirking into a smile.

Luke gave a slow nod as his gaze moved back to Trinity. "I am. I'm doing exactly that."

Skylar laughed and gestured with the tortilla she was holding. "You could cut up the onions for Trinity. She hates them."

At the mention of onions, Trinity's freckled nose crinkled and she pointed the knife she was holding at a bunch of green onions on the granite countertop. "Have at it, big guy."

"Sure thing." Luke ambled over to the sink and washed his hands. Trinity kept her attention focused on the tomato, dicing it into the smallest bits he'd ever seen. "You aiming to turn that into sauce?"

Trinity's cheeks burned as she stopped in midchop and stared down at the desecrated tomatoes. "I, uh, like them that way." She lifted the cutting board and scraped the tomato goop into a bowl with the knife.

Darned if she was going to tell Luke that she'd been daydreaming about him the whole time she was dicing the tomato. He was all she'd been thinking about, every minute, and it was going to drive her crazy.

"How would you like to join us for dinner first of the week, too, Luke?" Skylar asked from behind them. "Rylie's coming with her brother Levi, and we're playing poker afterward. You'd make it an even six."

Trinity cut her gaze to meet Luke's and he grinned. "Strip poker?" he said with a teasing glint in his eyes and Skylar laughed. "Count me in."

"Just be prepared to ante up, cowboy." Skylar banged the frying pan against a burner as she moved it off the heat. "And keep your clothes on."

Luke chuckled and gave Trinity a look that said he could see right through her blouse. Her body ached so badly for him she could hardly stand it.

"I'm finished with the taco shells," Skylar said, and Trinity glanced over her shoulder to see her sister shut off the stovetop burner. "I'll let Zack know dinner's about ready," Skylar added. "Back in a sec."

The moment she left the kitchen, Luke moved close to Trinity, his jean-clad thighs brushing against her as he murmured, "How was your afternoon?"

Luke's spicy aftershave flowed over Trinity, bringing back memories of the Christmas party and of the hot tub, and the way he held her today when he talked to her on their walk.

How was she supposed to concentrate on his words?

She looked away from Luke and slipped the vegetable knife into the dishwasher, barely able to think with him so close. "Ah . . . fine," she said as she shut the dishwasher door. "But I enjoyed my lunch a lot more."

He caught her chin in his hand, forcing her to look at him. His touch caused her skin to tingle and her nipples to peak beneath her blouse.

"You're beautiful," he said, his blue eyes intent. "And you know how much I want you."

"I . . . um . . ." Trinity could scarcely breathe the way Luke was looking at her. "Want . . ."

Yeah. That's what she was doing.

Wanting.

It was all she could do.

His smile was tight. "You think you're about over breaking up with what's-his-name?"

"Race," Trinity muttered, vaguely remembering her ex-boyfriend's e-mail. "Nothing to get over, really. It wasn't that kind of relationship."

Damn, she wanted to slide her fingers into the thick brown hair beneath his cowboy hat. She wanted to see his incredible body again, touch him and taste him . . . and finally, finally feel him inside her.

Cripes but she had it bad.

Lust. A serious case of cowboy lust.

Luke's smile turned sensual as he ran his thumb along her lower lip. "I can read those pretty green eyes, sugar. We're right for one another, but you're not feeling sure about that yet, are you?"

"You don't know what I'm thinking," she whispered. "And you don't know we're right for each other."

"It's the truth." Luke lowered his head, bringing his mouth inches above hers. "You're flat out too scared to admit it."

Trinity pressed her palms against his chest and almost groaned out loud. She could feel the play of his powerful muscles beneath his shirt.

"I—I barely know you," she finally said.

"Sugar, we already know each other better than some folks who've been together for years."

She shook her head. "We only met a few days ago."

"Doesn't matter." He brought his face closer and filled all her senses with his presence. She felt as though she was drowning, losing herself in this virile man, and *wanting* to lose herself in him. "Somehow, I'll give you another day—or two, if that's what you need to be sure."

"I want you now, Luke. I want you tonight."

His lips touched hers, then pulled back, sending shivers of pleasure across every inch of her skin.

"Not yet." His blue eyes pinned her where she stood. "Because

I already know this much—when I take you, I won't be letting you go."

The sound of Skylar's and Zack's voices snapped Trinity out of her Luke-induced trance. Pulling free of his grip, she grabbed the bowl of mutilated tomatoes and dodged to the other side of the kitchen just as her sister and brother-in-law entered the room.

Luke's soft laugh punctuated the pounding of her heart and she didn't know whether to fling the whole bowl of diced tomatoes at him, or throw herself into his arms.

Chapter 20

On Tuesday night, exactly eight days from when she first met the man, Luke moved beside Trinity as she dug out the playing cards from the china cabinet drawer. She shivered from his nearness. The light cotton dress she was wearing suddenly felt too thin, made her feel too vulnerable, like she was wearing nothing around him.

All evening during last Friday night's dinner, and then again tonight, Luke had taken every opportunity to brush against her, to touch her when no one was looking.

When I take you, I won't be letting you go . . .

Cripes, the cowboy didn't play fair. Not at all.

"What are we playing?" Rylie asked from behind Trinity as she finally located the cards, and Trinity almost dropped the whole damned deck.

"How about five card stud?" Luke said, the warmth of his breath caressing her ear.

Levi slipped past Trinity and Luke as Rylie tossed the deck onto the dinner table. "Sounds as good as any," Levi said.

Zack had removed the two middle table leaves a few minutes earlier, so that the table was much smaller and cozier for playing poker. Now instead of a long oblong table, it was almost circular.

Rylie's blond hair bounced against her shoulders as she punched her brother in the shoulder and she laughed when he grabbed his arm. The man's hair was as blond as his sister's, and almost as curly. "You ready for me to kick your ass, Deputy Levi Thorn?"

"Now this I gotta see." Zack pulled a chair up to the table, his gray eyes glinting with humor as he grabbed the deck of cards. "I always said local law enforcement was nothing but a bunch of—ah—" He cleared his throat and grinned at Skylar. "A bunch of bad card players."

"Watch it, Hunter." Rylie gave Zack a mock glare then kissed her brother on the cheek before slipping into the chair next to Levi.

Skylar carried in a tray from the kitchen, filled with bowls of pretzels, bottles of beer and wine, along with wineglasses. Blue followed at Skylar's heels, and then settled himself under her chair, his head on his paws.

Trinity helped her sister, and after everything was distributed, Trinity took her seat next to Luke, who was dealing out stacks of red, white, and blue poker chips. When she eased into her chair, he paused and gave her that dark, sexy look that made her ache. She had no idea how she was going to make it through this night without having him.

I won't be letting you go . . .

Damn, damn, damn, damn.

She wanted sex.

The handsome, sexy guy was the one who wanted something more serious.

In what world was *that* friggin' fair?

Trinity had already decided to stick around long enough to help Skylar—and DropCaps wasn't even expecting her to get going at full speed until after the holidays. They were shipping her gear to her, along with a brand-spanking-new high bandwidth satellite dish to stick in Skylar's back flower bed. With that puppy, she'd be able to send DropCaps files the size of Montana in about three seconds—so, really, she could work at the ranch as long as she needed to.

That meant she could enjoy a few rolls in the hay with Luke.

But it's not fair. I won't be staying forever . . . Besides, I'm afraid that I could lose my heart to this cowboy.

She'd never done casual sex or one-night stands. No. She couldn't have sex with Luke knowing that the relationship definitely wouldn't go any further.

Right?

Shee-yeah.

She was ready for all out heavy, wild, screaming sex with the man.

Trinity sighed and took a long sip of her Zinfandel, letting the liquid slide down her throat until it warmed her belly. She could feel Luke's eyes on her, but she refused to look at him. Every time those blue eyes met hers, she forgot all the reasons why it wouldn't work out in the long run.

Zack finished shuffling the deck. "Deuces are wild," he said as he dealt each player five cards, the first two facedown and the other three faceup.

Rylie and Skylar chatted about the new shooting range that had been opened up several miles west of Douglas, while Trinity, Levi, and Luke watched Zack deal the cards. It still seemed so odd that Zack was her brother-in-law now.

It was even stranger to realize how comfortable she felt with the six of them having dinner together, and playing cards.

Friends.

And family.

She could get used to this.

No surprises.

No mysteries.

But with Luke . . . well, yeah, there was lots of mystery in the man, but she knew exactly where she stood with him. He wanted her.

And damn but she wanted him.

It's time, Trinity.

She could barely look at her own hand, for looking at him instead.

It's time to tell him you're pretty sure you're ready.

It's time to be ready.

But was she?

"You heading home for Christmas, Luke?" Skylar asked as she looked over her cards. "Hey, no peeking," she added to Zack with a frown as he leaned back in his chair as though he might glance at her cards.

Luke gave a noncommittal shrug as he discarded one card and drew another. He was deep enough undercover that if a search was done on him, it would come up that he was born and raised in an obscure town in Texas, and had studied agribusiness at Auburn University.

Truth of the matter was he'd lived on a ranch outside Houston his entire life before heading off to the University of Texas to earn his bachelor's in Criminal Justice and then going into the academy.

He wondered what Trinity would think once she learned that he wasn't who she thought he was. Well, he'd just have to cross that cattle guard when he came to it.

"You don't have anyplace to go for Christmas?" Trinity asked after she tossed a card onto the discard pile. Her green eyes were wide, as though she felt concerned that he'd be alone over the holidays.

He smiled as his gaze met hers. Wouldn't hurt to tell a bit of the truth. "If I don't show up Christmas Day for some of my mama's roasted turkey, cornbread stuffing, and her special pecan pie, she'll never forgive me."

"And I'll bet you'd never disappoint her," Trinity said softly, looked to the cards in her hand. "You have a big family—I remember you telling me that. How many brothers and sisters?"

"Two of each." He grinned at the thought of them. "And between all of them, damn near a dozen nieces and nephews. Miss them like hell."

Her eyebrows raised in surprise. "I can't imagine what that's like." She gestured toward her sister with one of her cards. "For so long it's just been the two of us, except for Zack horning in now and again."

"Hey," Zack grumbled. "I don't horn."

Rylie snickered, and Zack acted like he was about throw his cards at her.

"Not talking about horns. TMI." Skylar nodded to Luke. "It's your turn, Rider."

He studied his cards. Two pair, not too bad. "I'll hold."

"Come on, Texas." Trinity's eyes played off his face. "I already know you're bluffing."

He raised an eyebrow. "Why do you say that?"

"Your drawl." Her eyes focused on Luke. "It gets worse when you're holding back on something."

Well, shit.

"Is something going on between you two that we ought to know about?" Rylie interrupted in her usual direct manner. "It's your play, Trinity."

Luke smiled as Trinity's cheeks flushed again and she studied her cards.

"I'll hold. I think." She frowned and looked at them again. "Yes, I'll hold."

Before Trinity had the chance to bug Luke about bluffing again, Luke asked Zack something about Satan, that spoiled-rotten bull of Skylar's.

As the night progressed, and more beer and wine had been consumed, the whole evening took on a surreal feel to Trinity. No one seemed to notice the times that Luke would deliberately brush her breast with his hand, or lean close to whisper in her ear.

Then Luke slipped one hand under the table and caressed her thigh.

She froze, her gaze locked on her cards. Afraid to move and afraid to make a sound, like someone at the table might notice that Luke's hand was creeping up the inside of her thigh under her dress. Even though everyone seemed wrapped up in the poker game, or tipsy from the alcohol, how could they not notice that Luke only had one hand on the tabletop?

Yet she couldn't get herself to make him stop.

While play continued, the chatter around the table was nothing more than a loud buzzing noise to Trinity's ears. She stared at her cards, not seeing them at all as Luke's finger reached the center of her panties. If anyone had asked her at that moment what she had in her hand, she wouldn't have been able to name the cards. No matter that she was staring right at them.

Luke slid his fingers inside the elastic, and touched the soft curls underneath.

She almost closed her eyes. Oh, jeez. She had to make him stop.

Mindlessly she tried to play the poker game as his finger entered her wetness and stroked. If it wasn't for Luke whispering suggestions throughout each hand, she would have lost everything within moments.

She could smell his flesh, could smell her own arousal. Could everyone else smell it, too?

The sensations in her abdomen grew stronger and tighter, and she knew she was close to climax. "You can't scream," Luke whispered in her ear. "You're gonna have to hold it in, sugar."

Trinity bit down hard on her lower lip as the orgasm took hold of her body and shook it like a mesquite tree in a summer storm. She braced her hand on her forehead and looked down, shielding her face from everyone at the table as her body trembled, and Luke's finger drew the climax out even longer.

"You all right, Trinity?" Skylar asked through Trinity's alcohol and orgasm haze.

Luke slipped his hand out of Trinity's panties and she fought to control her breathing, to let her heart rate slow to a normal pace.

"Too much wine," Trinity mumbled and rubbed her temples with her thumb and forefinger. "I think I'm done for."

Luke chuckled and murmured so that only she could hear, "Like I've already told you, sugar, we haven't even started yet. You just let me know when you're ready."

Trinity tossed and turned in her bed, slipping in and out of a misty dream world.

The poker game went on and on, like it was never going to end.

And then she was on her back on the table, her dress hiked up around her waist and Luke sliding deep inside her.

Everyone continued playing around them, tossing their now rainbow-colored poker chips onto Trinity's bare belly. Even as Luke took her, she realized the poker chips on her belly were actually condoms. Lots and lots of condoms across her stomach and scattered across the table, but Luke hadn't put one on.

He kept driving into her, the game around them never stopping. Skylar and Rylie repeated something that sounded like poison, poison, while Zack and Levi responded with fire, fire.

All Trinity knew was that she needed to come so bad she couldn't stand it. But the tension in her abdomen only intensified until she thought she'd lose her mind . . .

And then she was alone.

Utterly and completely alone. Standing somewhere dark and cold, like a cave, and she was entirely naked.

Where was Luke? Without him she felt incomplete, lonely even.

Trinity didn't know what had happened, or where she was, but something in her gut suddenly told her that Skylar was in danger.

She had to find her sister. Had to help her.

And then Trinity was out in the open. She ran across the dream desert . . . she dodged through tumbleweeds and mesquite bushes, hurrying toward the barn. Yes, that was it. She had to get to the barn. She had to hurry—

Trinity's eyes flew open and she stared up at the white canopy above her bed. Her heart raced like she'd really been running and she couldn't catch her breath.

Her limbs trembled as she sat up in bed and braced her back against the headboard with her arms on her knees. That horrible feeling that something was wrong wouldn't go away. She'd never been superstitious. Never been one to believe in dreams or intuition, but she couldn't shake the feeling that she should get up and go check on things. Why, she didn't know, but she just had to do it.

A sense of urgency took over. She hurried out of bed, pulled her nightgown over her head and tossed it onto a chair. After she yanked on her sweatpants and an oversized T-shirt, she stuffed her feet into her Nikes. She grabbed her jacket as she headed down the hall and toward the front door.

Someone had left on the Christmas lights, and they helped her make her way without stumbling. Blue stirred in the kitchen and Trinity heard the dog's nails click against the tile as he followed her into the living room.

"You sense it too, don't you, boy?" Trinity murmured as she neared the window.

Blue's ears pricked forward as he jumped up and rested his front paws on the windowsill and looked out into the night with Trinity.

Everything was still. Nothing moved.

And then Blue growled.

Trinity was about to look at him when she thought she saw a flicker at the far end of the barn, where the storage room was, and her skin chilled. There it was. Stronger now. Like a flashlight . . . but different.

Her heart pounded and she started to yell for Zack and Skylar, that there was an intruder, when she realized what the flicker was. *Fire.*

Blue growled and then barked, loud and sharp, and Trinity shouted at the top of her lungs, "Fire in the barn! Fire in the barn!"

She ran toward their bedroom door, still yelling, but as she reached it Zack came crashing out, pulling on his boots, his pants undone and shirtless.

"Fire in the barn," Trinity repeated frantically. She turned and ran for the front door, yanking it open and barreling into the night, screaming, "Fire! Fire!"

Blue barked at her heels and Trinity didn't stop yelling as she ran toward the barn. So many animals. She had to help get them out!

The acrid odor of smoke met her as she neared the barn. She coughed and choked as she tried to shout some more. The bell! Trinity dove for the ancient bell and grabbed the rope hanging down from it and pulled.

It started clanging, loud and clear in the night. Above the noise she could already hear the shouts of men and saw them running toward the barn.

Smoke poured from the barn and the horses screamed their fright from inside. She'd seen the fire at the opposite end of the barn, and so far no flames from the barn door.

Trinity released the bell's rope and dived for the lights, flooding the barn with a yellow glow that blinded her for a second. She yanked off her jacket and tied the arms around her head so that her nose and mouth were covered, but she could still see. Dodging inside the barn, she ran toward Dancer's stall.

Men shouted behind her, and Trinity thought she heard someone calling her name, but she didn't care about anything except getting those animals out.

Smoke burned her eyes as she reached Dancer. The mare was wild-eyed and frantically pawing at the stall door. Trinity climbed up the side of the gate, took the jacket from her face, and covered Dancer's eyes with it before releasing the bolt lock, speaking to the mare in low, steady tones and calming her down.

As she led Dancer out of the barn, the smell of smoke nearly overwhelmed her. She heard shouts, saw men rushing back and forth, and knew they were fighting the fire. Everything seemed to be a blur, a horrific kaleidoscope of sights, sounds, smells, and sensations.

When she finally made it out of the barn with Dancer, Trinity led the horse to the closest corral. The teenaged ranch hand Luke had been teaching helped her open the gate and put the mare safely inside. Clenching her jacket in her hands, Trinity rushed back to the barn, set to go in again.

Someone grabbed her from behind and whirled her around. "What the hell are you doing?" Luke's face was streaked with smoke and his furious glare focused on her.

"I'm getting the animals out!" She tried to pull away, but he wouldn't let her go.

"It's too damned dangerous in there." Luke gripped her arm and started dragging her toward the far end of the barn. "That smoke could kill you," he said as he brought her to where the men were fighting the fire with hoses and buckets and fire extinguishers. A sigh of relief rushed through her when she realized the fire was almost out.

"Get a bucket and help from this end," he said in a tone she'd never heard from him before. "If you try to go into that barn again before I say it's safe, I'll tie you to the fence post."

With that he strode back to where the men were still throwing buckets of water on the fire from the stock tanks, and spraying it down with the hose. Trinity's first instinct was to be furious with him for his high-handedness, but then she realized what it was she'd heard in his tone and seen in his eyes.

He'd been scared for her. Afraid something had happened, or that something would happen to her. Scared in a deep, real way that unsettled him.

It unsettled her, too.

The man really did care about her, didn't he?

Trinity watched Luke work to finish putting out the fire, and her thoughts kept focusing on one sentence.

I really think I'm ready.

Over and over again, she said it to herself.

I'm ready, Luke. When all this craziness settles down, when we have a chance to get our thoughts and minds and bodies together—

I'm ready.

If she'd thought it was all a blur before, it seemed even more so, later. By the time the fire was completely out and all the animals treated and returned to their stalls, dawn was breaking. Trinity was so tired that she could hardly see straight. Her muscles ached, her eyes and throat burned, and she felt like she'd sleep for a week.

While the men had fought the fire and made sure all the animals were safe and tended, Skylar had called the sheriff's office. Clay Wayland had arrived by the time the fire was out, and spent time going over the scene with Zack, Levi, Luke, and any ranch hand still able to walk and help.

Once they'd taken a good look around, Clay felt pretty certain the fire had been deliberately set. After Zack and Trinity put Skylar to bed, Zack, Levi, Clay, and Luke talked a lot about the postcard Skylar had found, and whether or not it was related.

Noah Ralston showed up after that, and the five men hashed out possibilities long past the point Trinity could understand, or even listen. Sure seemed like Luke knew a lot more about crime investigations than most ranch foremen would probably know.

Trinity tried to stay awake long enough to ask if anybody had found footprints for her to analyze, but she figured she was getting delirious. She could hardly keep her eyes open, and she didn't protest when Luke insisted she get back to the house, take a shower, and then get to bed.

He didn't say another word about her running into the barn like she had. Instead he escorted her into the house, kissed the top of her head, and then left her staring out the living room window and watching him walk away.

"But I'm ready," she mumbled after him as he went back to Clay, Zack, Levi, and Noah—and other men were showing up, too. Foremen from other ranches. Like Rios. Trinity recognized him as one of Luke's friends. Brad Taylor was there, and even Wade Larson.

If Guerrero had pulled this stunt—and for the life of her, Trinity couldn't figure out why he'd do such a stupid thing—the drug lord had stirred up a hornet's nest.

As Trinity dragged herself into the shower, she thought about Guerrero, and how he wouldn't even be expecting trouble until all the hornets came buzzing in to sting him to death.

Chapter 21

On Saturday, Luke stood behind Trinity at the firing range as she aimed the handgun at the target. "That's it, sugar," he murmured, even though she couldn't hear him through the protective ear coverings she wore. "You're doing fine."

She seemed to understand him, though, and her hands were steadier on this shot than they'd been during her first half dozen. Trinity had argued with him about not needing to learn how to handle a firearm. But after some heavy-duty convincing by Luke, she finally gave in.

He wasn't taking any chances.

Busting the damned rustling operation hadn't stopped the trouble, and someone was still trying to mess around with the MacKenna women. He and Zack planned to make damned sure nothing happened to either of them.

When Trinity finished firing the last round of bullets, she set the gun down, pulled off her ear coverings, and gave him a smile. "I think I did better that time."

Luke nodded and pressed the button that slowly brought the target back to them. "I think you're right," he said as he pulled the target off the clip. She had a tendency to aim a little high, most of her shots going to the target's neck, but it was a sight better than her first try. Those holes had been scattered all over the target— half of them not even close to the body.

Trinity rubbed the earrings along her left ear, something he noticed she did whenever she was deep in thought. "I don't under- stand why this person would do the things he's doing. Why the note? Why burn the barn?"

With a shrug, Luke replied, "I don't know, but Clay Wayland and Zack and Noah Ralston are aiming to find out."

Me, too, sugar. I'm on it like you wouldn't believe.

He'd pulled back from the main drug-running investigation, leaving Rios in charge of that, and of tracking Guerrero's every slimy move. He was handling the trouble at the Flying M with Zack, and Clay Wayland assisting whenever they needed him.

Whatever was happening at the ranch, it seemed to tie back to Woods and the rustling operation they'd destroyed, at least in some loose way. Guerrero-based, but not necessarily Guerrero himself pulling the strings.

That damned stooge Woods might be involved with this, and Luke had people leaning on him and his buddies already. This close to trial, they couldn't afford any more trouble.

Of course, neither Skylar nor Trinity would leave the Flying M and go stay someplace safe, no matter how hard Zack and Luke tried to push the issue. These women were not about to be run out of their home, and away from what mattered to them.

Frowning, Trinity looked as though she intended to say something else when she turned to glance at the shooter setting up right beside them.

Luke had to stifle a groan when he saw who it was. Joyce Butler.

Trinity turned away and started packing up the ammo, and then slid the gun back into its zippered case.

Yeah, sugar. That's it. Let's get the hell out of here.

"Won't do you a damn bit of good in there." Luke smiled and rubbed his hand over her back, trying to get Trinity to take the piece back out of its case. "You need to carry it around. Get the feel of it."

"It makes me nervous." Trinity eased the zipper up and around the case. "I feel safer using my bare fists and my feet."

"You're real good at it, too." He moved his fingers to her neck and she shivered beneath his touch. "I'd wager you could kick some ass if you had the chance."

She raised her brows. "So . . . you've watched me practice my kickboxing?"

"Every chance I get," he murmured, wondering if he'd ever confess what else he'd watched—and when.

Probably not.

But the memory—damn, it was a good one.

A commotion in the lane next to them caught Luke's attention and he turned his gaze toward Joyce Butler's target that she'd just pulled in.

"Wow," Trinity said, a touch of surprise in her voice. "She's really good."

Luke shrugged as he studied her target. The shots were all centered on the head. Apparently Butler liked the idea of blowing a man's brains out better than his heart.

When Luke and Trinity moved to pass the woman, Joyce Butler practically shoved her shot-up target in Trinity's face. Her smile was as thickly sweet as her perfume. "A hell of a lot better than your pitiful display," she said.

With more class than Joyce Butler could ever hope to have, Trinity nodded. "You're absolutely right. I could never be like you, Joyce."

Butler gave a smug smile and turned back to her next target, clearly dismissing Luke and Trinity.

Luke draped his arm around Trinity's shoulders as they headed out to his old Chevy. "How are you doing getting your thoughts about us together, sugar?"

She leaned into him, and for a minute, Luke thought she might answer him. That she might say, *I'm fine.* And then, *Yes, I'm ready.*

But for now, at least, Trinity MacKenna didn't say anything at all.

Trinity glared at the reinforced punching bag Zack had set up in a corner of the barn storage room, where she'd trained every day for almost two weeks. The heavy odor of smoke from the fire just wouldn't go away.

Her breath came in angry huffs and sweat trickled down the small of her back beneath her workout clothes. Her skin was warm and flushed from her intense workout, and she barely felt the chill in the air.

Damn the bastard. Maybe bastards. Whoever sent that postcard. Whoever started the fire in the barn. Somebody was trying to hurt her sister. She jabbed at the leather bag several times, a litany of *damn them, damn them, damn them* running through her mind with every punch.

Using skill obtained from four years of kickboxing practice, Trinity raised one leg, and with a powerful side kick she slammed her Nike-clad foot into the punching bag. Her ponytail slapped against her back as she followed up with five quick bare-fisted jabs, each punch feeling solid and good, and relieving some of her frustration.

A little, anyway.

Part of her frustration was sexual, and no amount of punching or masturbating was going to make that ache go away. Nothing and no one could—except Luke.

Even with the craziness around the ranch, she still found herself thinking about him. Thinking about them.

Thinking about the fact that no matter how hard she was trying not to, she was slowly falling in love with a cowboy. Christmas less than two weeks away, and she was having dopey fantasies of spending the holidays with Luke.

She gave the black leather punching bag another wallop.

Her learning of the job with DropCaps was going great so far. No pressure, since she wasn't officially starting until January.

Punch to the bag. It felt hard against her knuckles.

Finding the bastard who was after her sister—not so great.

Another punch to the bag. Clay and Noah and Zack were so pissed they walked around like dark clouds, storming all over the Flying M. Luke hadn't been much better—and he'd been gone a lot, too, out with his friend Rios, doing God only knew what.

One of the ranch hands had made a comment to another hand about Rios and Luke being heavy drinkers at a Douglas bar on their days off.

Trinity frowned. She couldn't picture Luke as a drunk. Couldn't picture it at all.

But she could picture herself in bed with him.

"I'm ready." Trinity smacked the bag again.

Just thinking about Luke made her ache all over, inside and out.

In a quick movement, Trinity spun and kicked the punching bag dead-on with her right foot. In a flash she nailed it with her left foot, then jabbed at the bag with each fist in rapid-fire succession.

Just as she was about to kick the bag again, hair prickled at her nape.

Strong hands gripped her shoulders from behind.

Wild thoughts tore through her mind—of the arsonist and the bastard who sent that psycho postcard.

Adrenaline pumped through Trinity, and she went on defensive autopilot.

She shot out her foot, low and hard, connecting with a booted shin. At the same time she twisted and broke free of the grip on her shoulders. She whirled, sending her fist into a hard muscled abdomen—

A fraction of a second before she realized it was Luke.

"You've got a helluva left, sugar." He grimaced and rubbed his abs with his palm. "That's certainly one way to greet a man."

"Yeah, well, serves you right." Trinity's cheeks burned as she tossed her ponytail over her shoulder. "Maybe that'll teach you not to sneak up on a woman."

He took a step closer, dominating her personal space, but she lifted her chin and held her ground. Beneath his dark Stetson, dirt streaked his stubbled face and he smelled of dust, horse, and testosterone. Sweat soaked his blue denim work shirt, and dang if he wasn't wearing a pair of well broken-in chaps.

No fair. A good-looking cowboy in chaps had always been one of her weaknesses. There was just something sexy about a man in all that leather.

Trinity shivered, her nipples hardening, her body already throbbing and tingling. She could picture him naked, with only his chaps on . . .

Luke's wicked blue eyes glittered as he moved so close that his belt buckle brushed her belly. "I've been dying to get a little uninterrupted time alone with you." He placed one hand on her hip and reached up to trail his thumb along her cheekbone with his other. "I can't hardly sleep at night, picturing you in my bed."

Heat suffused her body, starting from where his hand rested on her hip, flowing across her thighs, between her legs, up to her breasts and neck and on up to the roots of her hair.

Trinity swallowed hard past the dry lump in her throat. She licked her lips and a muscle in his jaw twitched. God but she wanted him to kiss her. Wanted to feel his sweaty naked body—against her own currently sweaty body.

His mouth neared hers and she braced her hands on his muscled chest.

"I'm through playing games with you, Luke." She shoved against all that strength and power. "I'm as ready as I'm going to be, so don't even ask me this time."

His deep rumble of a laugh made her that much hotter.

"I'm not sure I believe you." His words rolled through her body like thunder. "But at least you're starting to believe yourself."

"I'm not making you any promises," she whispered. "I don't even know what you really want from me."

"Yes, you do." Luke slid his hand from her cheekbone, roughly brushing her earrings as he reached for her sweat-dampened hair. Grabbing her ponytail in his fist, he pulled on it, gently bringing her closer to him. He swept his lips over hers and she tasted his breath as she moaned. He nipped at her lower lip and she sighed into his mouth. "I want everything. And I want it right now."

"Trinity?" A British man's voice called from the other end of the barn, shattering the hold Luke had on Trinity. "Are you in here?"

"Oh." In a confused haze, Trinity tried to push away from Luke but he kept his grip on her hip and her ponytail. *Oh, this is not good. Not good.* "Let me go, Luke."

His eyes narrowed. "Is that who I think it is?"

"Trinity?" Race called out again, the sound of his voice incongruous as Trinity cursed out loud and in her mind, double-time.

She could tell from the stunned look on Luke's face that he was thinking all sorts of things—like, maybe she hadn't broken it off with Race when she said she did, or maybe she'd been in touch with him, or having second thoughts the whole time she'd supposedly been getting herself ready to give herself completely to Luke.

Damn!

"Give me a minute," she said to Luke, but he didn't look like he was about to have that kind of patience.

"I need to do this," she told him. "And I need you to trust me."

Chapter 22

Trinity pushed against Luke's powerful chest again. He held on to her ponytail for a moment longer, then let it slide through his fingers as she broke away from him.

She couldn't seem to break eye contact, even though she needed to go talk with Race. Trinity had never felt so sexy, so attractive, and so secure as she did around Luke—while totally unbalanced all at once.

He was driving her crazy.

She was so ready for him—and now *this*?

Was life just playing one big long joke on her?

"Trinity?" Race sounded lost and completely confused.

"Coming." Cool air dried the sweat on her skin even before she grabbed her sweat jacket from a hook on the wall and slipped it on.

Trinity started to leave, then paused to glance back to Luke. With that possessive look on his face she could just imagine him pulling a Neanderthal routine and getting in the middle of things. She pointed her finger at him. "You—you behave," she whispered before turning. She jogged around the corner and spotted Race at the opposite end of the barn.

Trinity came to a dead stop, unable to make herself hurry toward the man she'd been with for the last two years of her life. Before she stepped back in time and started wrestling with her past.

It had been what, almost a month since she'd kissed Race goodbye at Heathrow Airport in London. A light, conservative kiss since he was a typical reserved English gentleman who never indulged in public displays of affection.

But when she saw him here, in the world she'd grown up in, it was almost like the last two years had happened to another woman. No excitement rushed through her at the sight of him, no fluttering of anticipation in her belly. Just a pleasant feeling of seeing a good friend . . . mixed with the twinge of uncertainty and a distant ache over not wanting to hurt someone she truly cared about.

"There you are, my dear." Race smiled as he strolled up to Trinity.

Yes, he was a devastatingly handsome man, fit and well muscled, and about as tall as Luke. His high cheekbones gave him an aristocratic look, but his sandy blond hair and deep brown eyes made him friendly and approachable, and definitely gorgeous and sexy.

Race's cobalt-blue polo shirt, khaki slacks, and brown loafers were glaringly out of place in the barn, but she couldn't imagine the sophisticated and refined man in anything more casual. Funny, but she'd never seen him in a pair of jeans. As far as she knew, he didn't own any.

"What are you doing here?" Trinity tried not to sound shocked or annoyed as he reached her and took both of her hands in his.

"I came to make my case in person." Race lowered his head and gave her a light kiss. His lips were cool and firm, and he smelled of the musk cologne she had given him for Christmas last year. "I hoped it might be a nice surprise."

As he touched her, she felt nothing. Nothing at all.

"I couldn't be more astonished." It was as if she'd lost the ability to smile as Race drew back.

It occurred to her that not only was she sweaty, but her hair was no doubt poking out of her ponytail, and her face probably streaked with sweat and barn dust from her intense workout.

A part of her couldn't help but analyze the difference between Race's greeting and Luke's. Even though she looked like a mess, Luke had made her feel beautiful, sensual, and wanted. If he'd had the chance, she knew Luke would have made love to her right there in the barn, dirt and sweat and all.

Race—Race would want her to shower.

The discomfort she felt no doubt showed on her face and mirrored his, because his smile faded away. "I've made a terrible mistake coming here, haven't I?"

Trinity had to admit she cared about Race a lot, but she wasn't in love with him, and he wasn't in love with her. Maybe it had taken him flying thousands of miles and seeing her in a barn to get a grasp on that, but she thought that's what was happening.

"I don't think it's a mistake." She finally found her smile, now that she was becoming certain he wouldn't misinterpret it. "We probably should have done this face-to-face before, to make it real."

"Well, then." Race's smile came back, this time a sad one. "Let's finish it properly, shall we?"

When the Englishman kissed Trinity, Luke gritted his teeth and clenched his fists. He had to fight the urge to grab the bastard by his collar and kick his pansy ass back to where he'd come from.

Trinity was Luke's woman now. If Race didn't back off, Luke was going to have to get in the middle of things in a hurry. He strode toward them as the man drew away from the kiss. Before Luke reached them, Trinity said something he couldn't hear and Race smiled.

When Luke came up behind Trinity, the Englishmen glanced at him. "Hullo," he said as he released Trinity and held out his hand to Luke. "Race Bentham. And you must be one of the, er, cattle herders?"

"Something like that." Luke shook the man's hand, surprised by his equally firm grip. "Luke Rider."

"He's the Flying M's foreman," Trinity said in a rush as her gaze darted from Race to Luke and back. "He, ah, works for Skylar."

"You two have some talking to do." Luke's eyes rested on Trinity, telling her without words that he would do his best to trust her, but it was damned hard. "I'll be out at the corrals if you need me."

He gave Race a nod and touched his hand to his Stetson, then strode out of the barn without looking back. His gut clenched and it was all he could do not to turn around, grab that woman, and cart her off by her ponytail like a damned caveman.

Trinity watched Luke walk away, his leather chaps framing his tight ass as he headed out the barn door. Dang but a cowboy in chaps made her hot. Although Luke definitely made her hotter than any man ever had—chaps, or no chaps.

"Would you like to freshen up, my dear?" Race asked, and she caught the note of concern in his voice. "I would like to do the same if you don't mind me doing so here."

Trinity snapped her gaze from Luke's retreating backside and met Race's warm brown eyes. He was so kind, gentle, and considerate. Everything that Luke wasn't.

Although that wasn't quite true. Luke had been considerate in his own way—he had given her time to understand herself, and what she really wanted. He'd tried to protect her, and teach her to protect herself better. And now, even though she knew it was hurting him, he was giving her space to talk with Race.

Race frowned, his brows furrowing. The concern made him look all the more regal and distant. "Trinity, are you quite all right?"

She clasped her hands together and squeezed them so tightly her knuckles ached. "This is awkward for me, but I feel like I owe you this conversation," she said so fast she stumbled over the words. "Two years is a long time for me just to end the relationship over the telephone."

Race's eyes held hers as he slid his hand into a pocket of his slacks. Sparkles flashed in the barn's dim interior when he brought out a diamond ring and held it in his palm. "Tell me I've still got a chance to change your mind," he said softly, the rich timbre of his accent lending the plea a special poignancy.

Trinity bit the inside of her lip as the diamond flashed and glittered. It had to be two carats—and the band was probably platinum. Race would choose such a symbol, a concrete statement of her worth—and his.

Emotions rolled through her like bouncing tumbleweeds. She had never come so close to having every material thing she'd ever wanted. Not to mention the one thing she'd never had in her childhood—an even-tempered, safe, dependable man.

In a handful of days, after a few blistering encounters with a man she barely knew, was she truly ready to throw away the security she had with Race?

Race stood before her, holding his ring, clinging to his hopeful expression even as his eyes hinted that he knew the truth. Trinity saw him completely in the prismatic diamond light—a wonderful, kind, and passionless prison of a man.

Regret flooded her and she lowered her eyes to the barn's dirt floor.

She knew what she needed, and it wasn't safety or propriety.

No. Not anymore.

Her future lay in risk, in leather, in the desert heat, and a cowboy's muscled arms.

At least for now.

For the first time in her adult life, Trinity MacKenna felt a real sense of freedom and anticipation for tomorrow. A tomorrow that wasn't studiously mapped or planned, or confined in the squeaky-clean manners of the corporate world.

She had to hurt this man all over again, probably even worse than she had on the telephone and in her e-mail, and that reality shook her deeply. With her emotions turned loose, she felt the sting of his pain even before she inflicted it.

No guilt, though. The real wrong would be pretending to love Race when she didn't. Giving him parts of herself that rightfully belonged to another man.

Trinity raised her eyes and met Race's. "I'm sorry, Race, but no. There's no chance. I can't marry you." With a rattling sigh, she reached up and closed his fingers over the ring. "You're an amazing man. Somewhere there's a woman who'll rock your world, but it's not me."

Race hesitated. For the first time ever, Trinity thought she saw a blaze of pure, raw emotion change the man's features. For a split second, he seemed younger. Fierce and lion-like.

And just as fast, the look vanished. Race had tucked his feelings back in their bottomless box. The corner of his mouth quirked in a resigned smile. "You did a lovely job of that. Rejecting me, I mean."

Trinity felt her insides coalesce and firm up. She knew she'd made the right decision, and thank God Race was taking it so well. "Your woman-to-be, I mean she'll *really* rock you. Not just shake you up a little."

Her former lover gave a hint of a smile and slipped the ring into his pocket. His expression told her he was hurt . . . but at the same time was that relief in his eyes?

But as was his habit, he didn't speak about it any further. The conversation was quite clearly over.

And yes, this felt more real. More final. More right.

Arm in arm, Trinity and Race walked out of the barn in comfortable silence, making the short trek to his red sports car with its rental sticker on the bumper.

"You're not returning to London," he said as though the statement were fact as they came to a stop next to the driver's side door.

Trinity cut her gaze to his and she started to tell him of course she was. But instead she said, "I haven't made any final decisions. My life, my career's been in England, but my sister needs me here right now. DropCaps will let me work anywhere—and the Flying M will do fine for the moment."

"Ah." He placed a light kiss on her forehead. "But you've found much more than your sister and your past here at this ranch."

"What? No—" Trinity's protest was silenced with Race's finger firmly against her lips.

"It's in your eyes, my dear." He glanced toward the corrals. "And I do believe I saw it in his."

Trinity's entire body tingled as she followed the direction of Race's gaze and saw Luke leaning against the corral's wooden railings. He'd folded his arms across his chest and pulled his Stetson too low for her to see his eyes, but she could make out the hard line of his frown. He was still dressed in his dusty clothes and chaps, and to her he'd never looked better.

She looked back to Race as he removed his finger from her mouth. With a smile he brushed his lips over hers then pulled back and winked. "And I'm sure that little kiss will put a twist in the chap's knickers. He seems the possessive type, as well he should be, this close to winning a rare prize like you."

Trinity wrapped her arms around Race's neck and kissed his cheek. He might be wrong for her, but he was one heck of a guy. "Watch out for the local girls while you're in Arizona." She released him and stepped back. "That sexy accent of yours is a killer."

Race smiled as he opened the door to the sports car and climbed in, then shut the door and buzzed the window open. "Dunno about that, my dear. Might have to sample the wares a bit, don't you think? I've always fancied American experiments."

She smiled, feeling almost giddy as the engine roared and he backed the car out of the driveway and headed down the road.

Trinity did her best to ignore Luke as she watched Race drive away, but the cowboy might as well have been right beside her rather than a hundred yards off at the corrals.

Instead she focused on the car's taillights and the growl of its engine growing fainter in the distance.

Race. In a little red American sports car. Threatening to sample the local wares. Too funny. Maybe she should give him Nevaeh's phone number. After all, turnabout was fair play. And Trinity had definitely been turned about. Upside down and inside out. Her entire life had changed, and in seconds, it would change even more.

Risk . . . leather . . . desert heat . . . a cowboy's muscled arms.

"I'm ready," she said out loud, wondering if he could hear her, and not even caring if he believed her—because she was damn well about to convince him.

Her heart hammered, and she shivered in the evening's growing chill. As if to protect herself, she wrapped her jacket tighter.

Who am I kidding? I'm way past protection. Jumped off the damned cliff the day I met Luke, and so far, I'm still flying.

The sunset seeped across the horizon in hues of orange and purple, and the air smelled crisp and wonderful—of winter around the corner and Christmas on its way.

Without looking she knew that Luke was striding toward her. Beneath her jacket her nipples beaded and ached, and a whole swarm of butterflies invaded her belly. Her skin tingled from her scalp to her toes and she felt alive in a way she never had before.

The moment Luke reached her, Trinity whirled to look up at him, a sense of breathless anticipation soaring through her. His eyes were still shadowed by his Stetson, but the tenseness of his jaw and the firm set of his mouth told her that Race's little show hadn't settled well with her cowboy.

"Well?" Luke demanded, still just as gritty and sweaty as before.

Dang but she had to have him.

"I want to have a word with you," she murmured and walked away before he had a chance to respond. She could feel the heat of his gaze on the sway of her hips, on the curve of her ass, almost as though he was touching her with those strong, callused hands.

When she was in the shadows of the barn's dusty interior she turned and saw Luke still standing right where she'd left him. She raised her hand and curled her forefinger toward herself, telling him to *Come and get me*, with just that little motion and a teasing grin.

His long legs ate up the ground so fast it made her heart beat like thunder, the sound filling her ears. When he was close enough, Trinity didn't think twice. She flung her arms around Luke's neck, climbed him like a tree, and wrapped her legs around his hips.

A sensual grin curved his mouth as he cupped her ass and held her tightly to him. She felt his leather chaps through the thin material of her sweatpants as he pressed his erection against her.

"I'm ready, damn you." Hunger and need surged through Trinity and she brought her mouth to his in a hard rush, a kiss that demanded he give her everything he'd promised and more. "I'm ready, and you can believe me or not," she murmured as she bit Luke's lower lip as he'd done to her, letting him feel the depth of her desire for him, her need. "I want you, Luke. I'm free and I'm ready, and I *need* you."

"You're not free." Luke kissed her back, fierce and uncivilized. "You're mine."

His?

God, he hadn't been kidding, about taking her, and not letting her go.

It did scare her a little, but she didn't care. She needed all the wild passion that only Luke could give her.

Holding her tighter yet, Luke groaned and thrust his tongue into her mouth, then pulled away and looked into her eyes. "I've got to have you," he said, his voice rough and filled with need so tangible that she felt the vibrations straight to her core.

Trinity kissed the corner of his mouth, his stubble rough against her lips, causing them to tingle. "I want you, Luke Rider."

A rumble rose in his chest, a sound of overwhelming need. "We'll take my truck and head away from here."

"No." She moved her mouth closer to his ear and darted her tongue along his lobe, tasting the salt of his skin. "The barn office. Right now."

Chapter 23

Luke didn't have to be told twice. He was done waiting. Trinity clung to him as he strode toward the office at the end of the barn. She nipped at his earlobe with wild little bites, making purring sounds that about drove him insane with lust.

When he reached the office, Luke yanked the door open with one hand and slammed it closed behind him. He took Trinity straight to the old-fashioned desk, sat her down on one end and eased her arms from around his neck and her legs from his waist. He kept his hips pressed tight between her thighs, though. That much ground he wouldn't surrender yet. Not until she was good and ready for him.

Even in the dim light coming through a part in the gingham curtains, he saw how heavily she was breathing and that her nipples were hard enough to raise the fabric of her light jacket.

She reached for his belt, her small hands brushing against his hard cock as she unfastened the buckle. "I need you so bad."

"Hold on." Luke reached over Trinity to flip on the desk lamp so that the glow illuminated her beautiful face. In a quick movement he grabbed her lapels and jerked her jacket down to her elbows so that her arms were trapped at her sides.

Her eyes darted to his and she ran her tongue along her lower lip, her eyes dark with passion. "What are you doing?"

"You know exactly what I'm doing, sugar."

Excitement and arousal swirled through Trinity at such a mad pace that she could barely stand waiting. Cool air rushed against her skin as he stripped away her shoes, socks, sweatpants, and panties. It left her naked from the waist down, open and vulnerable.

"Damn." Luke sucked in his breath as he ran his finger along the soft hair of her mound. "You're beautiful everywhere."

Shivers coursed her spine. "Hurry, Luke." She tried to move, but her arms were still bound by the sweat jacket.

"We'll get there." He pulled apart the snaps of his Western work shirt, yanked it off, and tossed it aside.

The sight of his broad, bare chest and his powerful muscles just about undid her. "Hurry," she begged again.

"Double damn," Luke murmured as he pushed her T-shirt up and then pulled down on the lacy cups of her bra, releasing her breasts, yet leaving them pointing high and out. "A pair of fine nipples on the most beautiful breasts I've ever had the pleasure of tasting."

He reached up with one hand to take off his hat. "Wait," Trinity said and his eyes met hers. "Leave your cowboy hat on." Her gaze dropped to the bulge at his crotch, and the chaps that framed his hips so well. "Leave those on, too."

Luke's smile was so carnal she knew it had to be outlawed in at least half a dozen states. He slid his belt out from the loops and tossed it on the desk beside her, the metal buckle clattering on the polished wood. After releasing the single button on his jeans and unzipping them, he freed his incredible erection. Trinity's mouth watered.

He palmed his cock and moved his hand up and down its awesome length. "You sure you're ready for me?"

Spreading her legs wider, Trinity arched her back, raising her breasts up to him. "If you don't get inside me now, I'm going to scream."

"Oh, I aim to make you scream. Plenty." Bracing one of his palms on her thigh, Luke moved between her legs. The feel of his leather chaps along the soft skin of her thighs, and the sight of his erection jutting toward her was such a turn-on that she could hardly keep from shouting for him to get inside her.

Luke rubbed the head of his cock up and down, teasing her with slow, sensuous strokes. Trinity gasped at the incredible sensation, unable to believe how close she was to exploding already, and he'd barely touched her.

"I want to make something real clear." Luke's deep blue gaze locked on her as he continued to tease her. "You're gonna watch me take you. And when I slide into you, sugar, you're mine. No more bullshit, no big-city games, no ghosts from the past, and no arguments. I'm staking my claim, for now. Maybe for always."

At that moment that whole darn barn could've been burning down and Trinity wouldn't have noticed. Her lips parted, and even with Luke's cock so close to sliding into her, she tried to find a way to deny him, to tell him that she wasn't a possession to claim.

But he had some kind of power over her. A way of making her

feel like she was an exquisite treasure he'd discovered, that he would cherish her always—but first he would insist that she give him everything . . .

Her body, her soul, and her heart.

Could she give all of herself to a man she'd known for just a short time? And a cowboy for cripes sake. A man who represented everything she'd thought she'd left behind long ago.

Luke moved the head of his cock to the opening of Trinity's core, causing her to gasp as it sent electric thrills of anticipation zinging through her. His sculpted biceps bulged, the veins along his muscles standing out like he was holding himself back with all he had. "So what's it going to be?"

Trinity took a deep breath, drawing in the strength to do what she needed to do. To say what she knew needed to be said. She ran her tongue along her lower lip, and the only thing that came out was, "Okay."

His eyes flared with satisfaction. He cupped the back of her head and gently forced her to look down to where his erection was poised to enter her. Her whole body vibrated as her gaze locked on his cock, so close to sliding in . . . So close to turning her life down another road—that road she knew she'd been approaching since the moment she'd met the man who'd become a wild card in her future.

"Watch me take you," he demanded, his deep voice rumbling through her like a freight train barreling toward its final destination.

Blood rushed in her ears and her body was so highly sensitized that she didn't know what would happen when he finally drove home.

Home.

Luke.

She didn't have time to think anymore as Luke rammed his hips hard against her, thrusting his thick cock deep inside her, *taking her*, just as he'd promised.

Trinity shrieked. The instant orgasm that rocked her body was so fast, so unexpected that it robbed her of her breath, of all thought.

"You're *mine.*" He clenched her ponytail and brought her mouth to meet his, hard and demanding, while he pressed himself against her, stretching and filling her like nothing she'd ever imagined. The kiss made the waves of her orgasm continue, her core contracting around the length of him.

Omigod. Unbelievable. She'd never had an orgasm during intercourse before, and for a moment she wondered if this mind-bending climax would ever end.

Trinity bit at his lower lip as she kissed him back, struggling against the jacket that still kept her arms pinned to her sides. Luke's masculine scent surrounded her, filled her senses. Their sweat mingled, their breathing hot and labored and sounding as one.

He tore his mouth from hers, kissing her chin and the length of her jaw, abrading her skin with his coarse stubble. "You feel so good wrapped around me like this."

"Take off the rest of my clothes," Trinity begged, trying to free herself and frustrated that she couldn't. "I've got to touch you. I've got to."

His gaze raked over her breasts jutting from above the cups of her bra. "I know exactly what I want you to do with your hands."

Even as Luke stripped her jacket, T-shirt, and bra from her body and tossed them aside, he kept their bodies locked together. His

192 | Cheyenne McCray

every slightest movement pressed against a pleasure button deep within her.

When she was completely naked, Trinity rubbed her palms over his hard muscled chest. "More, Luke." Her fingers trailed down to where they were joined and she slid them over the part of his shaft that was showing, slick with her juices. "I need it wild." Her gaze met his and she was so breathless she could barely speak. "I need it *hard*."

"Hang on." His smile was absolutely sinful. He reached up with both hands and freed her hair from the ponytail holder and tossed the band aside. "Yeah . . . that's better," he said while he raked his fingers through the long strands. She shivered as he let them slide over her shoulders in a sensual caress.

He eased her down so that her back was flat against the desk's polished surface. Then hooking his arms under her knees, he drew her wider apart, allowing himself to penetrate her even deeper.

Slowly he started thrusting and Trinity arched her hips up to meet him. "Faster," she demanded.

"Lick your nipples." Luke's strokes increased, and Trinity could hardly think with the sensations of pure pleasure flooding her body. "That turned me on when I watched you in the hot tub."

Luke's eyes were shadowed beneath his Stetson as he ordered her to touch herself. It made him look even darker and sexier and more dangerous than ever.

She caught her breasts in her hands and pushed them up as high as she could. It only took a slight rise of her head to flick her tongue over her nipples.

Oh, God, but it felt good . . . Luke driving in and out, her own tongue hot against her sensitive nipples, the feel of his chaps rubbing along the inside of her thighs, and the cool, smooth wood of the desk at her back.

She'd never experienced anything so erotic in all her life.

Clenching his jaw, Luke forced himself to keep from coming too soon. The sight of Trinity spread out before him and her tongue flicking out over her nipples—*damn.* He'd never been so close to losing control.

Even though she wanted more, he'd been reining in the desire to let all hell break loose and take her so furiously she'd be sore for at least a month. But he'd held back, afraid to chafe her delicate thighs with his chaps.

"Harder!" she demanded between licks.

"You want it hard," he said in a near roar, "then you're gonna get it hard."

Luke drove into her like he was hell-bent for leather. Trinity cried out, her eyes rolling back and she paused in what she'd been doing. "Yes, Luke. Yes!"

"Keep sucking your nipples," he ordered. "Don't stop till I tell you to."

She obeyed, pushing her breasts together so that she could swipe her tongue over each nipple even faster.

He focused on her jade eyes as he felt her channel start to contract around his cock. "I'm coming." She raised her head and spoke almost in wonder as her body trembled and her face flushed a light shade of rose. "Oh, God. I'm coming *again.*"

Her words nearly pushed him over the edge, but he held back, determined to give Trinity all the pleasure she deserved. The sound of her purring moans and the hard slap of flesh filled the room. "Come for me," he demanded. "Right now."

A scream tore from Trinity, so loud it was a wonder the barn didn't fall down around them. Her body jerked and she twisted, like she was riding a bronc.

Luke thrust twice, maybe three times more, as her channel contracted around his cock. With a hoarse shout he came, shooting his come into her with hard jerks of his hips against hers. He pumped his cock in and out of her, stretching out her climax and his.

When the last fragment of his orgasm settled deep in his loins, Luke eased Trinity's legs down from where he'd been holding them. She wrapped her thighs tight around his hips and locked her ankles behind him, keeping him snug inside her. "You're not going anywhere, cowboy," she murmured, her face flushed with satisfaction and her eyes heavy-lidded.

"Hell, no." He rubbed up against her, his cock growing rigid inside her in a Texas minute. "I've got plans to wear you out and then some."

Trinity smiled and wiggled her hips. "I like that plan."

Bracing his hands on the smooth surface of the desk, Luke worked hard to bring his breathing down to a normal level and to control the rawness of his emotions. He sure as hell had gone after Trinity from the moment he'd spotted her at Nevaeh's Christmas party. But he'd never expected to feel like a lovesick schoolboy with a crush on the hot new teacher.

Yeah, he'd known he had to have Trinity. And somewhere in the back of his mind he'd known that he intended to keep her. But he'd never allowed himself to acknowledge that he might fall for her so hard.

Damn.

Trinity's breathing was still rough, causing her chest to rise and fall and her breasts to jiggle. Her tempting dark-rose nipples bobbed up and down, drawing his attention and luring him in to taste them for himself.

Luke took Trinity's hands, intertwined their fingers together, and raised them above her head. He held her there while he nipped, licked, and sucked at the tight nubs that were still wet from her own tongue. He tasted the flavor of her mouth on her nipples, mixed with the salt of her skin. Her peaches-and-cream scent was stronger in the valley between her breasts, a perfect blend of smells when combined with the intoxicating scent of her juices.

Yep. He had it good and he had it bad.

This wasn't something he'd ever get over.

Shards of sensation sliced through Trinity as Luke bit at her nipples, and incredibly enough she felt another climax building within her. But then he pulled out of her and released her hands, and she whimpered in disappointment.

"I'm going to turn you over and take you from behind," he said, even as he rolled her onto her belly.

"God, yes," Trinity said, ready for him to thrust into her again. The desk felt warm and smooth against her belly and breasts, and the floor was cool beneath her bare feet. Deliciously wanton feelings surged through her as she splayed her thighs, exposing everything to Luke's eyes, and being unable to see him at the same time.

"You've got one hell of a sexy ass." His callused palms massaged her butt cheeks as he spoke. "I love these dimples right here." She felt the brush of his lips against the small of her back and she shivered. "And here."

"Come on, Luke." Trinity wiggled her rear, arching herself up to him. "Stop teasing me."

His fingers parted her butt cheeks, making her feel even more sensual, more exposed. "You ready to be fucked in the ass?"

Her heart pounded so hard she swore she could feel it against the desktop. The way he said that, and the thought of Luke sliding into her other passage felt forbidden, and all the more exciting. She licked her lips and arched up to him. "Oh, yeah."

Satisfaction surged through him at how she trusted him enough to take him any way he wanted to give it to her. "Hang on for the ride." Luke rubbed his cock against her slick folds, coating it in her juices.

On the desktop he spotted a bottle of lotion and reached for it, then squirted it on his hand. The stuff smelled like vanilla but was thick and creamy. Perfect for sliding into her ass.

Trinity made that sweet little purring sound as he used his fingers to spread lotion around her ass. He squeezed more of the lotion onto his palm and then greased his cock with it.

"I'm big and it's gonna be tight." He eased two fingers into her and she gasped. "Think you can handle me?" he asked as he reached around her with his other hand and found her sweet spot.

"Yeah." Excitement sounded in her tone, fueling his own, and she rocked back and forth against his hands. "Definitely."

Luke grunted with satisfaction as he withdrew his fingers from her ass. He placed the head of his cock against her tight hole and gently pushed inside the opening, slowly stretching her as he entered inch by inch. "How's that?"

"Different. Wild." A moan slipped from her lips as he slid farther inside. "I love how you feel."

When he was buried inside Trinity, Luke gripped her hips with his free hand and started moving in and out in a slow, methodical motion. "I could take you all day and all night." With his other hand he continued to fondle her button, drawing juices up and over the slippery nub. He circled it with his finger, gentle teasing strokes as he slowly moved in her ass. "I'll never get enough of you."

"Come on. More." Trinity squirmed against Luke's hand and his hips as he slid in and out of her. Although she'd been curious, she'd never imagined that anal sex could feel so fine. Luke Rider could take her any way he wanted and she'd take him—and she'd enjoy every minute of it.

"Is this what you want?" His strokes increased, his leather chaps rubbing against her butt. His fingers worked her center in a way that felt so good she could hardly stand it.

"No." Trinity thrust her hips back to meet him, the best she could do the way she was sprawled out on the desk, her breasts smashed flat and hurting so good. "Give me more," she insisted. She gripped the edges of the desk, holding on tight. Placing her cheek against the smooth surface she closed her eyes, the smells of lemon oil, vanilla-scented lotion, and sex filling her senses.

She reveled in the sensation of him, all him, everywhere him. She enjoyed how he demanded more of her. And she wanted to give it to him. Wanted to give him everything he asked for and more.

"Is that good enough for you, sugar?" he asked as he pummeled into her.

"Yes, Luke," Trinity practically shouted, unable to hold back. "Oh, my God, that's it . . . ooh, just like that!"

The tight coil of her climax expanded outward, larger and larger yet, growing beyond anything she'd experienced before. A different kind of climax that built to a wild frenzy of unbelievable excitement until it exploded within her.

Trinity cried out and her eyelids flew open as the orgasm rocked her.

That's when she realized two crucial pieces of information at the same time.

They hadn't used a condom, not at first, and not now, either.

And her sister was standing in the doorway to the office.

Chapter 24

As Luke thrust his cock in and out of Trinity's ass, Skylar was frozen, her jaw practically hanging to the floor, and her hand clasped so tightly around her heart pendant that her knuckles were white. As Trinity's gaze met her sister's, Skylar's face turned as red as a hibiscus bloom and in a flash she backed out the door, closing it quietly behind her.

"Yeah, that's it," Luke was saying to Trinity as Skylar slipped out of the office. "I want you to come again."

In that moment, Trinity couldn't decide whether the heat rushing through her in tandem with her climax was from sheer embarrassment . . . or that she was incredibly turned on because she and Luke had been watched. She had a strong feeling that Skylar had been standing there long enough to get one heck of a good show.

A sense of déjà vu sent goose bumps rippling along Trinity's skin as she thought about those moments she'd had her own wild performances to observe—a decade ago, with Skylar and Zack.

Another orgasm rolled through Trinity's body while Luke

pounded into her. It magnified as she recalled the couple of times when she followed Zack and Skylar and watched them have sex, back when the lovers first met. From a cave near their hideaway, Trinity would spy on them and give herself a little relief.

At the same time she'd bite her lower lip to make sure she didn't let a sound escape when she came. She could still picture Skylar on her hands and knees on a picnic blanket. Zack holding his cock with one hand, then guiding himself forward to thrust into Skylar. Watching those two together had made her hungry for sex, but she'd never found a partner who'd matched the intensity she'd seen in her sister and Zack.

Until Luke.

An even more powerful climax whooshed through Trinity as Luke took her where she'd never gone before. She rocked so hard against the desk that her mound and thighs were probably bruised. But she didn't want it to end. She wanted more.

"You feel like heaven on earth, woman." Luke's cock was as hard as steel, hard enough that he was sure he could thrust into *his* woman forever.

He had almost paused when from under the brim of his Stetson he'd seen Skylar open the door, catching him getting it on with her younger sister. But when Trinity hadn't said anything, and Skylar had just continued standing there like she was hypnotized, Luke hadn't been able to stop.

Hell, if the boss lady got off on seeing Trinity and him going at it, let her watch.

Luke focused on the beautiful woman that he was driving into. Damn but he loved how she took him. "Your ass is so tight. Everything about you feels good."

"Oh, God." Trinity cried out again with yet another climax.

His balls drew up, tightening in a rush, and then his orgasm sped through him like a bull out of a rodeo chute. He bellowed as he came, every part of his body throbbing in time with his pulsating cock, adrenaline rushing through him and making him feel so high that he was positive that sex with Trinity was some new kind of aphrodisiac.

From the corner of his sex-fogged brain, Luke suddenly realized he'd screwed up big time. Holding back a groan, he rested his forehead between Trinity's shoulder blades.

He'd just done something he'd never done before. From the time his dad had taken him to that whorehouse in Reno and Luke had lost his cherry to the well-worn brunette, he'd always used protection. *Always.*

But this time, with the one woman who really mattered to him, he'd forgotten to use a condom.

Trinity sighed with pleasure as Luke braced his hands to either side of her, pressing his chest to her back. Her core continued to contract from her multiple orgasms, and his cock still felt fine right where it was.

"I'm sorry," he murmured near her ear and he kissed her softly. She could feel the sweat running down his face and chest and mingling with her own.

"Why?" Trinity wriggled her hips and she swore she felt him harden inside her ass. "That was better than I'd imagined."

"I didn't protect you." Luke sighed and eased his cock out. "I forgot to use a condom."

"Yeah . . . that makes two of us." Trinity grabbed a handful of tissues from the box on the shelf above the desk, and handed them to Luke when she turned to face him. "Forgetting protection was as much my fault as it was yours."

Instead of cleaning himself first, Luke picked up Trinity by her waist and set her on the desk. "It was my job," he muttered as he pressed her thighs apart and gently started wiping the flood of juices. "I've never lost my head like that before. I promised to protect you, and I screwed up."

"I went kind of crazy, too." Trinity smiled and took off his Stetson so that she could see his face as he swiped at her folds with the tissues. "Just don't give me any of that 'I'll do the right thing' bullshit," she added as she put his hat onto her own head. The Stetson was so big it slipped down over her eyes, blocking her view of him.

"Hey." Luke stopped cleaning her and pushed up the brim of the hat with one hand, while moving between her thighs at the same time. He tossed the tissues into the wastebasket beside, then caught her chin in his hand and forced her to look into his eyes. "I thought I made it clear I don't intend to let you go."

An almost shy smile curved the corner of his mouth as he added, "If we just made a baby together, I'll be the proudest daddy there ever was. You got that?"

An amazing array of feelings swirled through Trinity as she stared up at her man. She barely knew him, yet she felt like they were interlocking pieces that fit perfectly together.

And *wow*, the way he was looking at her, the way he talked about having a baby together . . . *omigod*.

Jeez. What had one of her first thoughts been when she'd met this man?

Can I have your baby, too?

Trinity reached up and wrapped her arms around Luke's neck

while pulling his head down until his lips met hers. Their kiss was slow and sensuous as they tasted one another as if for the first time. Gentle strokes of their tongues and light nips with their teeth.

When they finally pulled apart, Trinity slid her hands into Luke's thick brown hair. "You have hat hair." She gave him a teasing grin while she fluffed a few sweaty strands. "And cowboy forehead," she added as she observed his face was grimy from a day working the ranch, but his forehead was free of dirt from where his hat had rested.

Luke returned her grin and brushed away a streak of dirt on her cheek. "I'd say we could both use a shower."

Easing her hands through the light sprinkling of hair on his muscular chest, Trinity nodded her agreement. "I'll bet we can come up with some interesting ways to get each other squeaky clean."

"I do like the way you think." He chuckled and reached across her to grab a few more tissues out of the box. His hard biceps brushed her nipples and she tingled all over from the contact.

He straightened and wiped her juices and his come from his now semi-erect but still impressively sized member. "There's something you probably ought to know."

Luke's remark barely registered as she watched him handling his cock. The sight of his thick length in his own hand was something she found unbelievably arousing and she could already imagine him sliding into her again.

His voice lowered. "Your sister walked in on us."

"M-hmm," she murmured. But then she realized what he'd said and her gaze shot up to meet his. "You saw Skylar?"

He raised a brow as he tossed the rest of the spent tissues into the wastecan. "Out of the corner of my eye."

Trinity reached for Luke's chaps and pulled him closer between her thighs, needing to feel him next to her. "This is sure going to make things awkward."

That sexy smile of his just about turned her to mush as he settled his hands at her waist. "Not a thing wrong with what we're doing."

When Trinity nodded, his hat slipped over her eyes and Luke had to grin. She looked so sexy in nothing but his Stetson that it was all he could do to hold back from taking her again, *right now.*

She pushed the hat up and he could see her green gaze. "I—I used to spy on Skylar and Zack." Color rose in her cheeks as she spoke. "Back when they first dated."

"You watched your sister and Zack?" Now that was interesting.

Trinity waved one hand toward the east. "Up in those mountains, behind the ranch. They had a special spot, and I found a cave nearby, where I could hide and watch."

"Oh, yeah?" He grinned at the image of his woman watching another couple having sex.

Trinity's face was so red that the light dusting of freckles across her nose stood out like copper sprinkles.

He swooped down to kiss her, hard.

"Hell," he murmured as he pulled back, his erection jutting up again. "You've always been a hot little thing, haven't you?"

"Yeah," she whispered against his lips. "But I've never been like I am around you. I want you again. Right now."

Luke released her to slide his fingers into his front pocket and pulled out one of the three condoms he'd stashed there.

Her gaze met his, surprise in her eyes. "You carry those things around with you when you're working the ranch?"

"You bet your pretty ass." He gave a slow nod. "Every minute since that night at the hot tub."

"Real good answer, cowboy." She took the package from him and tore it open. "*Real* good answer."

Anticipation and excitement skittered through Trinity as she rolled the condom down Luke's huge erection. When she released him, he moved the head of his cock to the opening to her core, and in one quick, hard stroke he buried himself inside her again.

Right where she wanted him.

Right where he was supposed to be.

She moaned as she dug her fingernails into his biceps and wiggled her hips. "God that feels good."

"Grab onto me and hang on," Luke said as he slid his hands under her ass.

Trinity's pulse doubled as she obeyed and he easily picked her up off the desk, their bodies fused together. She wrapped her legs around his waist and clung to him. His torso was rock hard against her chest and belly, and his chaps and jeans were rough against the sensitive flesh of her ass and thighs.

Luke's gaze locked with hers as he used his powerful muscles to move her along his length.

Trinity had a hard time forming a coherent thought, so exquisite was the feel of him riding her on his cock like she weighed next to nothing. With every thrust he hit that pleasure center deep inside her, and it was about to send her over the edge. "You like me like this—helpless in your arms?" she asked, her words coming out in rough gasps.

"Oh, yeah." His voice was hard yet filled with sensuality.

Trinity gave in completely to the sensations of him taking her while he was standing. He lowered his head and grasped one of her nipples between his teeth, and she moaned. When she tilted her head back and arched her breasts toward him, begging for more, his Stetson tumbled off her head and onto the desk behind her.

She'd had so many orgasms, Trinity didn't think she'd be able to come again so quickly. But in only moments she shot toward the peak and screamed as she toppled right on over the summit.

Luke followed her moments later. As his cock pulsed inside her, she rested her head against his chest. He held her close and murmured, "I'm never letting you go, sugar. You can count on that."

This time, Trinity didn't feel any urge to argue at all.

By the time Luke and Trinity had dressed and left the barn, it was well past dinnertime and warm yellow light glowed through the curtains of the ranch house. Trinity had stalled as much as possible, enjoying every moment of their time together, not wanting to leave her cowboy stud.

A sense of belonging—feelings of being wanted and of being *home*—surged through Trinity when Luke draped his arm around her shoulders as they headed toward the house. The night was still, the gentle lowing of cattle floating from the corrals along with a horse's whinny in the distance. Her steps slowed when they approached the front porch, and she wished the two of them could just take off and spend time somewhere, anywhere alone.

What would it be like to wake up in Luke's strong arms? To feel his big body wrapped around hers?

"Sure you don't want me to go in with you?" The low rumble of Luke's voice tickled her ear, bringing her back to the moment and to the cowboy at her side.

Trinity shook her head and felt his lips brush over her hair. "I think I'd rather face my sister alone and get it over with."

He squeezed her tighter to him while they walked up the front porch steps and he said, "No regrets."

When they came to a stop on the porch, Trinity tilted her head back and smiled up at Luke. "The only regret I have is that we didn't lock the door."

"I was too anxious to get inside you." The corner of his mouth quirked and his words made her knees weak. "And now I can't wait to get you back into my bed."

Trinity slid her arms around his neck and reached up to brush her lips along his jawline. "We didn't exactly make it into bed, you know." Smells of their sex and sweat filled her senses, making her ache. Where Luke was concerned she was insatiable.

He gave a soft chuckle as he settled his palms on her hips. "No, we sure didn't." Sliding his hands lower, he cupped her ass and squeezed. "But we sure as hell had some fun."

Trinity purred as Luke pressed his hips against hers and she felt the hard line of his cock. He was just as insatiable as she was. She felt sore and well ridden in all locations, and yet she couldn't wait to saddle up that cowboy and take him out for another hard ride.

He gave her a soft lingering kiss that left her breathless and wanting more. It took all her strength to force herself to break away from him. "I—I'd better get inside."

Luke raised his hand to her ear and skimmed his knuckles along the row of gold earrings. "Sure you don't want me to come?"

Oh, she wanted him all right. And she could think of lots of ways for him to come.

Instead she caught his hand in hers and pressed it close to her cheek. He opened his hand and she turned to press her lips against his palm and flicked her tongue against the callused skin.

Luke's fingers shot into her hair and he dragged her to him for a bruising kiss. He bit at her lower lip, just hard enough to cause her to cry out in surprise.

"Damn, woman," he muttered when he finally released her. "I'm tempted to haul you off and have another go."

Oh, my.

"In fact, I think I know exactly where I'd like to go." Now the man had the devil in his eyes. "You take me to that spot on the mountains, where you used to spy on your sister. You take me to the cave where you learned about sex, and we'll see what all you remember."

Trinity's knees wobbled as she backed away.

That was just about the most erotic proposal she'd ever had.

Going to have wild sex in that place—

Damn.

It didn't get any more perfect-fantasy than that.

"I'll meet you in the barn tomorrow, in front of Dancer's stall." She opened the front door with one hand, her eyes still fixed on Luke as she slipped into the house. Just before she shut the door, she gave him a sultry smile and said, "I'll bring lunch. You bring the condoms."

Chapter 25

Holding her breath, as if that might help her slip inside without being noticed, Trinity shut the door quietly behind her. Yes, she needed to face her sister and get it over with, but first she'd like to shower and change. She smelled like sweat and sex and barn dust, and she knew she looked like hell.

Of course Skylar *had* just seen her looking a lot wilder.

She released her breath and rolled her eyes to the ceiling. Jeez. At least when she had spied on Skylar and Zack, they'd never caught her.

Pausing for a moment, she listened for sounds from the kitchen and heard nothing. After she quietly kicked her shoes off at the front door, Trinity walked as silently as possible through the living room. The tile felt cool beneath her sock-covered feet as she stole down the hallway and passed Skylar's and Zack's closed bedroom door.

She slipped away into her own bedroom, locked the door behind her, then stripped off her soiled clothing and tossed it all into the hamper in the adjoining bathroom. While she ran the shower until the room filled with steam, memories of her wild evening with Luke continued to scroll through her mind.

Cripes.

No doubt she was becoming some kind of sex fiend. That's all she'd been able to think about from the moment she'd met Luke. Not to mention that tonight she'd gotten off by knowing Skylar had watched them.

Water pelted Trinity's skin as she climbed into the shower, the warmth chasing away the sweat of exercise and sex. From head to toe her muscles had the pleasant ache of being well used and sweetly tender, all over her body. Even her ass felt different—like she missed Luke's cock there, too.

The comforting smell of her peach-scented shampoo filled her senses as she squirted a generous dollop into her hand and then washed her hair. When she rinsed it out, streams of lather flowed over her sensitized breasts and nipples, down her flat belly, and over her mound. Traveling over her like Luke's hands had.

She hadn't been entirely honest with him about wanting to face Skylar alone. Once she was away from the heat of the moment, away from her need to have him inside and his arms around her, fear had started to replace the desire. She needed space away from him, needed time to think about the future, *everything.*

What if she was pregnant? She definitely wasn't ready to be a mother. Luke claimed he wasn't about to let her go, but was that what she wanted?

He was still a cowboy for goodness sake. What would they do? Live here on her sister's ranch and raise a passel of kids? Not that he'd asked her to marry him, but what if he did . . . would she be expected to be a good little ranch wife who cooked dinner for her man?

Okay, so that was a bit stereotypical. Trinity had to smile at her own generalization. She knew plenty of women ranchers, like her own sister, who ran an entire ranch operation on their own, or side by side with their men. Heck, on the other side of the mountain she knew of two women who ran their ranch together, as partners in *every* way. Renee Duarte and Shannon Hanes had one of the most profitable operations in the county.

Closing her eyes, Trinity turned her face to the water, letting it splash over her forehead and down her face. She'd worked so hard to get to a position like she'd accepted with DropCaps. Four years of busting her ass, working countless hours to rise to the top, and she had the job she wanted now. Her perfect dream job. Staying in Douglas—it would be hard to keep her position, so far away from the main hubs of activity in the company.

She'd already made one monumental decision and had walked away from the caring man she'd dated for the past two years. Tossed that relationship right out the door. She'd left security and her comfortable world and headed straight into the wilds and the unknown.

What, am I insane?

With a groan Trinity opened her eyes, grabbed the luffa sponge and squirted peaches-and-cream-scented shower gel on the pad. As she scrubbed her body, thoughts of Luke tried to push aside her doubts and fears. Memories of how he'd touched her, how he'd filled her.

Was sex enough?

Yet it wasn't just sex that attracted her to Luke, or the way he looked at her and made her feel as though she was the most important thing in the world to him. Since she'd been at the ranch, she'd taken what opportunities she could to watch him interact with the other ranch hands, observe his leadership and fairness. And even though he'd been mad as hell at the arsonist, she'd seen the concern in his eyes for her the night the barn was set on fire.

But was that enough foundation to begin building a relationship? And was it worth leaving everything that she'd worked so hard for?

No matter how she tried to fight it, though, Trinity knew she was falling in love with one cowboy named Luke Rider. What she was going to do about it . . .

At this moment she didn't have a clue.

After Luke walked Trinity to the front door of the ranch house, he headed straight to his cabin. If his quarters weren't so close to the bunkhouse where the half-dozen ranch hands lived, Luke would have hauled Trinity out here with him and kept her all night long.

Course the night wasn't over yet.

When he faded into the darkness, out of sight from the house, Luke stopped and quickly retrieved the small firearm from the top of his boot. Even though he couldn't stop thinking about his woman, he wasn't so far gone that he would fail to ensure his building and surroundings were secure.

With practiced skill he listened for any unusual sounds, but all he heard was the faint creak of his leather chaps and the light brush of his boots over dirt as he continued toward his cabin and up to the front door.

As he checked to make sure his cabin hadn't been entered since he'd left that morning, an impression in the dirt by his doorstep caught his trained eye. After a quick glance around, his senses on full alert, he examined the print.

Easily about the size of a woman's booted foot, but a little larger than Trinity's or Skylar's, he'd wager. He frowned as he dug his key out of his front pocket and checked the thin strip of paper he'd lodged between the door and the frame, close to the threshold. Still there, so likely no one had been in his place. Who the hell had been snooping around his cabin, and why?

After he'd done a quick sweep of the apartment and locked the door, Luke yanked his cell phone out of his pocket and dialed his partner.

"Rios," the man answered after one ring.

"Denver here." Luke ambled into the kitchenette as he spoke. "I'm going on a field trip tomorrow. It's mostly personal—for pleasure—but there's a cave I want to check out in the mountains behind the Flying M."

"Yeah?" Rios said over the whinny of a horse. The man must be doing some fieldwork.

With his free hand, Luke yanked open the fridge and grabbed the carton of milk. "Got a gut feeling we're getting close to something again. Maybe right on top of it."

"Yeah, well, we're definitely on top of something with your friend Gina Garcia. Get with me tomorrow, so we can go over everything that's come in. And watch your ass, Denver."

As Luke popped his phone shut, he slammed the carton onto the counter and let the fridge close.

Gina Garcia came out of the darkness behind the refrigerator door like a blond avenging angel, only she wasn't carrying a flaming sword. She had a Ruger SR9, 9 millimeter, and she had it gripped in both hands, aimed like she knew how to use it.

Luke let go of the carton on the counter and raised his arms enough to show her he wasn't carrying. He was pissed as hell that she got the drop on him just like her brother. Only, Gina Garcia and her pistol looked a lot more serious about causing him pain than Brad Taylor had been.

"I thought my brother asked you to stop digging around in my life, Luke Denver." The sarcasm in Gina's tone was unmistakable, and the pistol in her grip didn't so much as wobble. "I should have known you're law enforcement. What are you? Fibbie? ICE?"

Luke kept his arms up. She'd heard him talking to Rios. No reason to bullshit now. "DEA."

Gina's expression stayed flat and deadly. "It's all the same to me. You and your partner made inquiries about my past."

Luke leaned against the counter slowly, careful not to give the woman any reason to pull that oh-so-sensitive trigger. "How do you know that?"

"Because a friend called me to give me fair warning." Her green eyes went from furious to something like tired. "Cruz Rios got the scoop on me—and I'm figuring you'll meet with him tomorrow to find out the juicy details. Want to know what you'll learn?"

Luke didn't say a word.

Gina was about to tell him what she wanted him to know, and as long as she kept talking, he kept breathing. Sometimes, the little victories mattered the most.

"You're gonna find out that I was young and stupid and impressed with bad boys, so I married one." Her accent got a little rougher, a little more northeast as she went. "I hooked up with a man who killed people for money, only I didn't find that out until Lola's sixth birthday. I barely got out of New York City alive, and now, thanks to you, the fucker I ran away from has a pretty good idea where I am—and worse, where Lola is. I should shoot you for that. I should shoot you right between the eyes."

Luke couldn't argue that point with her, if what she said was true. "All we did was check around under your real identity."

"You sent an inquiry that went to New York and then to New Jersey where I'm from. When it hit Jersey, the FBI field office handled it as a favor." Gina sounded sure of her information, and that tiredness he had sensed in her eyes, came through in her tone, too. "Because all inquiries involving my name get routed there. Want to guess why?"

A sinking feeling made Luke lower his arms, but not too much. "Your ex is FBI, and he has a trap and tracer on your name?"

Gina's laugh made his heart hurt. No humor in it. Only animals in pain made that kind of sound.

"My ex is James Scorcise," she said. "He's a made man in the Cordano crime syndicate, and yeah, he's FBI. The mob infiltrates you assholes just like you infiltrate them—so now maybe you're getting it. I've got nobody to protect me, and you just fucked up any chance I had at some peace in this place."

"Let me get you and Lola out of town. At least let me give you some contacts to help you before you blow my head off." He felt like shit over this. He really did. "Can't say as I'd blame you for it, and I mean that."

Gina started to cry—not sobbing or sniffling. Just angry, frightened tears, sliding down her cheeks as her grip on her gun seemed to become surer. "I don't want your contacts, and I don't want to shoot you any more than my brother did. I just want you to understand—things aren't always what they seem."

Luke tried to think fast, to figure out why Gina had come here, if it wasn't to kill him for wrecking her life. "Did you set Skylar's barn on fire to try to get my attention or make your point?"

Gina thrust the pistol closer to him, and her tears flowed faster. "I haven't done anything to Skylar or the Flying M, and I never would."

"Sorry. Had to ask." He had his arms down now, but he gripped the counter behind them to keep his hands in plain view. "There's a lot going on in Douglas."

"Look after Brad. I'll get in touch with him once I'm settled somewhere, but we won't be able to see each other for a while." She was keeping Luke sited, had the barrel aimed right at the sweet spot where his heart thumped—steadily for now. "Brad's in a mess there at Fenning's. You want to make this up to me, get him out of it, and get him out of it clean. I don't want to be calling my brother in jail. He's all I've got."

Now they were getting to it. She did want something from him—maybe even something he could give her. Luke risked folding his arms to give his chest a little cover, and Gina didn't squeeze her trigger.

"What's going on at Fenning's?" he asked.

"If you're hoping I can hand you Guerrero, keep dreaming." She blinked her slowing tears out of her eyes, leaned back, and rested her shoulder blades against the cabin's kitchen wall, near the slot between the refrigerator and the wall where she'd probably been hiding when he got home. "Fenning got lit on the anniversary of his wife's death and blew away an illegal he caught sneaking across his front yard. Stuffed the body in his meat locker, then sawed it up and left it there. Brad found out about it a few weeks after it happened, and he helped the old man get rid of the body."

Trinity's analysis was dead on target, Luke thought, then didn't like his own word choice. "That could be a problem for your brother, but it's something we can work with."

Gina's face reflected a little relief. "Brad doesn't want anything to happen to the old guy, and he didn't want anything to disrupt us here in Douglas, but it's more than that. Fenning's children won't want to keep the ranch—and who do you think will be waiting to buy it, just like he bought Zappati's?"

Luke had felt some respect for Gina before, and what she must have gone through to get her daughter out of danger. That respect increased as he realized her grasp of the situation in Douglas.

"Guerrero," he said, because all the bullshit in town, one way or the other, came back to that smooth-talking asshole.

"If you're planning to take down Fenning, you better damned sure have a play ready to keep the land out of that drug lord bastard's hands, or Douglas will be screwed even worse than it already is." Gina's tone suggested she hated Guerrero as much as everyone else, and Luke realized he probably reminded her of everything she had fled in New Jersey and New York City.

And as long as she was talking—

"Do you know anything about competition for Guerrero, encroaching on most of the Douglas and Bisbee areas—or where Guerrero's moving his product?"

Gina flexed her elbows without changing her pistol's position, but she didn't have Luke sited anymore. "I don't, but I'd wager Joyce Butler does. She was hot for that deputy who went down in the rustling scheme—what was his name—Woods?"

Luke nodded, then felt a wash of relief as Gina finally lowered her Ruger. She kept the grip in both hands, and he didn't make any moves.

"At some point, my husband will show up here searching for me," Gina said. "If I were you, I'd stay as far away from him as you can get. Tell your friends in local law enforcement. I don't want—" She let out a small, pained sigh. "I don't want any more blood on my hands."

Luke met her gaze, noting the fresh tears trying to push out of her green eyes. "Are you sure you won't let me give you some names? I know some honest men, Gina. I'm an honest man."

For a few long seconds, Gina actually seemed to be considering his offer, but then she frowned and gave her head a single, sharp shake. "I'd bet my life on that, but I won't bet Lola's."

What could Luke say to that?

Nothing at all, so he didn't try.

The most he could do for Gina now was be still and let her get finished—then work his ass off to keep her brother out of Clay Wayland's jail.

"I'm leaving now, Luke Denver," Gina said. "If I ever see you again, I'll kill you."

Luke didn't answer that either, because no answer was necessary. The lady had just made him a promise he figured she'd keep—and he didn't aim to find out if she meant it.

Gina holstered her weapon and slipped out of his kitchen—not toward the front door, but toward his bedroom. He heard the rasp of his window sliding upward, then a second rasp as she closed it behind her.

How the hell had he missed the marking at one of his window

frames? He allowed himself three seconds to be irritated that he'd have to postpone his lunch with Trinity, and that trip to the cave where she learned all about sex and fantasies and dreams.

Work again. It always came back around to that, didn't it?

Luke unfolded his arms and got on the phone to Rios in one big hurry.

"Yeah. Get Wayland and Ralston, and head to Bull Fenning's place. We've got a lot more than footprint data now—a real break on the UDA murder. If you can call it that. I'll brief you when I get there."

Chapter 26

Trinity never got the chance to keep avoiding her sister and Zack. She finished taking her shower, combed out her wet hair, yanked on a comfortable pair of flannel pajamas and slippers—and Zack came knocking on her door to look at the final printouts from her body temp overlay analysis again.

"I'm heading to Bull Fenning's," he said, stepping back from her worktable. His gray eyes seemed intense and focused. "I, ah, want Luke to go with me in case this goes bad for Fenning and Brad Taylor needs some extra help. He asked me to tell you he might not be back in time for lunch tomorrow."

"I understand." Trinity smiled in spite of the burst of disappointment. Running a ranch and working in law enforcement had a lot of similarities. Some things just couldn't wait. "But, Zack, wait a minute, okay?"

She shifted the papers on her desk and pointed to the last analysis she'd been working on, but hadn't finished yet. "This one set of prints here, the ones you and Wayland's people didn't think were related to this crime scene. I've been giving them a second look."

"We think Fenning had a man helping him. Those tracks probably belong to him, checking up on Fenning." Zack was heading toward the bedroom door. "Making sure the body disposal went like it was supposed to. We'll find out soon enough."

"I think those are female prints," Trinity called after Zack, and she heard his mumbled response.

"We'll look at it later."

Trinity slid the paper back toward her laptop and sighed. She didn't much feel like fooling with any of it tonight. She still felt embarrassed. Unsettled. And . . . hungry.

Time to head to the kitchen.

It was close to ten but she had a good feeling she'd find Skylar there.

Trinity's stomach growled as she padded down the hallway— she hadn't eaten since noon and she was starving. She passed the twinkling Christmas tree, rounded the corner, and headed into the kitchen, and sure enough, there was Skylar at the breakfast nook with a half gallon of Rocky Road and two spoons sticking out of the ice cream. Her sister appeared to be deep in thought, playing with her spoon in the Rocky Road.

The kitchen was spotless, but Trinity caught the delicious smell of roasted meat—probably pot roast—and her stomach grumbled again. It was so quiet that the rumbling of her belly was the only sound Trinity could hear other than the ticking of the kitchen clock.

As she approached her sister, Trinity felt heat rise to her face. "Save any for me?" she asked as she sank into the chair opposite Skylar.

Skylar looked up and smiled as she gestured toward one of the spoons. "Dig in. Unless you'd rather start with dinner."

Thankful to have something to do with her hands and mouth, Trinity shook her head and grasped the spoon. "This is most definitely the dinner of champions," she replied as she dug out a particularly large chunk and then stuffed it into her mouth.

"So . . ." Skylar's voice trailed off, and Trinity knew what was coming next. "You and Luke, huh?"

Trinity shrugged, her face burning hotter than ever while she studied her spoon and slowly chewed the chocolate ice cream filled with marshmallows, nuts, and fudge. The taste was welcoming and comforting, and somehow it had always made it easier to talk with her sister.

After she swallowed, Trinity glanced from her spoon to her sister. "It all started that first night I came home. I met Luke at Nevaeh's Christmas party."

Skylar raised one eyebrow. "You've been seeing him that long?"

"Well, sort of, but not exactly." Trinity dug her spoon into the softening ice cream. "He's been working on me, and I've been fighting the attraction," she said before taking another bite.

Shaking her head, Skylar replied, "That sounds awfully familiar." She winked at Trinity. "And knowing Luke, when he sets his mind to something, he doesn't give up. Not for anything." She licked her spoon, a thoughtful look on her face. "So what about Richard, or Rocky, or whatever his name was with the British accent and the corny rented sports car?"

Trinity swallowed the mouthful of Rocky Road and snorted back a laugh. "Race."

"Whatever." Skylar pushed the ice cream carton aside and leaned over the table, closer to Trinity. "I knew you said you'd cut it off by phone and e-mail, but when he came to the door, I wondered."

"He needed to hear it face-to-face. So did I, really." Trinity dug into the ice cream again. "Felt more final after that."

"That accent alone's enough to give any woman the shivers. And he's one *fine*-looking man." Skylar pointed her ice scream spoon at Trinity. "When he started talking, it was all I could do to find my tongue."

Trinity smiled. "I sure fell for that refined British accent." Her smile faded as she considered the reason why their relationship hadn't worked. "I really think the world of Race, but the problem was that he's *too* reserved. I know he cares about me, and probably loves me in his own way, but something happened in his past that caused him to lock away his emotions and feelings."

Trinity toyed with the spoon as she spoke, studying her upside-down reflection on its shiny surface. "It wasn't until I met Luke that I realized Race was truly passionless. I realized that I need someone who's able to feel and *live*." She raised her eyes to meet her sister's. "And I wasn't the right woman to set Race free. Just like he couldn't set me free."

"Sorry about walking in on you and Luke." Skylar's cheeks went pink and her hand moved to the peridot heart pendant at her throat. "I was feeding the horses and that devil Satan, when I heard noises in the office. After the postcard and the fire—"

"We should have locked the door." Trinity was sure her own face was Christmas red. "It was our first time, and we went kind of wild."

Skylar's eyebrows shot up. "Your first time with him and he gave it to you in the ass?"

Resisting the urge to duck under the table and hide, Trinity nodded. "Well, actually, that was after we did it the, ah, usual way."

Her sister leaned forward on the table again. "So tell me. How did it feel? In the ass, I mean."

Trinity laughed and before she thought better of it, she said, "As wild as you and Zack have always had it, you've never tried anal sex?"

Skylar frowned. "I've never told you about our sex life."

"Oops." Trinity chewed the inside of her lower lip, then decided to spill the beans. "You know, back when you and Zack were dating . . . before he left?"

Skylar's spoon clattered to the tabletop and she clasped her pendant tighter. "You didn't."

Trinity hid a grin and gave a solemn nod instead. "Up at that place you called your hideaway. There's a cave hidden behind some bushes. I was curious and hid out there and watched you guys."

"Oh. My. God." Skylar slowly shook her head, an expression of disbelief on her features. "I can't believe it."

"Let's just say it was a real education for a teenage girl." Trinity stuck her spoon into the ice cream that had softened to the point of turning into a mudslide instead of Rocky Road. "Better eat up. It's melting."

Laughter escaped Skylar and she raised her hands in an *I give up* gesture. "Well, I sure don't feel so bad walking in on you and Luke now."

Trinity snorted and giggled and then in the next moment the

sisters collapsed into fits of laughter. Tears rolled down their cheeks, and Trinity laughed so hard that her stomach ached.

God, but it felt good to laugh.

And even with all the stress, even with all the craziness in Douglas and at the Flying M, it felt really good to be home.

Chapter 27

In the near darkness, the Bar F looked like a kicked beehive full of flashing lights. When Luke got there, he counted half a dozen law enforcement vehicles, marked and unmarked, and more were coming up fast behind him. Floodlights had been set up in the yard, making the sidewalk and porch bright as noon. Crime-scene tape marked an area to the right, leading to an outbuilding where Luke presumed Bull Fenning kept his meat locker.

Luke got out of his truck and put on his black Stetson, and made his way to Clay Wayland, who was standing by the front door making notes on a pocket-sized pad. Clay Wayland's deputies were already leading Bull Fenning away from the massive stone ranch house in handcuffs, and the big man had his head down so low his chin seemed to be part of his chest.

"Damn shame that boy from Mexico had to die." Clay Wayland lowered his pad and adjusted his tan Stetson as he greeted Luke. "I'd like to get my hands on the fucking coyote who cut that poor kid loose and sent him wandering across Bull's land in the middle of the damned night."

"Something has to change." Luke watched as the deputies helped Bull into the back of a marked car.

He knew stopping fuckheads like Guerrero was key to ending scenes like this. Before the American people and the people of Mexico would ever embrace immigration reform, the drug lords had to be put out of business. Everything along the border, all the issues— sooner or later, they meshed together. Couldn't fix one without fixing the others, too. Not really. Sometimes it felt a lot like shoveling shit out of a manure pile the size of Canyon de Chelly.

Wayland rubbed the corners of his dark moustache. "We talked to Fenning about Guerrero, and Fenning thinks his oldest son might step up to the plate with the Bar F after all. He signed a quitclaim to transfer the property to him, and he gave Brad Taylor the cash to wire his son what he'd need to cover this year's taxes and operating expenses."

"Damn." Luke whistled from surprise. "That's a lot of capital to have lying around."

Wayland's mouth twitched into something like a smile. "The old man had it in waterproof safes, sunk down in his well. I've heard tell Fenning's father was like that—but you know, after the market crash bullshit and all the failed banks, they don't seem that crazy after all."

Luke thought about how the federal government and other nations were busy busting up tax havens in Swiss banks and offshore accounts. He thought about all the hours of forensic accounting the DEA hired and paid for, day after day and week after week. They got a ton of intel from watching where the money moved, but there would always be a Bull Fenning somewhere, burying—or drowning—his cash off the radar.

A few seconds later, Cruz Rios came out the front door, hustling Brad Taylor in front of him. Luke was relieved to note the lack of cuffs on Taylor, and he pulled off to the left with Wayland and Cruz, away from the growing crowd of officers and technicians, to talk to the man.

As they reached a clutch of pines near the edge of the yard, Taylor's brown eyes looked wide and wild, hunted, not unlike his sister's when she'd come to Luke's cabin earlier that evening. Luke felt a twinge of guilt, especially when Taylor smashed his fist against a pine tree trunk, then wheeled on him.

"You should have listened to me, Rider—if that's even your name."

Luke didn't volunteer anything about his cover. "You should have told me the whole story, Brad. Especially if you suspected I was law enforcement."

Cruz and Wayland stayed silent, obviously realizing Luke had enough of a relationship to pull off defusing the situation and getting Taylor where he needed to be.

"Christ, I may never see her again." Taylor rubbed his bruising knuckles against his jeans and stared at the gray dawn sky. "And Lola—they're really on their own now."

"I tried to get her to go to some of my friends," Luke told the man. "She wouldn't do it."

"I sent Levi Thorn after her," Wayland said in his quiet, matter-of-fact voice, surprising Luke and Rios, too, by the look on Rios's face. "I had him headed out to question her at the K and K based on the info the DEA had received. When he found her and her daughter gone, Levi tracked her to the Flying M."

"Not bad," Rios muttered, giving Luke a look, no doubt about the Flying M connection.

Luke quickly explained about his encounter with Gina, and how she'd come to the Flying M to ask him to help Taylor.

Taylor's mouth came open, and his already red face got a little darker. "Your deputy won't ever catch up to my sister, Sheriff Wayland. She's good at running. She has to be."

"Don't underestimate the man," Wayland said. "Levi's former special forces, and he worked for the U.S. marshalls for his first four years out of the service. Last I heard from him, he'd picked up her trail again, on the edge of Cochise County, heading north and east."

Taylor shook his head and smacked his damaged hand against his leg. "Call him back. How do you know you can trust Thorn not to get Gina killed like these DEA assholes almost did?"

Rios winced, and Luke didn't even try to defend himself. A crime syndicate hit man working for the FBI wasn't anything he could have prepared for.

Wayland's reassurance came out smooth and simple, and completely convincing. "Levi's got plenty of money—his own, and from his family. Trust me, he doesn't owe anybody anything, and he's not corruptible. He'll take care of your sister and niece."

That seemed to help Taylor settle down, at least a little bit. Luke had to admit he felt better, too, thinking that Gina and Lola had a good man like Levi Thorn on their side. Seemed like they'd need that help—and a lot more—to escape Gina's past.

"When we're sure all of this is settled," Wayland added, "when we're positive Gina's ex can't do her any harm, Levi will bring Gina and Lola home."

Luke picked up the cue from Wayland's voice and the glance he fired in Luke's direction. "Taylor, we want you to wait for them at the K and K, keep it fixed up for them."

Wayland looked at Rios, who brought it home with, "And we want you to give us whatever information we need, whenever you hear or see anything related to Francisco Guerrero."

Taylor cut his gaze in the direction the squad car had taken, the one that had carried Bull Fenning off to jail for murdering the UDA, then trying to cover up his crime.

His non-response let Luke know what Rios and Wayland no doubt saw, too. Taylor understood his position, that he was staying out of jail for Gina's sake—and to be useful to the DEA and local law enforcement. He didn't yet know what they'd be asking him to do, or all of what they'd demand, but whatever it was, Taylor would do it. For himself, and for his sister.

Luke didn't much like this aspect of his job. Cultivating informants was one thing. Conscripting them—another. But in its own way, the border situation *was* a war, after all. And Taylor's other options weren't viable for him, or for Gina.

"All right." Taylor rubbed his knuckles again.

"Better let me get somebody to look at that hand," Wayland said, right about the time Luke's phone buzzed.

Luke pulled out the little cell and glanced at the display before answering.

"Denver?" Noah Ralston's tense voice boomed across the sensitive connection.

Shit. This already doesn't sound good.

"I'm here," Luke said, motioning for Rios to take Taylor out of earshot.

"Is Wayland with you?" Ralston asked as Rios led Taylor back toward Fenning's big stone house.

"Yeah, and half the county's resources. We've got a situation at the Bar F—"

Ralston cut him off without so much as a wait-a-sec. "I'm at the Rocking B. You and Clay—get over here. Now."

"I'm sorry, Noah." Clay Wayland's green eyes had a grim, dark cast as he studied the destroyed ranch house with Luke. "I know Joyce meant something to you."

Ralston said nothing as Wayland turned away and got on his phone, and Luke couldn't blame the man. Ralston barely had his temper and reactions under control.

Joyce Butler had gone missing.

Somebody had really trashed her place, and apparently taken her with them when they left.

Everywhere Luke looked, he saw busted furniture, walls with big smashed holes, no glass intact—like somebody had taken a sledgehammer to every inch of the place. The walls that hadn't been knocked to smithereens contained a variety of messages and slurs, painted in garish red that Ralston had already determined to be paint, not blood.

Puta had been used most often, but Luke saw a fair number of *chingada madre* and *chocha*, and some death threats.

At first blush, the whole scene could be taken for vandalism, maybe even a random attack by a group of delinquent UDAs. The more reactionary racists in Douglas and along the border would no doubt take this crime for exactly that.

Luke knew better, and so did Wayland and Ralston.

This attack had been deliberate, and planned, and designed to leave a powerful message for any enemy of the Guerrero drug cartel.

This is what happens to people who cross us.

Ralston must have been right all along. Joyce Butler had gotten in over her head with Guerrero, and now she had paid the price. He hated to think what her body might look like when they found her—*if* they found her at all.

Even though Noah Ralston's interest in Joyce Butler had been purely the loyal-old-friend variety, it had to kill him inside, knowing what the woman was probably going through right now.

"Her father's given permission for us to search every inch of border dirt he owns." Wayland snapped his phone shut. "He's kicking in equipment and volunteers. If there are any corridors or tunnels on this land, collapsed or still standing, we'll find them."

A little too late, Luke thought, and cursed their lack of resources. Every agency, from local to federal and everything in between, needed more technology, more people, more money, and they just didn't have it.

"I'll head straight to the field office," he told Ralston. "You know the DEA will be in this eyeball-deep, right beside you, like we have been."

When Ralston turned to face Luke, Luke saw a full version of the flash of hot, steely rage he had first seen from Ralston at Nevaeh's. "Guerrero's going down. If you and your people don't take the bastard out, Denver, I will. Count on it."

Chapter 28

Trinity hadn't gotten to play out her fantasy in the mountain caves with Luke. In fact, she hadn't gotten to spend much quality time with Luke for days now, not since Bull Fenning got arrested. Skylar and Zack kept telling her how Luke was helping Brad Taylor on the Fenning spread, and at the K & K, too, since Gina Garcia had to leave town suddenly.

When she'd actually gotten to see Luke, he was so covered with dirt and exhausted, she could swear he'd been helping to dig up half of Cochise County.

I'm sorry, sugar, was the best he could do. *Sometimes, this is my life.*

As for Zack, he'd been absorbed with the rest of the world, in the hunt for Joyce Butler. Which is why he'd interrupted her work again after her morning shower, to go over her analysis of the unrelated prints at the Fenning crime scene.

"I still don't know who this would be," Zack said, his gray eyes tired as he evaluated the printout and her theories that the prints could have originated from the direction of Fenning's house, or from Gina Garcia's K & K. "Maybe a female UDA in the wrong place at the wrong time."

"The prints are my size." Trinity rubbed her hair with her bath towel, glad she'd already been dressed when Zack came banging on her door. "The woman would have to be about my height."

Zack actually gave her a grin—rare these last few days. "Other than you and Sky, that leaves, what, half the females in Douglas? If we don't count Bisbee."

"But this woman knew where she was going, I think. Or what she was doing. Not much hesitation." Trinity pointed to her list of print depths. "See? She didn't press in and turn often. She just walked up, stopped, then walked away."

Zack folded up the printout to take to the ICE field office, and share with the other agencies searching for Joyce. The prints were her size, but like Zack pointed out, that didn't mean much.

"Sky's going to town for a feed run since Luke's tied up," Zack said as he got up to leave. "You'll be okay?"

Trinity knew that was code for, *Is your gun loaded?*

"Fine," she told him, glancing at the zippered pouch on her nightstand where she kept the pistol.

They hadn't had any trouble on the Flying M since all the chaos at Fenning's Bar F, and Guerrero wasn't even in town. Trinity figured the drug lord would keep himself way past quiet until all this died down, but she supposed he might have henchmen, or minions, or whatever the hell she was supposed to call his hired help. She knew she couldn't be too careful.

"Rider's here today, by the way," Zack said as he reached the door to her room, sounding almost casual even though his smile told Trinity he knew how that news would affect her. "He's, ah, taking the day off, and he asked me to tell you he'd meet you at noon in front of Dancer's stall, if you're still up for a ride."

Zack took off down the hall, leaving Trinity standing there with her hair in a towel and her heart racing.

Luke . . .

Day off . . .

Ride into the mountains . . .

Trinity's entire body seemed to catch fire at the same time, a slow delicious burn that touched her everywhere. The ache she'd barely been ignoring for days took her over, and she wanted to run straight to Luke's cabin, beat down the door, and climb on top of him.

But . . . she'd promised to make them lunch for the trip, back when they first planned it.

Crap!

She didn't have much time.

Dressed in a comfy pair of old blue jeans, a jade-green T-shirt, Nikes, and a jacket to keep out the chill, Trinity hurried from the ranch house toward the barn to meet up with Luke. She'd French-braided her hair to keep it out of her face and had kept her makeup light. After all, she was hoping he'd be kissing off all her lipstick anyway.

Flutters stirred in her belly in anticipation of seeing Luke. She shrugged the lunch bag higher on her shoulder and entered the dark recesses of the barn. The acrid smell of smoke from the fire was finally starting to fade, but it still surprised her every time she entered the barn, reminding her that their little world wasn't as safe as she'd always thought it to be.

Except today.

Today, she refused to think about Guerrero or Joyce or Drop-Caps or decisions or anything at all, save for Luke, and spending time with him.

As she walked past Satan's stall, she caught the sound of Luke's voice at the same moment she saw him ahead, standing next to Dancer's stall. The mare was already saddled up, and Tequila, Luke's sorrel mount, was right beside Dancer.

Trinity's pulse rate picked up and those flutters in her belly magnified. Lord, oh lord, he looked good wearing his black duster, black Stetson, jeans, and boots. Dark and dangerous-looking, that was her man.

". . . if you don't hear from me in four," Luke was saying into a cell phone as she got closer. "Just stay back." He caught sight of Trinity as she drew closer. She saw a flicker of something in his eyes, and then he gave her a brief smile and a nod as he listened to whoever it was on the other end.

"Uh-huh," he said into the phone, his gaze focused on Trinity. "Gotta head on out," he added and then took the phone away from his ear and punched it off before stuffing it into his duster pocket.

Trinity wanted to ask who he'd been on the phone with, but she knew it was none of her business. Instead she placed her palms on her hips and gave him a teasing look. "Cowboys and cell phones . . . somehow that just seems *wrong*."

With one finger, Luke beckoned to Trinity to come closer. "I'll tell you what's wrong, sugar." When she reached him, his eyelids lowered as he settled his hands at her waist and brought her hips flush with his. "Waking up every morning without you in my bed where you belong . . . that's a serious problem in my book. The world needs to get sane again, in a hurry, so I can give you the time you deserve."

Trinity realized he sounded worried. That he looked worried. "It's okay, Luke. I miss you—but I understand. I'm not a preschooler you have to amuse or anything. I do have other things to keep me occupied."

He pulled her closer, and closer still, his gaze doubling in intensity. "I don't want to lose you," he murmured. "Now, or ever."

The lunch bag fell to the dirt floor of the barn as Trinity sucked in her breath. She moved her palms to his chest, feeling the tenseness in his muscles through his denim shirt. "You won't. Not like that."

Luke's blue eyes flashed with sensual fire as he lowered his mouth to claim hers, and he sank his teeth into her lower lip. Trinity moaned into his mouth, and then took him deep as he thrust his tongue inside. He tightened his grip on her, rubbing his erection against her belly at the same time.

She ached all over as she tasted his unique flavor. His masculine smell, spicy aftershave, and the clean scent of soap wrapped around her. She couldn't think . . . she could only feel as he kissed her absolutely senseless.

When Luke drew away, Trinity was so dazed that she just stared up at him. He gave her that sexy grin of his that brought out the dimple in his cheek.

"Office," she said. "You. Me. *Now.*"

He grinned down at her. "We'd do just that if three ranch hands weren't already in there helping Skylar with her record-keeping."

With a sigh, Trinity replied, "Yeah, well, they can't possibly be having as much fun as we did."

Luke chuckled softly as he captured her mouth in another searing kiss. Trinity was so hot for him that she was ready to take him in a stall and have her way with him, no matter that someone might come by.

Hot breath blew across her cheek and a soft muzzle nudged the two of them apart. Trinity laughed and rubbed the nose of her black mare, Dancer. "You looking for some attention, old girl?"

"I don't know about her, but I sure am." Luke tweaked the end of Trinity's braid. "Let's head on out. Maybe we'll find ourselves someplace a little more private."

The ride into the mountains behind the Flying M was a form of torture, Luke decided. While he rode Tequila, the slow and easy gait of the roan mare only added to his sexual discomfort. He swore he caught Trinity's peaches-and-cream scent over the smell of horses and piñon, and could hear her heartbeat over the creak of saddle leather and the sound of hooves against dirt and stone.

His lawman's senses remained on high alert, always on the lookout for danger. These mountains had been used for decades to smuggle not only drugs and other contraband, but illegal immigrants as well. He needed Trinity to show him that cave before the day ended, but he wasn't taking a chance on anything happening to her. He'd get the location, then take her home before he came back and did any serious poking around.

While their horses traveled higher into the mountain, Luke rested his hands on the saddle pommel as he studied Trinity. An Arizona December breeze stirred the tendrils of hair that had escaped her braid. Her cheeks were flushed and her jacket was open, and he could see her nipples poking against the T-shirt that matched the jade of her eyes . . . Eyes that were so full of passion it was all he could do not to stop the horses and take her now. Hell, if it wasn't so chilly and she was wearing something a little less constraining, he'd have tried his hand at lovemaking on horseback.

Luke's cock throbbed against the tight denim of his jeans and he shifted in his saddle.

"Not much farther," Trinity said, answering his question before he asked it.

"Good thing." He gave her a smoldering look. "I don't know how much longer I'll last before I have to have my hands on you."

Her eyes widened and she ran her tongue along her lower lip. "I can't wait to get my mouth on you."

Luke clenched his reins in his fists. "All right. Your teasing's gone far enough."

Trinity laughed. "Hold your horses, cowboy. It's just around that piñon tree."

"Wait a sec." Luke reached out and grabbed Dancer's bridle and brought both horses to a stop. "Let me go on ahead and check it out first."

"Why?" Trinity gave him a puzzled look. "I was up here dozens of times, and nobody other than Skylar and Zack even knows the place exists."

"Things have changed." Luke swung one leg over his mare and dismounted, his black duster swirling around his legs. "Never know what's in these mountains these days." With a firm look, he added, "Sit tight and stay with the horses. I'll be right back."

She frowned and folded her arms across her chest, but didn't argue as Luke let Tequila's reins drop to the ground. The mare was well trained and would wait for him until he returned or until he gave the piercing whistle that was Tequila's signal to come at a gallop.

On silent booted feet, Luke moved through the trees and bushes until he came upon the secluded area surrounded by oak and piñon. From higher in the canyon a small stream tumbled over the rocks and down through a small ravine.

At first glance the place seemed empty. Bushes rustled to his right and in a flash he withdrew the gun from beneath his shirt, hidden at the small of his back. He trained the bead at the bush, but a second later a jackrabbit bolted out and sped across the clearing.

As far as he could tell, the area was secure. Now where the hell could that cave be—

The snap of a twig sounded behind him. Luke whirled, gun in his hand, only to point it directly at Trinity.

Her face whitened at the sight of his firearm and he quickly lowered it and tucked it back under his black duster. "I told you to stay with the horses."

Trinity swallowed, a confusing range of emotions swirling through her. What the hell was going on here? "I—I knew there was no way you'd find the cave without me."

Luke's features were hard and his voice cut right through her. "It's not a good idea to sneak up on a man like that."

"I didn't know you were carrying a gun." She shifted her feet, feeling for all the world like she wanted to run straight back to the ranch house. "Why would you need to bring one?"

"You should have brought yours, too. It's for your protection, and doesn't protect a damn thing zipped up in a pouch back at the house. We could find anything—including rattlesnakes."

Trinity frowned. "It's winter."

"There are a lot of different types of rattlesnakes out there." He scrubbed his hand over his face and his tone softened. "Why don't you show me that cave?"

"Okaaaaay." She forced down the niggling of irritation as she skirted the clearing, not bothering to see if Luke was following her. For a big man he sure walked quietly. Pebbles and dirt crunched under her shoes, but she heard nothing from him. She was tempted to turn around to see that he was behind her, but she didn't have to—she could *feel* his presence.

When she got to the back of the clearing, she started climbing up the boulders, higher into the canyon and to the right of the stream. Her jacket protected her arms as she shrugged by spindly trees and scrawny bushes on her way up the hidden path.

Flashes of memories came back to her, memories of watching Zack and Skylar have sex down below. She'd had such a perfect view. It had turned her on, making her want to experience wild and exciting sex like those two had shared. Trinity never had . . . until she met Luke.

Watching Trinity's pretty little ass as she climbed up the rocky incline was giving Luke a screaming hard-on. He kept close on her tail, ah, literally, but fell back a bit when she reached a ledge above the clearing. "Let me go in first," he called to her, but in the next moment she vanished.

His gut clenched and he rushed ahead to reach the ledge in a few strides. At first glance he saw only another boulder that easily topped seven feet in height. But when he rounded the boulder, he was suddenly in the cave, and Trinity was waiting for him with her arms folded across her chest.

With trained precision, he quickly scanned the cave and his eyes and senses told him it was clear as far as humans or animals were concerned. To his surprise it was big enough for him to stand up in, even with his Stetson still on his head. The floor was littered with leaves and a coating of fine dirt, and cobwebs clung to the ceiling. No sign of recent occupation by bats, wildcats, or any other critters.

He walked to the back of the cave and saw that it wasn't too deep and there wasn't any more to it than met the eye. Luke's muscles relaxed and he blew out his breath. He wasn't sure what he'd been expecting, but whatever it was, it wasn't here.

"Satisfied?" Trinity asked from behind him. He turned to look and she had one eyebrow raised. "I'd say there's more to you than you've let on."

Luke moved in front of her and caught her by the shoulders. "What if there is, Trinity MacKenna?"

For one second she wished he wasn't touching her, wasn't so close. Her brain always seemed to go on standby when he was near, and her libido on overdrive.

The hell with it.

Trinity threw her arms around his neck and pulled him to her. Luke groaned as she bit at his lip, her hunger for him driving her on in a flurry of touching, sensation, and feeling. He pushed open her jacket and shoved up her shirt and then his big palms found her naked breasts beneath. Trinity's hands reached under his duster for his Western shirt and she ripped the snaps apart with one tug. While he fondled her nipples, she went for his belt buckle. Their mouths never parted, their kiss wild and frantic as she undid his belt and zipped down his pants.

She tore away from him, her breathing so ragged that for a moment she was afraid she'd hyperventilate. "I want you in my mouth, Luke."

"Whoa, sugar," he murmured as she dropped to her knees on the dirt-covered floor and pulled out his cock. "I need to—" he started, but then sucked in his breath as she went down on him.

His hand clenched her braid as she slid him in all the way to the back of her throat. She stroked him in time with the movements of her head, her hand sliding down to the tight curls at the base of his cock and up to the thick tip. His masculine scent exhilarated her, made her anxious to please him, to taste him.

"That's good . . . so good." Luke's hand gripped her hair tighter, moving her more forcefully along his erection. She loved how she made him want her so badly he became even more masterful, more demanding, yet giving her everything at the same time.

Her shirt was still pushed up above her breasts and the cave's cool air brushed her nipples and caused them to ache beyond the point of pain. She brought her free hand to first one nipple, then the other, pinching and rolling each between her thumb and forefinger as she sucked and stroked him.

Yeah.

This was it.

This was what she'd wanted all those years ago, when she'd pleasured herself in this cave all alone, watching her sister bind her heart and soul and body to Zack Hunter.

Trinity had wanted her own match, her own equal, her own chance to fall that hard—and that hot—for somebody.

She'd wanted this.

She'd wanted a man named Luke Rider, even if it took her years to meet him.

Luke groaned out loud, the sensation of Trinity's mouth and hand on him sending all rational thought straight out of his head. And all irrational thought straight down to his other head. The feel of her hot, wet mouth sliding up and down his cock, that soft purring sound she made when she was turned on, the way she watched him as she sucked, and the way she tugged at each of her dark nipples in her excitement . . . *damn.*

"I'm gonna come," he said as he watched himself thrust in and out of her mouth. "Can you handle that?"

Trinity purred and sucked even harder. He choked back a cry as his hips bucked against her face. She kept on working him till he had to grab her head with both hands and say, "Hold on."

With a satisfied smile, she allowed his spent member to slide out of her mouth and slowly licked her lips. "Mmmmm," she murmured. "We'll definitely have to do that again."

From zero to fully functional, Luke's cock shot back to attention. How the hell did she do that to him?

It was like being sixteen again.

Worse.

No.

Better.

He gestured with one hand for her to stand up. The moment she was on her feet, he helped her pull off her jacket and yank her T-shirt over her head, tossing them both to the cave floor.

"Yeah, that's more like it," he said. "Now kick off your shoes."

No questions asked, Trinity obeyed. Her eyes and her face, though, were fevered with her excitement, her eagerness for him.

He yanked down her jeans and she stepped out of them in a hurry, leaving her in only her socks and nothing else. She looked so beautiful with her jade eyes almost black with passion, her strawberry blond hair sticking out of the braid, her nipples dark and swollen, every part of her, just waiting for him.

He'd given it to her hard last time and he'd wanted to take it nice and slow, but right now all he could think about was driving into her until she screamed and kept right on screaming.

"I want you now, Luke," she said, and that was all it took.

"Grab hold," he said even as he cupped her ass, raised her up, and brought her down hard and fast on his pulsing cock.

"Yes!" she shouted as she gripped his shoulders, wrapped her legs around his waist beneath his duster, and arched her back. "God, you're just perfect."

Luke lifted her up and down, her bare ass rubbing against his jeans every time he buried himself deep inside her.

Harder and harder he rammed into Trinity, and she only begged for more. He'd never in his life been so crazy, so frantic—so in love with a woman like this.

Trinity's cry tore through the cave as her walls pulled tight around him. Luke thrust again and again and again, and she shuddered and rode out every wave of her orgasm.

Sweat poured down his face, down his chest, and down his abs, to the place where they were joined. A burst of sensation exploded in his loins and he came inside Trinity in a heated rush.

Trinity collapsed against his shoulder, her breathing harsh and warm upon his skin. He held her tight, keeping himself firmly inside his woman as they both held on like they never wanted to let go.

Shit. They'd done it again—no condom. Damn, but this woman made him crazy.

"Luke," Trinity said against his shoulder, her voice husky and filled with passion. "I'm in love with you."

In the next instant he heard an all too familiar click, and he froze as ice chilled his spine. Luke pressed Trinity tightly to him, keeping her back to the cave wall and shielding her with his body.

Laughter came from behind them and then a familiar woman's voice said, "At least you got that out of your system, honey . . . before you have to die."

Chapter 29

Fuck. Luke's gut clenched as Trinity gasped and stiffened in his arms. His cock was still lodged deep inside her, and she was completely naked and vulnerable.

And right beside them, there was a gun-wielding bitch with her sites trained on them.

Luke turned his head and focused his gaze on Joyce Butler while protecting Trinity the best he could with his body. "We're a little busy here," he said, trying to stall for time as he formulated a plan to get him and Trinity out of this.

Trinity peeked over his shoulder, her eyes wide. "Joyce?" Her gaze rested on the slim semiautomatic in Butler's grip, and Trinity audibly caught her breath. "Half the world's out searching for you. What's going on?"

Butler smiled and rested one shoulder against the cave wall, her grip staying firm on her Colt .45. "Just to remind you—you've seen me shoot. You already know I'm an expert marksman, so don't fuck with me. Two shots. That's all it'll take."

Luke didn't waste words. Instead he sized Butler up . . . the unwavering confidence in her eyes, the egotistical curve of her mouth, and her relaxed stance.

"Where have you been?" Trinity asked, and before he could stop her, she eased her legs from around his waist. His cock slid out of her core as she stood in his embrace. "And why are you here now, doing this?"

"I rather liked you in that position." Butler aimed her gun at Trinity's temple. "Make another move without my permission and you'll be one dead little slut."

Forcing his arms to relax around Trinity, Luke said, "Let Trinity grab her clothes and leave. Whatever you've got going on, this isn't about her."

"Oh, sure. Like *that's* going to happen." The woman grinned, and she actually looked like she was having a little fun.

Egotistical bitch thought this was all a game. Well, he sure as hell could use that to his advantage.

Butler's gaze lingered for a moment on his cock and her tongue flicked against her lower lip. "Nice firearm you've got there." Her cold gray eyes moved to Trinity. "What a waste, firing your bullets in *that* hole."

Luke ground his teeth as he clenched Trinity's arm tighter and felt her tremble beneath his hand. He didn't know whether it was from cold, embarrassment, or anger, but figured it was probably a little of everything.

"Toss me your weapon." Butler turned her gun on Luke. "The one you keep under your duster. And you know how it works . . . nice and slow, cowboy."

Luke released Trinity and started to ease his right hand toward his back.

"Uh-uh." Butler shook her head. "I've seen you shoot at the firing range, too, and I know you're right handed." She indicated Trinity with a nod. "Hold on to the slut's arm with your shooting hand, where I can see it. Use your left to bring out the gun."

Luke tensed at her continued insults to Trinity, but obliged and gripped Trinity's arm with his right hand. He could feel her shaking even harder, and sensed her fear and confusion.

Very slowly he moved his left hand beneath his duster. Course, he was just as deadly a shot with his left as his right, but he wasn't about to take a chance with Trinity's life. He'd have to find another way to deal with this bitch.

Sorry again, Ralston, but I'm afraid you read this one ass-backward. We all did.

Butler pointed her gun toward Trinity's head again. "You know she's dead if you make me the tiniest bit suspicious."

"Wouldn't dream of it," he said as he slid one finger along the cell phone in his holster and pressed button number one, hoping like hell the cave didn't block the signal . . . all in the same motion it took to move his hand to the butt of his gun.

Keeping his movements as slow as possible, Luke brought out the gun and held it up where the woman could see it, barrel pointing down.

Butler indicated the cave opening with a jerk of her head. "Throw it all the way up there."

Luke tossed his weapon.

It clattered, spun, and came to an abrupt stop at the boulder that guarded the entrance.

Her eyes never left his. "How does it feel to be left alone and defenseless with your cock hanging out, Agent Denver?"

She stared between his legs again.

God damn it. How far would she take this?

Trinity gasped as she stared at Joyce, unable to believe what the woman had just said. "Agent Denver?" she repeated as she looked to Luke and almost reflexively started to step away from him.

"Don't move," he commanded her, tightening his grip on her arm.

Butler giggled and propped one hand on her hip, her nails bright red against her jeans and her pale gray eyes filled with mirth. "Sorry to spoil those feelings of love, *sugar.*" She gestured at Luke with her gun. "Your sweet innocent cowboy isn't what he seems to be at all."

Trinity had felt cold and vulnerable as she'd stood there in only her socks and looking down the barrel of the gun. But now the slow heat of anger and confusion crept through her, melting away the frost.

She couldn't for a moment believe that Luke had kept something that major from her.

"You're lying." Trinity clenched her fists as she glared at Joyce.

"Go on." Joyce smiled at Luke and gave an encouraging nod. "Tell her that you're DEA, undercover. That you hired on to the Flying M to investigate Skylar, among other things."

Trinity's gaze shot to meet his. "Luke?" she whispered, feeling like she was caught up in the middle of a kaleidoscope. Her whole world seemed to turn upside down and every which way with only a few words, and nothing was what she thought it was. "Are you—is this . . . true?"

The grip he had on her upper arm lessened and he rubbed his thumb along the soft flesh of her inner elbow, as though to comfort her. "I am with the DEA, and yes, your sister was part of the initial investigation, but—"

She jerked her arm away.

"Be still," Joyce shouted, her voice echoing throughout the cave. "Time to get you two down to where the action is. You're both going to be my saving grace, so to speak. Wayland and Hunter are far too close, just like you, Denver. Hell, even Noah's got pieces of this puzzle, and he's trying to put them together. I need a smoke screen fast, so thanks for coming way up here. I figured it would be Skylar and Zack—seen them up here at least once a week. That's who I was waiting for, but it's no big deal. I can still solve a bunch of problems at once with you two."

Luke gave Trinity a measured look, as though that was meant to clear up everything he'd neglected to mention.

Like his real name.

Like his real job.

If there wasn't a gun trained on them right now, she'd have socked him in the gut, like she'd done in the barn when he scared her during her workout. This time she'd make sure it would hurt like hell.

Luke turned away from Trinity, every possible scenario running through his mind as he fixed his gaze on Joyce. "Let's see . . . Trinity and I are going to have a lover's quarrel. I'll have supposedly shot her with my weapon and then turned my gun on myself.

That'll keep everybody stirred up and distracted while you shut down this pipeline and move your operation elsewhere."

Joyce's lips tightened and her smile seemed forced. "My, what a smart agent you are."

A muscle twitched along his jawline. "Not very original, Butler."

"Whatever." The woman gave a bored look and braced her shooting arm with her opposite hand. Looked like she might be tiring a bit. "With the extra groundwork I've laid storing my stock in this cave's back chamber and running three sizeable tunnels under the Flying M—well, that gives me some advantages, too. It'll be a big help when the feds think they've found the pipeline and the bitch who's been helping Guerrero. I can make my 'escape,' and nobody will be bothering to investigate me anytime soon."

"You're gonna try to make it look like Skylar was letting Guerrero run his drug operation off the Flying M all along," Luke said like it was cold fact. "Then you'll quietly wait until everything dies down, and help him open up shop again."

Smile broadening, Joyce replied, "Something like that."

"Your family has money and major political connections." Luke narrowed his gaze. "Why the hell are you helping a psychopath like Guerrero?"

"I'm not helping him, you stupid fuck." Joyce rolled her eyes, but then focused on Luke in a flash. "I'm carving out his territory."

A new coldness swept through Luke as he finally got a grasp of the full measure of Butler's insanity. "You've hooked up with another cartel to compete with Guerrero."

"Had to do something when the market crashed. My daddy's campaigns need a lot of money."

"Does he know about this?" Luke had to fight not to charge toward Joyce Butler, grab hold of her, and shake the shit out of her. "Does your father have one clue what you're doing to his good name?"

"Leave my father out of this." Her face darkened, and Luke knew he'd struck a nerve.

He took advantage of her distracted anger and stuffed his cock back in his jeans and zipped them up as he spoke. He knew now she wasn't planning to shoot them until she got them out of the cave, and probably near the entrance to one of her tunnels. Luke would be too big a body to drag far, and she couldn't afford an evidence trail that close to the cave. Not until she found other options to stash her stock, and got some new tunnels built. Besides, her plan would lose its impact if his body and Trinity's didn't point the way toward the tunnels Butler wanted law enforcement to find.

"You think killing us will keep Guerrero off your ass?" Luke risked prodding the woman, looking for any other opening he could find. "He's probably got an army out looking for you now. He's already trashed your house."

Anger turned Joyce's face an odd shade of purple. "I'm not some pussy he can scare off by painting *puta* on a smashed wall and breaking a bunch of glass. I've made this operation bigger than he ever dreamed. Hell, my men are smuggling double the drugs his boys are bringing out of Mexico. That's why he's buying up property like crazy, looking for any advantage to up his transport and production."

Luke fastened his belt and dropped his hands to his sides. "He'll kill you. That's what Guerrero does."

"We'll see. If he moves on me after I implicate Skylar MacKenna, he'll just be tipping his own hand." Joyce's eyes regained some of their focus, and her grip on her pistol tightened. "I think he'll spend his time planting evidence to implicate rival cartels, distancing himself from the tunnels, and chasing after my UDA mules. Francisco Guerrero is all about appearances. It's his weakness—and by the time he gets back down to business, I'll have most of the border property in this area sewn up. He'll have to pack up shop and move on down the road."

Trinity folded her arms across her naked breasts and stared at Butler, an incredulous look on her face. "How do you intend to pin your drug smuggling on Skylar?"

"Well, you see . . ." Joyce's expression was like a wicked little girl who always got her way. "Skylar MacKenna will be getting an urgent message from her kid sister to meet her right away. Near the tunnels, of course." Sighing, as though with great pleasure, Joyce continued, "Your sister will find both of your very dead bodies about the same time the sheriff's department arrives to investigate an anonymous tip."

Trinity's thoughts spun and she hugged herself tighter, her body shivering as she grew even more numb from the cold. "So you were the one who sent the postcard," she said, her voice harsh. "But not to get revenge for your ex-lover Woods getting caught rustling cattle for Guerrero. To make it look like my sister had pissed off her drug-running partners?"

"Good job, Meaty. I'm impressed." The woman's giggle was really getting annoying. But for once the nickname didn't. Joyce's voice was almost singsong as she went on. "The fire—now that was just for kicks. I'd hoped to cook a few of those horses and that damned prize bull, but oh well. It was fun enough to watch all of you run around screaming and moaning. I sent Skylar another postcard about that, from her drug buddies, telling her the next time it'll be her house."

Trinity had no idea what to say to this psychotic bitch, but she didn't have to talk, because Joyce was filling up all the air space.

"So, Sheriff Wayland will find not only bodies, but threats from Skylar's gang, plenty of drug residue in this cave, the tunnels—and in one of those tunnels, meticulous records that show Skylar's been running this operation for the past two years."

"They'll never buy it," Luke said. "You're wasting your time."

"I've bought the best forgery in the country. So good, in fact, that Skylar MacKenna will be locked away for a very long time." Joyce stuck out her lower lip and shook her head. "Sad, really. Grieving in jail for her dead sister, and for her husband who will have lost his life in the line of duty, not long after. And that leaves another border ranch open, and I'll beat Guerrero to it when it hits the auction block. If I can't run him out of town outright, I'll shut off all his access points, one way or another.

"*Bitch*," Trinity said with such venom that she was sure she was going to sprout fangs.

Joyce eyed Trinity's naked form and smirked. "Amazing. From such a fat cow to a skinny slut. What did you do, have head-to-toe lipo?"

Luke forced himself to remain calm and to keep from reacting to Butler's barbed tongue. His heart twisted as he saw how blue Trinity's lips had become, and the red blotches on her skin. "Let Trinity put on some clothes."

"I *am* getting sick of looking at that ugly body." Butler nodded toward Trinity's clothing. "Go ahead, but just remember the 'no sudden moves' rule. Not that you're capable of doing anything more than screwing the ranch hands."

Trinity's body wracked with shivers as she moved to put her clothes on, and Luke's gut tightened. If he'd been close enough to her, he'd have taken a chance on disarming the bitch. She was getting tired, and she was definitely overconfident.

Butler waited until Trinity had dressed herself, then the bitch waved her gun toward the cave entrance. "Start walking. Hands up where I can see them, yadda yadda yadda."

"Too bad we won't get to finish what we started in the barn," Trinity said with an odd note in her voice. Luke cut his gaze to her and she gave him a look that said, *Listen to what I'm not saying.* "You know, what I was doing—what *we* were doing—before Race interrupted us."

"Shut the hell up," Butler said. "I'm not interested in hearing or for God's sake seeing any more of your fuck-a-pades."

Luke wanted to tell Trinity *no,* don't try it, but she had that look in her eyes that said she'd made up her mind. Without smiling, Luke winked at Trinity, so that only she could see, telling her he got her message. At this point, since backup hadn't arrived, this might be their only chance. He had no idea where the tunnels were, but when Butler got them close enough, she'd shoot them both, and fast—and the bitch was a good marksman.

Luke raised his arms, palms forward, and started toward the cave entrance.

Hope you're as good as I think you are, sugar. Both of our lives depend on it.

Heart pounding like a herd of wild horses galloping across the desert, Trinity followed behind Luke, keeping enough distance between them that she'd reach Joyce about the same time he got clear of the cave.

Joyce Butler watched them coming, her eyes mostly on Luke, whom she perceived to be her only real threat.

Trinity was counting on that.

She clasped her two hands together, and thought about all the times Joyce had run her down, all the pain she had suffered from the bullying Joyce instigated.

For that, Trinity actually forgave the bitch.

It didn't matter anymore.

What she couldn't forgive Joyce for was threatening her sister and the man she loved.

This little murder plan of hers, that just wasn't going to happen.

"I love you, Luke," Trinity shouted at the same time she swung her fists up and under Joyce's gun arm.

Contact.

Trinity felt the jolt of her fists hitting Joyce's hands and the gun butt all the way through her skull.

Joyce screamed and the weapon fired as Trinity forced the woman's hand up toward the cave's ceiling. Rock shards rained down on them, landing on their heads and faces, getting in Trinity's eyes. Her eyes stung as she followed her first swing with another one, this time slicing her fists against Joyce's wrists and knocking the gun from the woman's hand.

Another shot fired. Trinity didn't know if it was from Joyce's gun, and she didn't stop to think about it.

"You fucking bitch!" With a shriek, Joyce raked her nails along Trinity's cheek, but Trinity didn't flinch.

Years of kickboxing training and Trinity went on autopilot. She landed a punch to Joyce's jaw, snapping the woman's head back. In a flash of movement, Trinity positioned herself for a side kick and slammed one Nike-clad foot down on Joyce's thigh, just above her knee.

Joyce Butler screamed again and fell back against the cave wall. Her face was a sickening shade of purple, her eyes glittering with fury. Her brown hair stuck up like horns, making her look like the demon she was. "You're gonna die now, slut," Joyce spat as her hand shot to her back pocket where she probably had a second gun.

With a powerful right jab, Trinity buried her fist in Joyce's belly, her hand sinking deep into the soft flesh.

Air rushed from Joyce's lungs in a loud cough, doubling the woman over until she dropped to her knees. Trinity snatched Joyce's extra gun from her back pocket. She backed up a few steps, and just like she'd learned at the firing range, she cocked the weapon and aimed it at the bitch's head.

The way Joyce was rolling around the floor and screaming in obvious pain, though, it wasn't likely she was going to be making any moves toward Trinity.

Sparing a glance toward the front of the cave, Trinity saw Luke casually standing with his own gun back in his hand.

Trinity's gaze met Luke's.

He smiled, and the look he gave her pumped the volume on every word he spoke. "I love you, too, sugar."

Chapter 30

The next few days passed by in a virtual blur for Trinity. It was worse than after Fenning's arrest and Joyce's supposed "disappearance." She'd hardly had a chance to see Luke with all that he'd had to do to wrap up those pieces of his investigation, and they hadn't had a second alone. Her body ached to feel him again, to be wrapped up tight in his arms and stare into his eyes for hours.

The moment she got him to herself, she was gonna jump him. After she beat him to death for not telling her he was a DEA agent.

He'd explained that.

Zack had explained it.

And Noah, and Clay Wayland, and even Skylar had taken a turn—but Trinity still thought a kick to the gut was in order.

His name wasn't even Rider. It was Denver.

With a sigh, she perched on the small stool at the vanity table in her bedroom and ran a brush through her strawberry blond waves. But she didn't even see her own reflection. Instead she couldn't help but relive the incredible sex she'd had with Luke in the cave. And then the terrifying moments that had begun immediately after.

Thank God they had made it out alive.

When Luke had reached behind him for his gun, he had managed to press a button on his cell phone. It had opened a line to some kind of special setup that notified his partner, Rios, and gave him Luke's coordinates, along with letting him in on the conversation in the cave.

Rios had called for backup, but had gotten sidetracked when he'd run into a group of Joyce Butler's men on his way up the mountain, illegal immigrants they'd been using as mules to smuggle cocaine into the United States from Mexico.

After Luke had secured Joyce's hands behind her back and bound her ankles with strips of material he'd torn from his denim shirt, he had whipped out his cell phone and reached Rios.

Thirty minutes later it was all over. The sheriff's department, the DEA, ICE, CBP—heck, it had seemed like everyone had arrived. Trinity had been vaguely embarrassed by the thoughts of the whole world snuffling around the cave where she'd just had wild sex—and gotten interrupted, of course, by that psychopathic bitch.

What was it, anyway, with people catching her having sex? Payback for all those times she'd watched Skylar and Zack?

Trinity sighed at the thought, feeling a twinge between her legs. Here it was, Christmas Eve, and she had no idea when she would get to see Luke, or where he even was right now.

Or even what she was going to do about the future.

Yesterday she'd contacted Human Resources at DropCaps and notified them that she'd be working from the Flying M until at least March. They had no problem with that, as long as she scheduled some time at the London, San Francisco, and New York hub offices, so she'd set up those visits. If things did work out for her and her cowboy . . .

She shook her head and smiled. A *cowboy* for cripes sake, and a lawman to boot. Anyway, if she and Luke were going to make a go at their relationship, she would try to get an estimate of how often she'd need to travel, and take it from there.

After all that had happened over the past couple of weeks, Trinity felt as though she had come full circle. She could finally leave behind the old, insecure version of herself and see where the future led her—even if that was back into some aspects of her past, like Douglas. She just needed to be herself, and being herself was all right.

Trinity sighed again as she set the brush down, grabbed her makeup compact, and popped open the lid. She patted a little more foundation along the four long scratches marring her cheek, souvenirs of her encounter with Joyce Butler.

A smile of satisfaction crept across Trinity's face. She'd kicked some serious butt in that cave, and it had sure felt good to let that bitch have it. No doubt, with all the evidence the various branches of law enforcement had gathered, Joyce was going to spend a very long time in prison—and the cartel she'd been working with had vanished like coyotes in the night. Guerrero might still be in business, but the bloody turf war Luke had described to her, that was history for now.

After Trinity finished putting on her makeup and had fastened earrings in all of her piercings, she slipped into an elegant strapless dress that she'd bought in Paris. It was a deep shade of emerald green, reached two inches above her knee, and hugged her slender figure. It didn't come near showing the amount of skin as the dress she'd worn at Nevaeh's. She felt sophisticated, sexy, and beautiful in it.

Too bad Luke wasn't going to see her in the dress—unless he made it to the party at the Gadsden Hotel tonight. She hadn't felt like going without him, but she'd promised Skylar.

Trinity struggled for a moment with the zipper, but finally managed to get it up. The shoes she chose were a matching green, but a decent height. Not like those death-on-sticks heels Nevaeh had talked her into wearing at that Christmas party where Trinity had met Luke. The stupid thong she was wearing was too tight, sliding up her crack, but she could handle that.

The hell with it.

Trinity hiked up her dress, peeled off the thong, and tossed it aside before pulling the dress down again. Just the feel of the outfit's silky material brushing against her bare ass was enough to give her ideas for about a dozen fantasies, all of them involving Luke.

A knock sounded at the front door—probably Rylie, here to take her to Gadsden. Skylar and Zack had left earlier, needing to take care of a few things before they attended the party.

Trinity grabbed her handbag and headed out of her bedroom, down the hall to the living room. Her heels clicked against the tile, and she wondered why the house was so dark. She could swear she'd left the lights on in the kitchen. Only the colorful, twinkling bulbs on the Christmas tree illuminated the living room, giving it a soft holiday glow.

Trinity fixed a smile on her face and yanked open the front door—

To see Luke standing there with his sexy grin and that adorable dimple. "Merry Christmas, sugar," he said in his deep, vibrant tone.

"Luke." Trinity's voice was only a hoarse whisper as she threw her arms around his neck and pressed her body to his.

Their mouths met, frantic, urgent, and demanding. He yanked up her skirt and groaned with obvious satisfaction when his palms rested on her naked ass. The next thing she knew, he'd picked her up and she'd wrapped her legs around his hips. Her head spun as he swung her around and backed her against the wall, never breaking contact with their kiss.

He felt so good, smelled so good, tasted so good.

Somehow he unbuckled his belt and she felt the coarse brush of denim against her thighs as he unfastened his jeans. Their hands and their mouths didn't stop moving. And when he freed his cock, he drove inside her right there, right then, no teasing, no waiting.

Oh, God. It felt so good, him taking her like that, his tongue plunging in and out of her mouth. Hard and fast he thrust into her, hurtling her so fast toward the peak that she could barely breathe.

Trinity purred her pleasure and her climax blasted through her in a flurry of incredible sensation. Luke swallowed her cries as his hips jerked against hers and his hot fluid filled her completely.

Lights blazed on, sudden and blinding.

At the exact same moment several voices shouted, "Surprise!"

And then the room went completely silent.

Trinity tore her mouth from Luke's and buried her face against his shirt. "Oh. My. God."

"Shit," he muttered.

"Um . . . oops." Skylar's voice came from behind them. "Um, guys, let's head back into the kitchen. We'll break out the food while these two, uh, say hello."

Giggles, laughter, snorts, and scattered conversation faded as the crowd moved out of the living room and into the kitchen.

"Sorry," Skylar said, and then the living room went dark again, leaving only the twinkling Christmas lights.

When the room was quiet, Trinity tilted her head to look up at Luke. "Think we'll ever be able to have sex without someone walking in on us?"

"Maybe." Luke grinned and pressed his forehead to hers. "At least until we have kids."

As far as Luke was concerned, they didn't need to join any damn party—but that was purely for selfish reasons. He'd wanted to keep Trinity all to himself. But despite her embarrassment, she'd told him that they might as well get it over with.

Somehow that sounded familiar.

While Trinity had "freshened" up in her bathroom, Luke took her overnight bag out to his truck where he'd left a bag packed with a few of his own things. Once they escaped from this mandatory shindig, Luke was going to steal her away for some serious time alone.

Turned out that everything had been a setup—other than them being caught in the act. Again. Rylie had asked Luke to pick up Trinity exactly at seven, to take her to the party at the Gadsden. "Something came up at the last minute," Rylie had said.

Hell, something had come up all right.

Just, ah, not quite what anyone expected.

When Trinity was as ready as she'd ever be, she and Luke joined the party that was now in full swing.

"Nice of you to make it," Zack said with a grin as they reached the living room.

"I'm really sorry." Skylar shook her head, a blush creeping up her neck as she reached for her heart pendant. "We had planned the surprise party out so well . . . it just never occurred to me . . ."

"I can assure you that we were definitely surprised," Luke said with a straight face and Zack snorted with laughter.

"What is this all about?" Trinity asked, sweeping her arm to encompass the room and all the guests.

"I planned this ages ago." Skylar shrugged. "It started off as a welcome home party, then became a celebration that you two idiots survived to see another Christmas—and then, when you said you were staying awhile, Trinity—"

Skylar broke off, obviously trying not to cry. "I really missed you, all those years you were gone."

Trinity smiled up at her older sister. "Thanks. It means a lot to me. *You* mean a lot to me."

For the next couple of hours, Trinity and Luke mingled at the party. The whole time he kept her close to his side, his arm around her waist in a protective embrace. She was grateful for his support as they talked with one person after another . . . all of whom had seen her with her dress hiked up to her waist and her legs around Luke's hips.

"Nice ass," Nevaeh said with a snicker after she and Trinity hugged.

Trinity gave her a mock frown. "I keep telling you to stop eyeing my ass."

With a wink, Nevaeh replied, "Well then, keep it covered, sweetie."

It seemed like most of their friends had made it. Of course Sheriff Clay Wayland, Brad Taylor, Cruz Rios, Noah Ralston, Wade Larson from the Coyote Pass Ranch, along with Renee Duarte and Shannon Hanes from the valley on the other side of the Chiricahuas.

And Race Bentham.

"Good show," Race said with a wink at Trinity and kissed her flaming hot cheek.

Great. Her ex-almost-fiancé had seen them, too.

"Thanks." She reached up and brushed her lips over his cheek. "Merry Christmas, Race."

Race's smile turned into a frown as he focused his deep brown gaze on Luke. "If you hurt Trinity in the slightest, I shall be forced to don my old sparring gloves, and . . . how do you Americans say it?" Race pursed his lips and then continued, "Oh, yes. I shall beat the shit out of you."

Trinity snorted and then burst out laughing. Race, saying *shit?* Maybe his wild side *could* be unearthed.

Luke raised an eyebrow and grinned. "You can rest easy, partner."

"Race was called 'Rock' back in his boxing days," Trinity told Luke. "During his career he won all but one of his matches."

"Is that so?" Luke looked surprised, and suitably impressed.

"Yes, well." Race shrugged and studied his wineglass. "A long time ago."

"Rock." Nevaeh joined them, a full bottle of beer in her hand. "It suits you. Much better than Race."

Race's gaze lifted from his wineglass, fixed on Nevaeh, and his nostrils flared. His expression was one that Trinity had seen only a handful of times, when he was ruthlessly pursuing a future client for Wildgames.

Looked like maybe he'd just found himself a new American experiment.

Nevaeh broke eye contact with Race and turned to Trinity and Luke. "Have a merry Christmas, you two." She gave an impish look and added, "Just try to keep your clothes on in public, okay?"

Trinity groaned and rolled her eyes. "We'll never live this down."

Luke grinned and pinched Trinity's ass, causing her to yelp in surprise. "Maybe we need to give them something else to talk about," he murmured close to her ear.

"My apologies," Race said to Nevaeh, his expression intent as he studied her and extended his hand. "I didn't catch your name."

She offered her hand in return, and when Race clasped it, her eyes widened. The electric currents between them were so tangible that Trinity could feel them.

"Nevaeh." Her gaze moved from Race's face and slid down his lean but well-muscled body. When her eyes met his again, she casually reached out and took the wineglass from his hand and replaced it with the bottle of beer she'd been holding. "But you can call me Heaven, Rock. It's a place I plan to take you."

And then she turned and walked away.

Race raised one brow, his eyes focused on the gentle sway of Nevaeh's retreating backside. "Excuse me." He spared a quick glance for Luke and Trinity. "I do believe it's time for me to move on."

Trinity smiled and nodded in the direction Nevaeh had just gone. "Hurry up. I think it's about time you found your wild side."

"Indeed," he muttered as he strode into the crowd.

"I think he's got the right idea." Luke scooped Trinity up in his arms so fast her head spun.

She shrieked and grabbed onto his neck. "Luke Denver!"

"Get a room this time," someone shouted from the crowd and everyone burst into laughter.

"You can count on that," Luke said as he strode to the front door. "This time there'll be no interruptions, and no peep show."

Chapter 31

The twenty-minute drive to the Gadsden Hotel in Douglas was twenty minutes too damn long, as far as Luke was concerned. He'd barely had the presence of mind to grab the overnight bags they'd packed from out of his truck, then the wait at the check-in and the time it took to ride up in the elevator to their room was unbearable.

They couldn't keep their hands or mouths off one another in the elevator, and if there'd been the slightest chance they could have gotten away with it, he would have taken her right there.

But this time Luke intended to have Trinity all to himself.

No more damned interruptions.

"Hurry," Trinity demanded when he slid the card key in the lock.

The moment the door was open, Luke swept her up in his arms and kicked the door shut behind them.

He needed to be in her so bad it was all he could do not to rip that sexy little dress right off her. Trinity was just as frantic. She kissed his stubbled jaw, his ear, his lips—anything she could get her mouth on while he carried her to the king-sized bed in the middle of the room.

Somehow they both ended up tumbling onto the bed, their kissing wild and frenzied. He'd wanted to make love to her slow and easy this time, but just like always, all he could think about was driving inside her and possessing her in every way.

Mind, body, heart, and soul.

Trinity's head spun. She hadn't had any alcohol at the party, yet she felt intoxicated, drunk with her need for Luke. One of her shoes slipped off and her dress hiked up to her waist as they rolled across the bed. In the next moment she found herself on top of Luke, her thighs straddling his hips.

He'd lost his hat and his hair was a sexy mess, his eyes like blue fire as she looked down at him. "You make me crazy, woman," he said as he reached down and teased the soft hair between her legs with his thumb.

"Then at least we're crazy together." She pulled his Western shirt out of his jeans and ripped the snaps apart, baring his sculpted chest.

Luke's hands were just as busy as hers. He yanked down the top of her strapless dress so that she was completely exposed, save for the material bunched up around her waist.

Trinity scooted down onto his thighs. Her fingers didn't even falter as she unbuckled his belt, undid his jeans, and freed his cock.

His palms were like fire as he cupped her breasts, kneading them and pinching her nipples as she wrapped her hands around his erection and rose up on her knees.

"Take me," Luke ordered as she placed his cock at the opening to her channel.

Coming down in a swift movement Trinity filled herself with his long, rigid length and cried out with the pleasure of feeling him so deep. And the way his cock curved slightly, it hit her g-spot, dead on. "You fit me so perfectly," she said as she wiggled.

"Oh, yeah." He gripped her hips. "That's it, sugar. Now ride me hard."

Trinity raised herself up so that he almost slipped out of her, then plunged back down so that his cock pressed against her pleasure button, and then she did it again and again. Her breasts bounced as she rode him, the slap of flesh and the creak of the bed frame an echo of her moans.

Luke thrust his hips up to meet her, pounding that spot that felt so unbelievably delicious deep inside. His jeans were rough against her ass and the inside of her thighs, the scrape of the denim adding to her excitement.

"I—I'm coming," Trinity said as her eyes locked with Luke's. His tense jaw and his wild blue gaze somehow tightened the spiral in her abdomen, and when the power of her climax unleashed itself, she totally and completely came undone.

"Damn, that's it," she heard him say through the storm of sensation lashing through her. He shouted something she didn't understand and then his hips bucked against hers, driving his cock still deeper yet and forcing the whirlwind of her orgasm to go on and on.

His cock throbbed and pulsed inside her sensitive core and she collapsed against his chest, totally exhausted, spent, and satisfied.

Luke woke with Trinity curled up on his chest and his cock still inside her—and it was hard as a steel rod. Her peaches-and-cream perfume blended with the smell of the rich cream between her thighs.

He craned his neck to get a better look at her face and smiled at the sight of her sleeping. That cute freckled nose, the dark crescents of her lashes against her cheeks, her smudged makeup, and her wild hair spread across her cheek and tumbling onto his chest . . .

She had never looked more beautiful.

Carefully he brushed the hair from her face with his fingers and tucked it behind the ear with all those glittering gold earrings. He frowned as he studied the scratches he'd just revealed along her cheek from that bitch Butler. He'd never been so terrified in all his life as he had when he'd heard that gun go off. But he'd been so damn proud of Trinity, too, for taking that woman down the way she did.

Stirring in his arms, Trinity purred, a soft smile curving the corner of her mouth. Her lashes fluttered open and then her jade green eyes met his. "Hi," she said.

Luke brushed another lock of strawberry blond hair behind her ear. "Have we met, sugar?"

"I hope so." Trinity covered her mouth with her fingers, holding back a small yawn before adding, "Otherwise a strange man has a very long and hard tool inside me."

He pumped his hips a couple of times. "You mean this?"

Her eyes rolled back and she moaned. "Oh, my. Yes."

In a quick movement, Luke flipped over. Trinity squealed and laughed as he pinned her beneath him and braced his arms to either side of her arms. "You ready for another round?" he asked with a small thrust of his hips.

"Whoa, cowboy." She squeezed her thighs around his waist and gave him a mock frown. "Now that we've finally enjoyed each other without someone walking in on us—"

"This session's not over yet," Luke cut in with a grin.

Trinity laughed and went on, "Why don't we try sex with *both* of us naked? Entirely naked. As in no socks, no dress around my waist, and you with every last stitch of clothing off." She pursed her lips as she eyed him, before adding, "Well, you could wear the hat."

He chuckled. "One problem."

She raised an eyebrow. "What's that?"

"How do I get my clothes off without taking my cock out of you?"

With an unladylike snort she braced her palms against his chest and pushed at him. "Don't make me get mean with you, cowboy."

"Now that I'd like to see." He didn't budge as she giggled and kept trying to shove him off of her. "You're about as mean as a potato."

"What? Ooooh . . ." Trinity gave him a pretty fierce look for a spud. "Just you wait."

"All right." Luke laughed and eased away and then stood beside the bed. He kicked off his boots and peeled off his socks as Trinity slid her crumpled dress from around her waist and tossed it across the room.

"I was wondering," Luke said as he shoved down his jeans, "if you'd fly with me to Houston tomorrow for Christmas dinner with my mom and the rest of the Denver clan."

"I'd love to." A radiant smile spread across Trinity's face. "Definitely wouldn't want you to disappoint your mother. And I'd sure love to taste some of that special pecan pie you said she makes for Christmas."

"It's the best." He gave her a quick grin. "Can't wait for Mom to meet you, sugar."

When he was naked, Luke stood beside the bed, his hungry eyes taking Trinity in. She reclined on her side as she watched him. Her long hair spilled over her breasts, her nipples peeking through, and the soft hair between her legs glistening with their juices.

Damn. It took every shred of his control not to slide between those pale thighs again, right this very second.

Whoa, Denver. He ground his teeth. *Take it slow this time.*

Trinity's heart beat a little faster as her man studied her as though she was a seven-course dinner he was about to devour. Her nipples tightened and she got impossibly more aroused. "What are you waiting for?"

He didn't answer, and she swallowed hard. Cripes but he was gorgeous—that broad chest, those well-defined muscles, and lord, oh lord, but those powerful thighs . . . *yummy.*

Luke reached down and grabbed his overnight bag that had been dropped on the floor, and she got a fine view of his tight ass. After he dug through the bag, he tossed it back on the floor and then slid onto the bed beside her. He was just inches from her, and she could feel his body heat and caught the warm smell of their sex. Both his fists were clenched, and when he opened one she saw that he had a bright red condom package in his palm.

"We seem to have a problem remembering these things," he said, his voice and expression serious.

Biting the inside of her lower lip, she glanced down at the package and then looked back to him. "You make me so crazy I can't think past wanting you inside me."

With a slow nod, he said, "Could be we've already made a baby. Then again, maybe not. But we need to decide now if we're ready to start our family if we don't start using condoms."

Her eyes widened and her heart pounded faster. "We haven't even talked about our future, Luke. Much less starting a—a *family* for goodness sake."

He uncurled his other fist, and her pounding heart shot straight up to her throat and lodged itself there. A ring. A gorgeous solitaire diamond in an antique gold setting.

All along her skin goose bumps sprouted and she began to shiver. Her gaze met his again and he was smiling. "Marry me, sugar. I know we've got a lot to work out. What we're both gonna do about our careers, where we'll live . . . when we want to start our family. We'll work it out. Just say you'll marry me."

Trinity swallowed hard, but couldn't get past that throbbing in her throat. She pushed herself to a sitting position and just stared at him.

"Of course," he added, and the corner of his mouth quirked, "asking's just a formality. Like I said before—you're mine and I'm never letting you go."

"Wow," she finally got out. "Everything you said . . . wow."

Amusement glittered in his wicked blue eyes. "And . . ."

"Yeah, I'll marry you," she told her wild card and gave him a teasing smile. "As long as you promise to wear those chaps for me. Frequently."

"You've got yourself a deal." With a soft laugh, Luke took her left hand and slid the diamond onto her ring finger.

Sparkles flashed and glittered, and Trinity sighed at the beauty of the flawless diamond. "Perfect fit."

"Your sister was a big help," Luke said as he rubbed his thumb over the back of her hand.

"Recruiting my family now, are you?"

Expression completely serious, he nodded. "Helps to have informants well positioned."

Trinity laughed and then quieted when he held up the red condom package and said, "It may be too late already to have a choice in the matter. I'm ready to start a family and have a couple of kids or more. But I'd like to know how you feel about it."

"I didn't think I was." She sighed and reached out to run her fingertips down his chest. "I'm still not sure I am. I know I want to be a family with you in every way. But maybe we should use these for now, and then if I'm not pregnant I'll go on the Pill until we're both ready."

"Damn, but I love you." Luke ripped the package open and sheathed himself in a hurry. In the next moment he had her flat on her back and he was between her thighs.

He slid into her core and she gasped and arched up to meet him. "I love you, Luke."

Slowly Luke thrust into Trinity, making love to her just like he'd said he'd wanted to, and just like she'd dreamed of since her days spying on her sister in that mountain cave—body, mind, heart, and soul. Their pounding hearts seemed to join as one, so loud that it all but surrounded her. Their mouths mated and they swallowed one another's cries as their climaxes blended and swirled and fused into one.

As tremors wracked her body, and through the haze that shrouded her mind, Trinity heard the door to their hotel room open, just before a voice called out, "Housekeeping!"

Take a sneak peek
at Cheyenne McCray's
next urban fantasy novel

No Werewolves Allowed

COMING SUMMER 2010
ST. MARTIN'S PAPERBACKS

Is it so difficult to grasp the concept of *By Appointment Only?*

I met the alpha Were's tawny-gold eyes and tried not to let irritation show in my gaze. And hoped Olivia would keep her mouth shut.

As usual, my hopes were futile.

"Your appointment is for nine tonight at the Pit, Furry." Olivia stood in front of Dmitri Beketov, her hands propped on her hips, her five-two to his six-four forcing her to look up. Way up.

Beketov scowled.

Touched by the afternoon sunlight that spilled through the window, Olivia was as stunningly beautiful as ever. From her Puerto Rican and Kenyan ancestry, she had rich golden skin and sharp black eyes. Add high cheekbones and striking features, and she could have been a model—if she was about a foot taller.

A petite package, Olivia was usually underestimated. But not for long. A third degree black belt and former officer on the NYPD SWAT team, she kicked major ass.

Right now Beketov and Olivia were having a scowling contest.

She looked up at the Were with total confidence and not an ounce of fear. "We don't take drop-ins, no matter how important they think they are." She gestured toward the front door where that fact was presented in iridescent purple and blue on the door's window.

Nyx Ciar

Olivia DeSantos

PARANORMAL CRIMES

PRIVATE INVESTIGATORS

By appointment only

When she put her hands back on her hips, the movement pushed aside her New York Mets sweat jacket. The vivid green T-shirt that stretched across her melon-sized breasts was classic Olivia—

DON'T MAKE ME BREAK OUT THE FLYING MONKEYS.

I wanted to grin, but managed not to. Beketov didn't smile. He probably hadn't "gotten" Olivia's T-shirt. It was hard to imagine the big Were kicking back and watching a vid of *The Wizard of Oz* or sitting in the audience at the Broadway show *Wicked*.

Beketov shifted, widening his stance. His Werewolf scent of woods and fresh air mingled with the smells of spicy Kung Pao chicken. The almost-empty cartons of Chinese takeout were perched on my desk in the midst of a bunch of bright-pink sticky notes from a case I'd been working on.

"I do not have time for this." His muscular biceps, revealed by a sleeveless beige leather shirt, flexed as he folded his arms across his chest. I had to admit, the Were was mouthwatering delicious despite his scowl and his harsh, angular features.

His eyes were deep set and, combined with his high cheekbones and striking features, he was Slavic in appearance. His long hair, which fell to the middle of his back, was the most beautiful shade of bronze I'd ever seen.

I imagined him in his pure wolf form. No doubt as a wolf he would be large, sleek, with glossy fur that shone like rich bronze in the sunlight.

He slid his tawny gaze over Olivia's petite but voluptuous frame. He had that arrogant alpha Were expression down pat as he assessed her.

"Give it up, Furry." Olivia gestured to the door again, this time in a manner meant to tell him to get the hell out.

Yeah, we liked business, but neither one of us tolerated arrogant assholes. However, this was a client that Rodán—my Proctor, friend, and former lover—had referred to us, so we couldn't completely send the Were away.

Beketov turned to me, blatantly dismissing Olivia. She narrowed her eyes and slid her fingers along her waistband so that her hand was closer to her Sig Sauer that was secured in her shoulder holster.

This was getting ridiculous.

"We have business to discuss. Immediately." Beketov's Russian-accented English added to his knife-edged tone. His accent was strong, so it was possible he was over a hundred years old. That was nothing compared to a Drow, such as my father, who had lived for a couple of millenniums.

He stepped closer so that he towered over where I sat behind my desk. His intimidation tactic was not fair.

To show I wasn't impressed by his show of dominance, I kept my expression calm and my fingers relaxed on the opening of my Dolce & Gabbana gold evening clutch. It was just big enough to hold my 9mm Kahr and my smallest Elvin-made—but very wicked— serrated dagger. I could have had either weapon in my hand instantly.

I knew his was a missing persons case, but I didn't have to mention that. We didn't usually handle missing persons, our competition did. We had bigger paranorms to fry.

"I'll determine how important your business is," I said in a cool and calm tone. "During your appointment tonight."

He said in a guttural tone, "We are going to discuss this matter now."

Again, I tried not to grip my clutch tight, this time out of sheer irritation. Dominant males who like to intimidate people make the hair on the back of my neck bristle.

"*No*, we're not." I met his gaze head-on. I had to calm myself to keep the dangerous white light from flashing in my sapphire eyes.

A predatory growl rose up in the Werewolf's throat and his own tawny-gold eyes brightened.

Nothing scared Olivia—not that she had ever shown—even though she was one hundred percent human.

Of course as a Night Tracker, I had dealt with Beketov's kind for over two years. That included taking care of more than my fair share of Werewolves during the full moon. I had no reason to be concerned about his show of dominance, other than retaining a good dose of irritation.

Although, Beketov was an alpha. A big one.

"Our PI firm is closed for the day, Mr. Beketov." How many times did we have to tell the bastard? I was running out of time before Nadia would be there. I couldn't disappoint her again.

Considering I was wearing a short, black, low-cut and backless evening dress, you'd think that would have given the Were a clue. If I made it to the matinee at the Metropolitan Opera House, the Thursday performance of *L'Elisir d'Amore* was early enough that I could be in and out before my change.

"Unacceptable." Beketov's tone caused me to bristle more, my skin prickling.

Beketov braced his hands on my desk, bringing his Werewolf scent of woodlands closer, richer, as he added, "This matter is far more important than whatever you have planned."

An angry, hot flush rose from my chest. I set my clutch on the desk, managing not to slam it on the surface, but kept it close enough that I still had access to it.

I slowly stood, never letting my gaze waver from his as I rose to my full five-eight height. My long straight black hair swung around my shoulders as I leaned forward, getting in his face.

He glared. "Don't fuck with me."

"As if you'd get so lucky." Olivia moved beside me and she leaned her hip against my desk, bumping into a haphazard pile of files on my desk. Despite my anger I winced as the pile rocked, and hoped the files didn't slip off my desk. Olivia crossed her arms over her chest. "Nyx doesn't do furry critters."

I wanted to laugh, but held it back.

The Were straightened and his massive chest rose and fell as he inhaled then exhaled. It must have killed him not to try to put Olivia in her place.

Beketov studied me for a long time. We had a lovely staring contest.

Finally, I saw the realization in his eyes. He understood that his behavior wasn't going to get him anywhere with Olivia and me. We weren't the type to back down no matter how much of an arrogant asshole we were facing.

The Werewolf sighed, harsh and audible, as if letting out the anger and frustration he'd been exhibiting. He unclenched his fists and his jaw tightened then relaxed, as if he was forcing a decent expression on his face.

His expression shifted so quickly that it startled me into frowning. He now looked like he was going to choke on a huge chunk of stringy raw meat because his following words were so hard to get out.

"My people's lives are at stake." He spoke in a tone that was dark, but with an almost humble quality that didn't fit the Big Scary Wolfman. "I need your assistance."

"My, my." Olivia's sarcastic tone brought Beketov's attention to her. "An alpha Were admitting he needs help." She picked up her XPhone and pretended to dial. "I'll alert the media."

His gaze darkened.

"Members of my pack are disappearing." Pain flashed through the big alpha's eyes. "And turning up mutilated . . . and dead."

My scalp prickled and the feeling traveled down my spine. I pushed aside my clutch and slowly sat again, my palms flat on the glossy Dryad wood desk as I stared at Beketov. "You have my attention," I said.

Veins stood out along Beketov's neck and one pulsed on his forehead. "After they disappear, my pack mates are eventually found, but always dead, their skin nearly in shreds."

My stomach churned at the image and the horror of what he was telling us. In a habit I'd developed years ago, I ran my finger along the band around my neck. The collar engraved with Drow runes announced my position as royalty among the Dark Elves.

I hadn't been informed yet on the case, just that it was a missing persons. But to hear Beketov now, explaining the Weres were mutilated and murdered . . .

"Each time, the mutilation occurred while the Were was still alive." Was his body shaking? With anger? Fear for his people? "This has been confirmed by our pack medical staff," he added.

"Shit." Olivia shifted her stance against my desk and one file folder slipped onto the floor with a plop and a whoosh as it landed then skidded a couple of feet on the wooden floor.

Beketov clenched his fists so hard I saw small wells of blood appear from where his nails dug into his palms. "From my pack, a total of six Weres have disappeared. All but two have turned up dead."

Chills scrabbled up and down my spine. "Here? In Manhattan?" The thought this could be happening without Trackers or Rodán— especially Rodán—being aware was virtually unfathomable.

Beketov shook his head and a lock of his thick bronze hair fell across his forehead. "From the places we feed."

"Where do you feed?" Olivia's tone was sharp, her expression focused, all antagonism and sarcasm gone.

Beketov's intense gaze flicked from me to Olivia. When he

spoke, he did so with the recognition that my partner was all business now, as was I. "Catskills. We've changed encampments several times but it's not enough. There are only so many places we can go. We must stay close enough to the locations where our pack members disappeared so that we can continue to search for them."

His chest expanded as he took in a deep breath. "We must also feed without endangering the wild animal population in any one area with a prolonged stay. Yet I cannot allow my people to stray."

Olivia raised her eyebrows.

"Weres rotate their feeding grounds to make sure they don't eliminate their food source in any one area," I said to Olivia. "The packs also have great respect for the balance of nature."

Beketov gave me an approving look before I swear his eyes clouded, almost misty, as he added, almost softly, "Two pups have vanished."

My lips parted. "Children?"

"Neither have been found, dead or alive." He looked away. "One of the pups is my son."

More chills prickled my skin and I spread my fingers on the cool surface of my desktop.

The thought of children being kidnapped and possibly murdered made me bite the inside of my cheek to control my anger. Dmitri Beketov's son's disappearance made it seem all the more real.

Beketov turned his face back to Olivia and me, looking as hardened as one of the statues in Central Park.

Then in his manner and bearing, Beketov returned to being one hundred percent alpha. An alpha who was beyond furious because his people were vanishing and turning up dead . . . but also a man who was damaged from the fact that his own son was one of the missing.

And an alpha who hated to admit he hadn't been able to help his people and was forced to ask for assistance. Likely it was even harder to have to ask two females who weren't of his kind. Weres are tight knit and aren't crazy about letting outsiders into their ranks, much less having to ask their help.

"Have a seat." I gestured to one of the black leather chairs in front of my desk. "We need details."

Olivia moved her hip away from my desk without upsetting any more file folders. "Instead of being an ass, you could have started with that information."

Uh, yeah. It sure would have made things simpler.

"That is of no matter." Beketov scowled. "What is important is finding out what is happening to my people and getting our children back."

Olivia rounded her desk before she sat in her black leather office chair. The wheels rumbled on the ceramic tile and the chair squeaked with the shift in weight as she arranged herself so that her forearms were on the desktop, in between her own piles of stuffed file folders and neon-green sticky notes. "Tell us everything. From the beginning."

Beketov didn't sit. Instead he began to pace and growl like the animal he was when not in human form.

Fae bells tinkled at the door and I cut my attention to see Nadia, a Siren, and one of my best friends. As usual she was absolutely gorgeous, but even more so in her thigh-length, glittering dinner dress that was a shade of sea foam. Strands of aquamarines sparkled in her upswept dark red hair.

Nadia pushed a loose curl of her luxurious, thick red hair away from her cheek. She looked from me to the Were to Olivia and back to me. Her musical voice sounded resigned when she spoke. "Not again, Nyx."

I grimaced. "Sorry."

Beketov stared at Nadia as if she was an annoyance rather than a gorgeous woman who most men couldn't take their eyes from. Of course if they knew she could kill them with a song, they might not be so anxious to get her attention.

Nadia focused on me. When the sun disappeared in the west, Nadia worked as a Night Tracker, like me. "This have anything to do with Demons?" she asked.

"The Demons are definitely gone. No worries."

Time to get off *that* incredible nightmare of a subject.

I took my XPhone out of my clutch. "Bring me back a program." I liked to look at the hot guys in the list of cast members.

She cocked her head. "Don't forget that you promised to go to *La Cenerentola* a week from tomorrow. Friday."

I glanced at Beketov, whose jaw was tight, his expression darker, before returning my gaze to Nadia. "I hope we'll have this case solved before then."

A frown looked out of place on Nadia who was almost always smiling. She directed her gaze at both me and Olivia. "Whatever this is, watch out for yourselves, okay?"

"As if we need to," Olivia said.

Nadia grinned, then disappeared out the door, bells tingling as the door shut firmly.

"No more interruptions." Beketov growled. "Lock the door."

Olivia studied Beketov who looked beyond irritated at the delay and she picked up her XPhone and stylus. "Tell us everything you can about these disappearances and deaths."

I was prepared with my own XPhone and stylus. Olivia and I had discovered over the last couple of years that when we took separate notes we often developed different angles with our cases.

Beketov dragged his hand down his face that was roughened with at least three days' stubble. "My son and his friend were the first out of the packs to vanish, two weeks ago. We haven't stopped looking for them."

My stomach was queasy, the Chinese takeout that I'd eaten before Beketov walked through our office door not settling well. As I'd proven when ridding the city of Demons, I have a weak spot for children. That weakness had almost killed me and I'd be dead if it hadn't been for T . . .

I was *not* going to think of T, even if he had saved my life. Twice. Bastard.

"An adult female from my pack disappeared after the children," Beketov was saying. "Then two more females before we lost an adult male."

Olivia took in an audible breath as she paused from putting notes on her XPhone. "Shit."

Beketov continued to look away from us. Then his waist-long bronze hair swung from a harsh jerk of his head when he returned his tawny-gold gaze to me. "I've sent out search teams and I have forbidden anyone from my pack to go out in groups of less than three."

"Any clues at all?" My own stylus hovered over my XPhone as I waited to write down more notes.

"Nothing matches." Beketov's Russian accent grew stronger, in tune with the growing anger in his voice. "The only thing in common is that they are all Weres."

Olivia tapped the end of her stylus on her desk. "Wolf or human form?"

Beketov's sigh was heavy again. "We are not sure."

"What about smell?" Olivia frowned. "Werewolves can detect the scent of anything. Humans, paranorms, and animals can't mask their scents. It just hasn't been possible no matter how many times it's been tried."

"Until now." Beketov bit out the two words like slicing them from the air around us. "Nothing beyond a scent like cotton balls on the Were's body when we find them. That smell does not lead anywhere from the body."

Olivia quirked her eyebrows. "Cotton balls have a smell?"

I ran my fingers along my neckband again. "Did the disappearances start during the last full moon stage?"

Beketov shook his head. "Two days after." He set his jaw. "I doubt anything could take on any member of our pack during the full moon stage."

Well, if I could take down a Werewolf as a Tracker likely something else could. All it would take was the right set of skills, such as the ones my fellow Trackers had. We all had different, but very powerful, forms of magic at our bidding, unlike most paranorms.

I didn't think Beketov would be pleased to discuss that I had slayed a few his kin when they went rogue. Packs were tight knit. If there was a rogue, the alpha would take it upon himself to kill it.

"The last full moon was over two weeks ago," Olivia said. "How close is your pack to civilization?"

"Too close," Beketov said. "We are camped near Devil's Tombstone, in Stony Clove."

"Well that figures," Olivia said.

It was my turn to raise my brows in question.

Olivia tapped her stylus on the table. "The Devil was supposed to have haunted that area way back when. Early settlement days. Men, women, and children supposedly frequently turned up missing." She was looking at me. "Considering what's happening, it couldn't be more appropriate."

"Nothing but superstition." Beketov's voice went deeper, closer to a growl. "And we have hunted in that location for years.

"We always go to the most isolated parts of the forest," he continued, "during the full moon so that we are not a danger to norms and paranorms."

Olivia turned her gaze on Beketov. "Anywhere in Stony Cove is way too close to civilization come the full moon."

"We may have no choice but to stay." He shook his head. "We cannot leave the area until the children are found."

"Uh, the during-the-full-moon thing near civilization—not good." Olivia held her stylus as she leaned back in her chair. "You'd be taking the chance of being seen and you might slaughter innocent people."

"Perhaps it is what's needed." He met Olivia with a hard stare. "We might take out whatever it is that is kidnapping and killing my people."

"Sure." Olivia tossed the stylus on her desktop and crossed her arms over her ample chest. "A Werewolf during full moon, a savage being not even aware of its true existence, taking care of this problem? I don't think so."

Instead of their natural wolf form, at the full moon a Were transformed into a hideous beast. Neither man nor wolf, but a walking abomination that would kill the closest thing to it with no awareness beyond the fact that it was hungry.

Always hungry.

Beketov's expression went darker, but I headed him off. "We have almost two weeks." I set my XPhone and stylus to the side. "We'll solve this atrocity before the next full moon."

For Cheyenne's Readers

Be sure to go to http://cheyennemccray.com to sign up for her *private* book announcement list and get *free exclusive* Cheyenne McCray goodies. Please feel free to e-mail her at chey@cheyennemccray.com. She would love to hear from you.